# Dangerous Desires

# Dangerous
## Desires

## PETER WELLS

VIKING

VIKING
Published by the Penguin Group
Penguin Books USA Inc., 375 Hudson Street, New York, New York 10014, U.S.A.
Penguin Books Ltd, 27 Wrights Lane, London W8 5TZ, England
Penguin Books Australia Ltd, Ringwood, Victoria, Australia
Penguin Books Canada Ltd, 10 Alcorn Avenue, Toronto, Ontario, Canada M4V 3B2
Penguin Books (N.Z.) Ltd, 182-190 Wairau Road, Auckland 10, New Zealand

Penguin Books Ltd, Registered Offices:
Harmondsworth, Middlesex, England

First American Edition
Published in 1994 by Viking Penguin, a division of Penguin Books USA Inc.

1 3 5 7 9 10 8 6 4 2

PUBLISHER'S NOTE
This is a work of fiction. Names, characters, places and incidents either are the
product of the author's imagination or are used fictitiously, and any resemblance
to actual persons, living or dead, events, or locales is entirely coincidental.

Pages 221-222 constitute an extension of this copyright page.

LIBRARY OF CONGRESS CATALOGING IN PUBLICATION DATA
Wells, Peter
Dangerous desires / Peter Wells.
p.   cm.
ISBN 0-670-85012-8
1. Gay men—New Zealand—Fiction.   I. Title.
PR9639.#.W43D36   1994
823—dc20   93-32419

Printed in the United States of America
Set in Bembo

To my brother, Russell

# CONTENTS

# Dangerous Desires

# PERRIN AND THE FALLEN ANGEL

*'Who has not been a slut, has not been human.'*

ERIC WESTMORE DID not consider himself either a beauty or a gorgon. People did not run out of rooms gagging: but, on the other hand, not too many were driven to distraction by his glance. This did not preclude great explosions of attraction: yet such was Eric's nature, ironic, self-mocking – or was it merely self-doubting – that he always put these frissons down to poor eyesight or a case of mistaken identity, which would almost inevitably catch up with him sooner or later.

He sat now in the brackish quiet of the Alexandra Hotel. It was 10 April 1986.

The Alex was a charmingly Edwardian hostelry on the outside, a wedding-cake of plaster arranged, tastefully, to snare passers-by on two back streets: it looked like the tiara, Eric always thought, of a minor Scottish peeress. It was the last week of it being a gay, or indeed any kind of pub. It was going to be demolished. All over the city, in a speculative frenzy driven by the stock-market, Edwardian and Victorian Auckland was being reduced to dust.

Even now, as Eric sat in the dullard moments of the quarter-hour before noon, demolition drills were attacking the air in nearby streets, a dull repetitive sound, drill to a toothache.

Yet it was a beautiful day, he said to himself, inclined to feel mellow (he was, after all, in the opening stages of, as he himself said, *a romance*, putting just the right ironic emphasis on what some might call a love affair and others might call a fuck). It was a superb day in early autumn: the crispness of winter had begun to lie like an essence over the lingering heat of summer. As if to symbolise his content, just as Eric walked down the street towards the pub, a yacht had serenely passed across the gap between two buildings, tightrope walker on his line of bliss.

*Yet.*

Eric, on the cusp of 38, aware that the tidal shifts of time were now beginning to run against him in a way that no amount of gym nor artful haircuts could entirely alter, knew there always had to be a *yet,* a determinant in his bliss.

The *yet* he was thinking of now, as he sat in the pub gazing thoughtfully at a block of sun on the carpet – 'like winter butter set out on a white porcelain dish,' he memorised for his column – was the phone call from Perrin that morning.

The phone had gone off at 7.30, aggressive as an alarm.

Matthew was still in the shower while Eric was standing in front of the stove, staring mindlessly at the milk he was scalding for *caffe lattè.*

Perrin's voice cut through his groggy sleepiness. 'Can we meet today?'

'Today?' said Eric, who was still adjusting the sensuality of the night before to the demands of prosaic daylight.

'*Yes, today,*' said Perrin without any of his customary humour. He sounded pissed off – or was it sour?

Did he suspect already, Eric wondered, about Matthew?

Matthew, as if an apparition appearing on cue, walked into the kitchen stark naked. Eric admired his body – which, of course, he was meant to do: his freedom, his flanks, his beautiful tassel-like cock. Matthew did a small coquettish whirl then sat down, forgetting Eric completely, and, picking up the morning's newspaper, began to study his horoscope.

'As soon as possible,' said Perrin's voice, again, in Eric's ear.

Eric had taken his eyes away from Matthew, unwillingly, and cast his mind ahead to his day. He thought of how much more work he had to do to get his daily food column readable. Then there was his guerrilla raid on an unsuspecting new restaurant, the one specialising in New Zealand game products.

'What about after six?' Eric suggested, looking tentatively at Matthew.

Matthew was, instead, investigating his pubic hairs with a monomaniacal scrutiny.

'*No. Earlier.*' Perrin was being relentlessly persistent.

'You could meet me at that new place – Faringays. I've got to *cruelle* it.'

Perrin and he always called Eric's reviews 'to *cruelle de ville*' it.

A pause.

Perrin's response was definitive. '*I don't feel like food.*'

Silence again as, in the background, Eric heard someone say good morning to Perrin and Perrin, crisply adjusting his tone to genial busy executive, batted back the greeting. Perrin said then, close to the phone: 'I want to see you, Eric.'

'*I need to see you baby,*' he said in one long breath of confession.

Oh no, sweetheart, you haven't been seeing Sweet Sixteen *again*, Eric was about to whiplash back. Sweet Sixteen was a troublesome, if nubilely splendid, Niue Islander Perrin was being relentlessly pursued by. But something about Perrin's tone told him it was not going to be their usual enjoyable slanging match, in which mutual insult and hilarious parody mounted up until Perrin, almost inevitably, managed to cap Eric off with a flourish of obscene absurdity. Perhaps it was too early in the morning.

Or perhaps, Eric thought more reasonably, Perrin had a hang-over. Or was it just that super-melodramatic flu which was casting Perrin into increasingly sombre moods: what Eric lightly dubbed his 'dame aux camellias' complex.

'*Please,*' said Perrin, who was not one to beg.

Eric had quickly succumbed. They would meet at the Alex a few minutes before 12. They would go on from there to somewhere 'quiet'.

Just as he put the receiver down, in that second before Perrin clicked off, Eric had an insane urge to put the phone back up to his ear, to listen harder, deeper, more faithfully to the textures of Perrin's silences, the underground music of his tone. But Eric was running late. His deadline for his food column was leering, the phone was already shrilling and then, of course, he had had hardly any sleep after his night with Matthew.

3

*Matthew.*

It was true, a good seven-eighths of his mind was given over to, willingly occupied by, thoughts of this young man who had suddenly, accidentally – impetuously – entered his life. Even as Eric now sat waiting at the Alex, 11 minutes before noon on that April day in 1986, he closed his eyes for a second, to reconnect with that world which still swirled, fragrantly as the scents of sex, through his consciousness.

Obligingly – or was it obediently? – he was wafted up to a serene and great height, as if he were in a glider which could not, would not, ever meet with catastrophe. And far below him he saw the body of Matthew, a vast landscape which stretched from horizon to horizon: a country he was beginning to be familiar with, his favourite destinations – Matthew's mouth, between his legs, his smooth buttocks like peeled grapes. Was it folly for a writer on food to conceptualise his new lover in terms of fruit, of vegetables? (His cock a courgette left on the vine too long and grown tautly too large, the pillows of his chest a perfectly ripe pawpaw he loved to lick and gnaw on, the cleft of his arsehole, well, not to be too ridiculous, moistly pink as perfectly cured Christmas ham. He could go on, his Matthew, his banquet, his feast.)

Perhaps this objectification, Eric lectured himself as he sat there, was simply defensive. It was part of his emotional defensiveness that he tried to picture Matthew in terms of appetite, keeping clear of that minefield, that scarred battleground of the emotions called love. Oh keep me clear of that, sighed Eric, seasoned trooper of the wars of the heart.

With a conscious effort – but also with a pang of regret that he must leave such a perfumed landscape, one with its own laws, its own hegemony over his unconscious – he tried to focus on the exact present.

He dallied with his glass of tonic, looking for a moment at the bubbles. Then a faint smile of anticipation softened his face. He longed for Perrin to arrive, so he could gently, as if accidentally, spill the treasure of his new romance before Perrin's eyes.

He had been seeing Matthew for over three weeks and, though Perrin and he, old friends, well, *ancient* friends, touched base at least once a week, he had carefully screened the event from Perrin, until the romance, affair, the series of fucks – whatever it was – had some stable *emotional* basis.

Perrin, meanwhile, had noticed nothing: neither Eric's soaring spirits, nor his pleasurable languor, nor even, on the one occasion he had managed to coax Perrin down to the pool, the expressive lovebites on the back of Eric's neck.

Perrin was inclined to be myopic anyway. His battles at the Equal Opportunities Commission, where he was a pugnacious lawyer, at times occupied all his fields of vision: when he wasn't, that is, pursuing remarkable pieces of Clarice Cliff, or unusually sensual young men whom he unearthed from unlikely situations, like post offices in small towns or half-empty laundromats – any of those situations which require a selective perception, tempered by endurance and fired by an almost fanatical flare of desire, and desirability. Or was it an unfillable capacity to be approved of, to be loved?

Perhaps that was why Eric wanted to torment Perrin, just slightly, at this moment. Perrin always had such spectacular success sexually (with, of course, its attendant moments of tedium, like courses of penicillin) that Eric felt drab and frowsy beside him. Eric always felt, in this situation, that his own desirability was diminished, a point he was not beyond getting petty about.

So now he carefully, and with a sense of epicurean enjoyment, selected his poisoned shafts. 'He (Matthew) is 23 (young), a student of architecture (a brain). He plays basketball (good body). And he's cute (rampant sexually).'

Eric toyed with the various ways he could casually, without undue emphasis, introduce this new persona to his and Perrin's life. Eric knew Perrin would want particulars: he would realise, as soon as Eric had introduced Matthew to him verbally, that it was merely a prelude to him meeting Matthew himself. Eric always regarded it as part of his lovers' educational process that they should meet someone as civilised, as exquisitely nuanced, as Perrin. Many a callow youth had learnt a correct table-setting in his presence.

Perrin would, perhaps, have him and Matthew round for one of his delightfully casual, perfectly produced Thai meals. Other friends would be there. They would range over politics, personalities, fashion, food. In this way Matthew would enter a mutual zone of friendship, that *terra cognita* Eric had relied on ever since he had discovered it, tremblingly, in a state of hilarious ignorance, in what he now called, with sardonic quotation marks around it, *his youth.*

He looked around appreciatively. It was in a pub like this, Victorian, slightly seedy, scented with all the beers supped by many forgotten drinkers - to drown what sorrows, evoke what dreams, nobody could any longer say - that he and Perrin had first met.

It had been Eric's first venture into a gay pub.

In a mood of determination which had about it the air of a suicide mission, Eric had bid farewell to his old self in his bedroom mirror and set out, one Friday night (15 May 1969, his old, deplorable diaries told him - marked with a significant X). He had presented himself, white-faced, at the bar. As far as he could see, there were only men there, apart from one extraordinary woman who appeared to be the hostess. She was dressed, head to foot, in a glittering black mumu, her most pronounced feature a suntan so intense it appeared less her skin than a form of basted flesh on which pieces of gold were placed, ornamentally, to great advantage. This theme was carried into her mouth where her teeth were bedizened in a similar precious metal. Overall she escaped, by a mere hair's-breadth, being spectacularly gaudy.

Eric went straight to the bar and asked for something he took to be a typically sophisticated 'gay' drink. 'A Negroni please.'

The barman had looked at him, was about to ask how old he was. Then something in Eric's face - his desperation, perhaps - made him hesitate and then, speaking almost *sotto voce* - say, 'Wait a sec.' He turned to serve two men who hung on each other's shoulders and, both casting conspicuous looks at Eric yet making him feel as if he wasn't quite there, continued to address each other in fluted tones.

Both men wore what Eric took to be a club uniform: white shoes, beige crimplene slacks and hair which appeared to be both subtly teased and unsubtly lacquered. Their faces, variously wrinkled, were glaucous with moisturiser. 'Two double gin and tonics, love,' one of them asked the barman, in tones not quite so orchestral.

His companion smiled tentatively at Eric, and Eric felt his face crack a little as he smiled back. His heart was beating so hard he felt sure they could hear it.

The men departed, and the barman casually came back. 'Do you know how to make a Negroni,' he asked quietly, without any suggestion of aggression or even undue attention in his voice.

Eric flushed. He did. His throat was dry when he started speaking: he coughed up air over sandpaper.

The barman waited. Eric nodded. 'Yes,' he said, and told him.

While the man proceeded to make it, Eric said to him: 'I looked it up.' Then he said: 'I like reading recipes.' As he said this, he felt a swoon overtake him, a flush begin to rise up his face.

The barman had turned to look over his shoulder at him, not so much sharply but as if to check out the ingenuousness of the remark. Seeing Eric's discomfort he slid the drink towards him and, shaking his head when Eric offered payment, solemnly withdrew.

Eric realised something nice had happened to him.

Safely in possession of something to hold, something to do, Eric slid his tongue into his drink experimentally. As soon as the alcohol hit his tongue, he had to try hard not to let his face react. It did not taste as he imagined the recipe would. Nevertheless, having obtained the drink in such special circumstances, he could hardly go back and ask for something else.

He must enjoy himself: that terrible imperative. He looked around the room to see who was looking at him. No one. It was extraordinary.

He looked around again, in panic. Nobody was taking the slightest bit of notice of him.

It was at this moment – this lacuna in his life – that Perrin McDougal walked in the door.

At this stage, before he had settled sublimely into his looks, wearing them with all the assurance of a bespoke jacket on carefully muscular shoulders, Perrin appeared a diffident, indifferent-looking youth. He was thin, high-nosed, dressed dramatically, head to toe, in black. He paused under a light, as if for dramatic effect, then threw his long amethyst scarf over his shoulder with a defiant emphasis.

This caused a momentary hush – almost of awe at someone contravening 'taste' so much. Then at the back a voice was heard to say something – thankfully, Eric thought, indistinct (it sounded like 'drama queen') – then there were guffaws or collapsed lungs of laughter.

Perrin, holding his profile in a distinctly Oscar Wilde manner (the young Oscar Wilde), as if he did not hear, obtained a drink and went into speedy exile – a miscalculation of effects? – by a wall.

Inevitably, it seemed, because they were the two people on their own, so spectacularly isolated, their eyes located each other. It was like radar – radar of the dispossessed.

It was Perrin who finally made the move across the room to him. Sidling up, he looked at Eric for a moment, radiant with silence.

Eric, panicking – was this his first pick-up? – said, with a dry voice, 'There's quite a crowd here tonight, isn't there?'

His new companion turned on him an eye from which satirical emphasis was not entirely absent. 'I *hate* crowds,' Perrin pronounced.

'Why . . . why do you wear black?' Eric asked, racking his brain for clever, unusual things to say.

'I'm in mourning for the world, of course,' Perrin said superbly.

Eric, who was not *au fait* with Edith Sitwell's autobiography, believed he found himself in the presence of acerbic genius. 'Are you from out-of-town?' he asked, looking into Perrin's thin face, pimples just visible by his nose.

Perrin seemed uncomfortable, even nervous. Nevertheless, so convinced was he of his superiority that he looked Eric up and down, then said drily: 'The unpleasant fact of the matter is, I come from a Rue Morgue called Hamilton.'

Eric's eyes widened. 'That has a lake, doesn't it?'

'In which,' said Perrin, who spoke as if always between parentheses 'the unhappy citizenry are driven to throw themselves, for their *divertissement.*'

Eric laughed, and Perrin congratulated him on his appreciation of wit, with a surprisingly shy, even tentative, smile. Then he turned to the room, sighing slightly.

'You see before you . . . a refugee. In fact, I clean dishes at the Hungry Horse.'

Eric saw that Perrin was by no means as self-assured as the turn of his scarf, the cut of his phrase. With this discovery, he felt himself to have attained a similar, happy refugee status.

A long, not unfriendly silence fell in which both did an inventory of the room, frequently and nervously sipping their drinks.

Eric was soon surprised to find his glass was empty: not a drop could be seduced from its shimmery viscous surface. Perrin's glass was similarly empty.

They both looked down at the diminution of their hopes and, as if in musical concert, sighed heavily together.

It was clear that, having created grand effects, neither had a penny.

'What were you drinking?' Perrin asked.

Eric, tentatively, told him. Perrin was thoughtfully silent (later he would admit he had never heard of the drink). 'I only ever drink Fallen Angels,' he said, with a high tilt to his nose which Eric read as instant glamour.

From that day on he would always think of Perrin - who later came to detest the drink as oversweet, the epitome of his early lack of sophistication, his suburban pretensions - as synonymous with that first occasion, when they had both tremblingly met and Perrin's mode of identification was, along with Edith Sitwell, a long amethyst scarf, a sense of the early Oscar Wilde, and a drink called Fallen Angel.

Later that night they left the pub, as if accidentally, together.

They walked to the bus stop still talking and each, on the point of saying goodbye, speedily allowed the other to understand that he could be found at the pub the following Friday.

Neither confessed it was his very first visit.

Now, sitting in the Alex so many years later, more mature, filled out into his body in a way which made him feel he knew himself, Eric glanced around the bar. The men there all knew they were men: the few women's names bandied about were always used, as it were in quotation marks, knowingly camp. The barman, fleshily muscular, with a tightly trimmed moustache, looked for all the world like a rudimentary Tom of Finland sketch requiring a few master strokes for sublime completion.

This world of the Alex now was light years away from that hotel, so long ago, in which Eric had nervously awaited his second meeting with Perrin.

That night Eric had allowed himself a small glass of beer. He was determined to keep sober. While he waited, anonymously, the crowd had swiftly grown. It was late summer and there was that lax, overexcited air of sensuality - of louche possibilities - in the air.

Eric relaxed his body against the wall.

'Everything OK here, darlink?' a voice said to the side of him.

Eric turned. Pushing through the crowd towards him, like a beaver, was a small man with waved pale blue hair and what looked like make-up on his face - or was it simply moisturiser? As he got nearer he closed his pink, slightly unguent lips together, cupid-fashion, and then laughed, revealing teeth which looked older than he was.

'Darlink! hold *onto* your funwig,' this man murmured to him, a mite melodramatically. His whole face was animated by a pleasantly puckish charm.

'Oh?' said Eric, not knowing quite how to reply. He broke out laughing.

Now, 'Call me Fay,' the little man said, pausing as if for breath. 'After the late great Fay Wray,' he murmured then, looking around the room in small darts and flicks, poisoned pricks of looks. 'We call her late,' whispered Fay, 'because she never comes on time! Famous for it!'

He looked around sharply, no longer smiling. 'Excuse me, dear, a dreadful clutch of old hags awaits,' declared Fay in a conspiratorial whisper, during which Eric felt his backside pinched, not unpleasurably – as if the man called Fay were a merchant and he was only taking a prudent feel of the fabric. Fay indicated with his head four men standing together, bodies turned, almost on display, to the constituents of the bar: 'We call them Boil, Toil, Struggle and Poke.'

'Ciao,' he called then, melting back into the throng. Eric imagined the departing remark was a Chinese codeword.

At this point Perrin appeared beside him, unwinding himself out of his long purple scarf, sweating and bad-tempered. He had missed his bus and had to hitch a lift, he said. He intimated it had not been a pleasant adventure. When his lift found out the nature of the pub, he had turned threatening. Perrin had opened the door while the car was still moving and run, he said with superb dramatic emphasis, 'for my very life'.

But he still had in his hands a gift for Eric: a 'borrowed' library copy of Edith Sitwell's autobiography. 'The beginning of your *aesthetic* education, my dear,' he said expansively.

Eric bought a round of Fallen Angels, nonchalantly, as if this were an everyday drink for both. They drank these perhaps too quickly. Then Perrin bought a round.

By this time the room, as crowded as an audience at a boxing ring, had taken on a certain hectic tone: at any moment, it seemed, the bell would ping, the lights would

11

lower, the main match would start. Obligingly, the bells began to shrill, urgent as the flutter of blood coursing through Eric's wrists.

Fay suddenly popped up beside him, almost with a suggestion of old-time vaudeville magic (later he found out that Fay had trained in Sydney as a show dancer before breaking his hip and ending up as a waiter). As the tidal swill of men swirled him past, Fay called out, 'Do you want to come to a party?'

'Oh,' said Eric, thinking.

'*Yes* ,' said Perrin quickly, '*I* would.'

Everyone was spectacularly drunk. People were walking about, banging into walls. A middle-aged man, unwatched by most, was doing an impromptu, slightly wobbly strip on a chair. 'Oh, *trust* Fanny,' someone was saying acidly. 'One *whiff* of alcohol, and *off* come her easies.' Another fanatically serious man circulated through the crowd, wearing someone's mother's best ming-blue bri-nylon suit.

Eric and Perrin stood together in a crowded kitchen. Fay was surrounded by people, as if he were a great courtesan holding court.

'And yes, they put me on the overnight from Wellington,' Fay was saying, '*escorted*' onto it by two large beasts. *Irish detectives.* They put me on and said, "Don't be in too much of a hurry to come back." Just to remind me they punched me. In turns.' There was silence. 'And then, after that, they said, "We've got some mates up in Auckland *waiting for you when you get in.* Just to make sure you don't cause any trouble up there, like." '

Fay left a brief, eloquent pause. 'So here I am, a poor helpless wretch,' he resumed, raising his eyes heavenward, in roguish imitation of a wilting Mary Pickford. He lisped softly, and with extraordinarily convincing pathos, 'Just doing the best that I can.' A particularly wicked look passed over his face.

Fay then rose with great dignity, the dignity of an Empress Eugenie receiving the news of the fall of the Third Empire, the death of her only son. He turned and, in a spectacular wavering motion, as if tilting to follow the impulse of his feet, he listed towards the door, finding it open almost by accident, so that, faintly surprised, even vaguely nonplussed, the man called Fay disappeared into the halloo-ing night.

Eric and Perrin had to walk home, as the buses had long since stopped. They walked through suburbs of spectacular silence. To entertain themselves each told the other a little about himself.

By the time they had parted – the first car was going to work – they had exchanged the same information: in order to cure them of their homosexuality, Perrin had had shock treatment, Eric aversion therapy.

They looked at each other, slowly smiling, in the diminishing night.

It had not worked.

Outside, in the street, there was a sudden crumbling sound, as a tidal wave of masonry came crashing down. In a few seconds, all that was left was a cloud, a hideous perfume, a perforation of memory almost.

The entire structure of the Alex had shuddered in that moment, as if in apprehension. Outside the windows, the air became frail with grit.

Pneumatic drills took up their sound again, a drumroll at once curiously undramatic yet relentless.

At that moment, as if blown in by the gust of energy from the latest demolition, a figure arrived, tentatively, and hovered by the door. The light was behind him yet Eric could see, immediately, the newcomer was not Perrin.

The man moved slowly out of the dust-filled sunlight, feeling his way, almost by toe, towards the bar. Eric felt a quiet claw of shock. The man was dressed with a certain hectic vivacity: his once-tight jeans were now winched in, painfully; over what was clearly a skeletal stomach, a belt with studs glinted with the eyes of a snake which had long ago lost its fury. And the man's face, gauntly handsome, haggard indeed, with deep heavy lines running from nose to chin, was shining with sweat, pale, white: he had not shaved, thus accentuating his dramatic pallor.

For one dreadful moment, Eric imagined he could remember the man: that is, he could recall a finer, fitter, indeed quite handsome man who seemed, now, like a distant, more healthy brother. *That* stranger - not *this* one, surely - had exchanged a few looks with Eric in the bar many years ago. Then *that* man, with his image of health and vigour, of whom this frail, too-old young man was a *doppelgänger*, had disappeared. He was rumoured to be in NY. He was either a waiter, according to one story, or, in the version preferred - because more apocryphal - he was the lover of someone very rich, very powerful and, to the public at least, very heterosexual.

Now this man had returned home and the sum of his voyage was making his way from the door to the bar in the Alex.

The occupants of the pub had grown briefly silent: then a series of falsely animated conversations broke out, like sweat on a forehead.

The newcomer reached a barstool but, suddenly relaxing his body against it, as if he had reached the end of what had become a too long and arduous mission, he misjudged its height so that, like a building collapsing sideways, his whole body began to topple down towards the carpet. At this moment, all pretence was abandoned.

The man beside him, a comfortable pool of flesh who propped up the bar from the minute it opened, getting slowly sozzled as the day went on, reached out an automatic arm, as if he had a spare limb set aside for the safety of drunks and others similarly incapacitated. Holding the falling man arrested for a moment, he got to his feet and, as if the other were a doll now, or a giddy child, plonked him down foursquare on the seat and held him secure.

At this the skeletal brother of the once-handsome man, once so much in command, the accruer of so many ardent looks, let out a wild laugh, its hilarity mocking everyone there in the gay pub, in its last days before being demolished. It was as if this man, so near his own end, clairvoyantly sensed that this place where so much life had gone on – where, indeed, rudimentary yet important transactions of a civilisation, a small branch of culture, had taken place – would be rendered faithlessly, by some dark law of anarchy, into a hole in the ground, an essential nothingness which might become, if it were lucky, the tarmac of a carpark.

Eric threw the last drops of his tonic back. Where *was* Perrin, why was he late when he had been so bloody melodramatic on the phone in the morning? And what was so bloody pressing?

Eric's contemplative eye, as if a needle within a compass of anxiety, returned to the man at the bar.

He was talking with an eerie, rambling gusto, telling the story of his travels. Eric could see from the faces of the listeners that they did not know whether to believe what he was saying, or believe something more profound, less acceptable.

Eric looked away quickly. He stared longingly out the door. The sun was still there, but it was gauzy with the dust of departing buildings. A huge demolition truck roared along the street, splicing everything abruptly into shadow.

He looked back into the room, quickly. He did not want to think of *that*.

He was prepared, of course, he used condoms, had studied the arcane codes of safe sex. (Come on him not into him, as the explicit ones said.) Yet, to Eric at that moment, the disease was still like a foreign war, happening, thankfully still, *over there*, a distant place from which occasional returned soldiers, like this one, emerged in the locals' midst, gnarled, bearing tales of defeat greater than anyone could possibly imagine. And to a certain extent it was unimaginable: this savage hewing down of men who had just climbed out of the darkness, emerging into light.

*What the bloody hell was keeping Perrin?* Suddenly Eric had an almost hysterical desire to flee the pub. He wanted to be outside, to be near the harbour or on top of one of the volcanoes where he could look down at the city, make some sense of his life. What was Matthew but a diversion; he was fooling himself by saying he wasn't falling in love. Of course he fell in love every time. What the fuck do you expect from someone who grew up with the fateful tunes of *South Pacific?* 'Somewhere across a crowded room . . .'

The drills suddenly swerved into closeness. Eric caught his own face in a mirror opposite: he was surprisingly, even insistently, physically *there* for someone who, at that moment, felt a peculiar see-saw of elation dipping down into black depression. He and Perrin had talked in the early days of having tests because, as Perrin had said, 'Let's face it, darling, we've both been utter sluts in our time . . . but then,' he had added thoughtfully, lifting his eyes up and looking towards a far distant point, as if he were delivering the eulogy for a generation, 'who has not been a slut has not been human.'

Eric had laughed.

Now he tried, with an almost fanatical need, to think of Matthew. He tried to conjure up in his mind those images of their love-making which acted, almost, as a way of banishing his anxieties. He began to wish, almost desperately, that Matthew was there with him, so that he might just casually brush by, knocking his body into Matthew's as if to recall what was real - against what could only be feared.

Yet at this moment, when he most needed him, Matthew refused to appear by osmosis.

It was now eight minutes past 12, on 10 April 1986.

At that moment, as if exactly timed to an acme of pleasurable lateness, Eric saw another figure arrive at the door.

At first, because of the light behind him, Eric couldn't tell whether it was Perrin. It was certainly Perrin's height, and approximate weight, but the person's body language was so different: slumped back, not pushing forward, standing there on the mat as if momentarily dazed, as if emerging out of a long black moment of introspection - thought - peregrination - a limning of the harsh white noon light, chalky almost, plashing and pouring down the side of, yes, it was Perrin's face.

He was still at the door, as if breaking off from some thought which possessed him. It was in his eyes as they searched the few people in the room, and the room went momentarily quiet *again* before, in quick shock waves, conversation took up, sealing over the startled apprehension that already, like an almost imperceptible drumroll, the words *again* and *again* and *again* were making themselves heard, explosions from the distant war landing closer and closer to that spot so that it was finally unavoidable that one day soon, or was it even now, a direct hit would be made and the whole culture, if it were not to be wiped out, would have to go underground again – disperse, change its nature – or else *fight*.

As if in the wake of this apprehension – or was it the beginnings of comprehension? – Perrin began to move slowly towards Eric. Each fraction of a centimetre closer he got, it was like a realisation being brought personally, without words, from Perrin to Eric, from Eric to Perrin, from Perrin to Eric.

Eric wanted to rise to his feet, he wanted to open his arms wide and put Perrin within them and hug him forever, till he could recover, get all right. The words were already forming in his mind, angry and furious: we will fight this bloody thing, it can't be allowed to win, *it won't, we won't let it.*

Yet already Perrin had raised his face to Eric's, as if he wished to intimate to him that he could sustain no thought, so deafened was he by the vast explosion which had, the day before, in a quiet doctor's room, blown away everything he believed in and held dear to his life.

So it was, in the pub, in the last weeks before its demolition, before the farewell party which everyone confidently expected to be halcyon, Perrin did what he would never have done, really, or only when completely drunk: he put his hand out and Eric, as if by accident, caught it.

Together, they began to hold on.

HE SAID HE was a brain surgeon and looked at Alan with the candid eyes of a liar. Alan looked at him long and hard then simultaneously they burst out laughing.

'You've got a lovely laugh,' the brain surgeon said with a voice of quiet longing. Their eyes, blue and brown, touched, touched, then swerved apart.

It had been like that from the start - an impossible attraction, an irresistible connection between an out-of-towner and a local.

When Alan came to think of his companion's body later he saw it in terms of a Michelangelo nude, that magnificent framework of limb, lovely musculature, symmetry. That he had the slight slutty voice of a small-town girl gave his huge body a kind of charm, like a flaw in a magnificent vase.

He was blond, slate-eyed, tanned. Alan's first impression of him was that he was a beach prostitute with a kind of Marilyn Monroe mind, light, flirtatious, with a melancholy layer of seriousness underneath. Sexual.

'I bet you're hard, eh?' the beach boy said, looking at Alan straight in the eyes. 'Why don't we do it in the bushes here, right behind me? *Now.* '

Alan looked around the sunken garden: the splash of the waterwheel, the salt-glazed annuals, the peeling paintwork of the bed-and-breakfast opposite. It was New Zealand at its most prohibitively prim.

'No,' Alan said with a short sigh. 'Not here. Come back to my motel. Come . . . back,' he said after a short pause of calculation, 'and we'll have a smoke. You smoke?'

'The minister said I shouldn't smoke,' the beach boy said with a high, wild laugh, 'but I've been totally out of it for three days. Haven't eaten for two.'

He proceeded to tell Alan about a minister who had picked him up one day on the beach. Just like now. Except the minister hadn't ostensibly picked him up. He said he was worried about the beach boy's soul. He wanted to help. So he went back to the minister's room. The minister went into the bathroom and came out saying, 'You realise I've already ejaculated?'

The beach boy said he went into a library and looked the word up in a dictionary.

They both laughed at that and Alan was aware he didn't have an erection. The talk of religion had removed his effervescence. The beach boy began to talk randomly about being mixed up, and was it wrong, and how he couldn't afford to be seen going into motels with strangers.

'Come back,' Alan said with a note of entreaty in his voice. '*Come back.*'

The beach boy looked at him: their eyes fused.

'You've got lovely eyes,' the beach boy said then. 'I could really go for a bloke like you.' He paused and did his own calculations. 'You'll have to walk ahead. Oh God.' He made a small gesture of self-rebuke. 'That's terrible, isn't it? But I live here.'

They sat together looking at the world they found themselves in.

'What's your name?' Alan said quickly, as they stood up.

'What's yours?'

'Alan.'

'That's mine, too,' the beach boy said laughing. 'A good name, Alan.'

A long time afterwards Alan wondered whether that was true, or whether Alan, the beach boy, had made it up on the spur of the moment. It probably made it easier for him to remember who he was with.

The room was lit by an orange curtain Alan had pulled along to kill the daylight. He had rolled a smoke and they paused a moment, breathing it in. They stood together, loosely touching. Their hands, bodies were hungry for each other. It went on like this, a feverish exploration which terminated in laughter as they rolled back onto the big flat motel bed.

For Alan it was a dream being in a motel with so handsome a stranger, having sex. Trying to have sex, because Alan was overtaken by a strange feeling of not responding to this beautiful, strange man who was more magnificent physically than anyone he could remember being with. It was a gift, a strange talisman, a sleight of hand like a rainbow seen very quickly then not there.

Alan the beach boy quickly established that he would not be kissed, sucked or fucked. This gave him even greater pause as he wondered what exactly they were to do. And he had no excitement. Or rather his sweeter excitement came from the warmth of flesh, the pleasure of touch.

They lay there, breathing heavily, sweating in the heat, a stalemate.

The beach boy said, 'Do I smell? Have I got a gooby at the end of my nose? Am I so ugly?'

'No no no no,' Alan kissed his arm lightly. 'We don't *have* to fuck, you know. It doesn't matter. This . . . this is nice . . . just being with you.'

The beach boy paused and looked deep into Alan's eyes. 'I could really lose my head over a bloke like you,' he murmured slowly.

They had a shower and acquainted themselves with each other's body. It was a quiet moment, almost introspective, as hand touched flesh, Braille of lost moments.

Underpants, shorts, T-shirt, jandals . . . little by little, like a film oddly in reverse, the beach boy slipped back into the guise of the stranger outside the room, on the street – till he stood, bag over shoulder, ready to go. But their eyes wouldn't leave each other's face as if, in the last seemingly casual moment, each was already remembering the other.

'Take my address in Auckland. Take my number,' Alan said without feeling the words belonged to him.

'What's the point?'

They kissed, for the first time, on the mouth, tenderly, slightly, softly, almost a child's kiss.

Alan let him out by the fire escape.

The following day, alone in his motel room, Alan sought to make order out of the confusion of the previous day. He was in the town delivering a consignment of books. He had only one day left. Yet already, almost against himself, he had begun looking for the beach boy.

One thing floated back into his mind which, at the time, he had hardly thought of. It was when the beach boy told him quickly, confessionally, with the complete frankness of strangers who meet accidentally and know they are unlikely to see each other again, his life story. That is to say, carefully not divulging where he lived, worked, what his surname was - though once, referring to himself, he used what Alan instinctively knew to be his real name. Terry.

His story was of such piercing sadness that for days afterwards, weeks, the memory of it would bring Alan to a halt in the middle of the street, in a traffic jam where, sitting in his car, the beach boy's face would return to him with an almost shocking power, his slightly sibilant voice tripping out his tale, his peculiar, poignant humour.

That day Alan gathered fairly quickly that Terry was married, had children, worked in one of the huge processing factories which surrounded the small city. Further, he gathered that Terry had one or two days a year when his wife visited her family. It was in one of these rare moments of freedom they had met: it was in those chaotic sudden shafts of freedom, like a sudden uplift of breeze, that Terry investigated his real sexuality.

Terry's story was that his homosexual life began when he was 22, pursued by a silent stranger. This other stranger, a man in the small town like himself, had not spoken to Terry but would silently turn up outside his house as he got into his car, eerily appearing beside Terry as he shopped inside a supermarket with his wife, parking behind him when he visited the neighbouring town.

Terry's own family never suspected, and the stranger, apart from one day leaving a note on Terry's windscreen, never attempted to talk to him. Life went on like this for two years, until finally the stranger came up and spoke. Would Terry fancy going for a drive in his car? Terry asked what for - he had his own car. Besides, he wanted to get back to his *wife and kids*. So the stranger disappeared.

Then a curious thing happened. Terry began to look out for the stranger. He began to feel a new emotion, a realisation that he himself had come to rely on the stranger's presence. He missed him. Painfully. Agonisingly. So badly that he himself began to search for the stranger who had so silently, and over so long a period, pursued him. *Two years.*

The strangers met, as if by accident. They argued, Terry denying that he was now in pursuit. Their argument ended in chaotic, furious love-making, hot with tears, blind with the fumbling realisation of feelings denied so long.

Their relationship after this was whatever two men can achieve in a small town full of eyes, where a mute dissatisfaction translates into a kind of rancour which forbids true happiness or ecstasy in others: in fact, sees it as a kind of reproach.

It ended badly. Without air to breathe - in a landscape of plain, mountain, ocean - no room to move: not even a room. The two men would meet on the wide shingle beach at night: it was there, under the clouds or stars, they made love. But it was bitter in the cold. And the excuses, the unhappiness, the dreams in the middle of the night when he reached out to touch his wife and murmured his friend's name.

That was the sum of the stranger's story: probably no different from a thousand other stories of gay men in small towns throughout the country, Alan thought later. But its potency fed into his life when he returned to Auckland. In the small town he had felt a rare, genuine connection, something more real than even his friends could provide. At the same time, the *tristesse* of the story lingered. Two years.

Slowly, as if forming in liquid, this powerful underlying melancholy came to focus on a shade of blue. Blue of hydrangeas, blue of radiant ink, jeans stiff after their first wash: cornflower blue. And Alan's first glimpse of Terry sitting on the beach, peeling his shirt over his head to reveal the body of a Michelangelo slave. It was one of those sharp tufty days, and out at sea there were beautiful blue-purple drifts, imprints of clouds. It was this passionate shade of blue he recalled.

With surprise, almost as if it wasn't himself, he began to whistle 'Blue Moon' so soulfully that, walking down streets, strangers would turn to look at him.

The chance came to return to the small town. His joy in going back was commensurate with a sense of getting closer to the place where Terry lived. He told himself, of course, he would not look for Terry: it would simply happen, as it had the first time, by accident, but as if it were fated.

He moved into his motel, carefully choosing one with an exit far away from the prying eyes of the owner. He washed himself carefully before going out, bought a bottle of Scotch, constantly glanced at himself in mirrors as if to see what Terry might see on first sighting him again. And he liked what he saw. He was happier than he had been for a long time. His eyes, hair, skin, all had the lustre of assured romance.

So he went about his work, all the time alert for the beach boy's reappearance. It was as if Terry might, at any second, walk through the door of the room he happened to be in, appear in a shop, simply emerge. This anticipation in itself became a form of enjoyment, for Alan, as if it was a liqueur to be smelt first, savoured.

Then swiftly, suddenly, the memory of two years ago revived and Alan began, almost against himself, to peer down the vistas of streets, searching for the stranger who he was convinced would soon appear. Gradually this feeling in itself changed into a kind of fretful waiting, an impatience: because the seemingly impossible had happened. The man called Alan, or Terry, had disappeared.

Alan began to rack his brain for clues he might have forgotten: he combed the phone book for likely names, he even began to walk around the streets, randomly, carelessly, without any design or motive other than the hope of running into Terry again.

He neglected his business.
He missed his plane back to Auckland.

It was a week later. It was as if Terry had completely disappeared: as if, in a way, he had been no more than an illusion, a phantom of beauty, longing, desire, summoned up by the vision of him unpeeling his shirt against the hydrangea-blue sea. A curious feeling of recklessness overcame Alan - he scoured hotel bars, toilets, sports clubs - but it was no use.

He rebooked his flight to Auckland.

He had an hour before his taxi took him to the airport. He retraced his steps and went down to the beach, to that part where he had first met the beach boy. He sat there, listening to the shingle roar. It was a hot day and the sun suffused the sky with a brilliant white glare. He grew drowsy, lost in his longing which had become almost a drug to him, sustaining him even while, silently, slowly, it was debilitating him totally.

He lay back, closing his eyes.

'*You've got nice eyes.*'

Alan awoke to see Terry's face reversed over his own. He was laughing, either at him or with him, Alan couldn't decide which. He felt the brush of Terry's fingers on his shoulder as he came and sat down beside him. Alan looked at him. They were silent, their thighs just touching.

'I was looking for you,' Alan wanted to say, 'all over town. I just wanted to see you again. I miss you.' Instead he said: 'Busy at work?'

Terry didn't say anything. He did an exercise with his legs, developing the tone of his calf muscles.

For a moment there was silence, Alan letting his eyes be dazzled, not by the man at his side, but by the sea. He noted how the hydrangea blue was changing, quickly, under cloud, into a deeper crushed purple, then back again, swiftly, into a piercing shade of aqua.

'You were just someone I met,' Terry said. 'You were nice,' he went on, continuing his exercises. 'Lovely.' Then: 'It was nothing.'

He stopped his exercises and turned to look at Alan with those eyes, the candid eyes of a liar.

'Nothing?' Alan said.

Terry smiled then, and leaning forward, his back shielding him from the eyes of the town, he kissed Alan on his neck lightly, affectionately, softly.

'Nothing,' he said.

# ONE OF *THEM*!

*'It hurts to be in love.'*

'I JUST DON'T get Dad,' says Lemmy in the flat tide-out voice he uses when he's thinking about something else. 'I *mean*, I just can't see why he won't get his eyebags surgically removed. They're so ugly, and I mean: *ug-leeee!*'

'Yes Lemmy,' I say, looking down at *Vogue New Zealand* which lies open on a cushion in front of us. We're doing research on what a facelift can do for you. I'm 14, Lemmy's going on 15 and he's fat. I don't ever say this to him, I wouldn't dare. He's four foot nothing, human dynamite.

I'm five foot 10 and thin. I like to think I'm Audrey Hepburn thin, sort of elegant. When I sit I try to cross my legs over, like I've seen in books.

When people see us together, they laugh. *We just don't care.* We laugh back. At least Lemmy does.

Lemmy's got eyeliner on, just the faintest line, and he's done his hair all spun gold and ironed flat, not a curl in sight, and he's borrowed some Stay Firm from Dianne, his sister. The faint smell fills the air, we breathe it in hungrily, like it's a perfume.

Lemmy wrote my note and I wrote Lemmy's note and we're hiding out back at his place, windows closed, door shut, we keep away from the windows. His mother's not at home, she was taken away. It happened last week. Now I look around the room, thinking this is where it happened.

Outside there's not a person in the street, not a car: nothing. I watch a blackbird spear a drowned worm. Beak slashes it aside, disgusted.

Lemmy's getting bored, I can feel it. Lemmy gets bored a lot, sometimes he does things just to stop being bored.

He goes over to the radiogram. Lemmy doesn't move a facial muscle as he puts on one of Dianne's records. I relax and wonder what's coming next.

The music swells all velvet around us.

*It hurts to be in love,*
*when the only one you love*
*turns out to be*
*someone*
*who's not in love with you.*

I look at Lemmy and Lemmy looks at me as the red velvet
unrolls all around us and we lie back into it; we loll.

Lemmy lights up a Bold Gold, blows out a stream of smoke.
He says: 'You know he's one of *them* ?'

He says it slow and husky, soft, like it's not a question really.

I just look at Lemmy, I'm almost frightened, I'm waiting.

*So I cry a little bit (to be in love)*

'*Him?*' I say soundlessly and I suddenly think of Gene's face on
the record cover and I get this overpowering waterfall of feeling
that I want to pull his fluffy poloneck jersey down, down round
his neck, I want to licklicklick and kiss him right under there,
where it's warm, it's hot, it's sticky. This shocks me. I see Lemmy
looking at me closely now, he's got this cruel look on his face.
*Don't laugh at me Lemmy*. Don't. *Please.*

I look back at Lemmy, forcing my eyes to look into his. His
eyes are hard. 'That's really disgusting,' I say. 'He must be *really*
sick.'

*And so you*
*die a little bit*

'I don't believe you,' I say desperately, wanting Lemmy to say it's
really true, and I pick up a book, any book, and pretend I'm
really interested in it. But as I flick through all I'm thinking about
is Gene's fluffy jersey and his soft parted lips. I can feel myself
getting red, slowly, like a stain all through me I can't get off. I can
hardly breathe now, yet I force myself to go on flicking through

the book, like everything's normal. *Normal.* I hate that word. Then I look down and see what I'm holding and it's *a sex book.* Lemmy just looks at me, blows out this cool veil of blue-grey smoke. He's watching me now, real close.

I act like I'm not surprised but my hand has turned dead on me, I can see it down there, a dead gull dried by the wind, eyesocket staring back at me, watching. 'Look at this,' my voice says for me. 'Look!' And I let out a strangled laugh. I wave at him the cover which says: *A Report on Real-Life Sexual Experience,* compiled by Dr Alfred K. Kitchsenburger, PhD (Med) (Hons) (Tuvalu Uni).

Now I've got Lemmy's attention and he's no longer looking at my face. He reaches over, snatches the book out of my hand, cruel, so I'm left naked again, with only my face to hide behind and I can't hide what's in my face. I'm not like Lemmy.

Lemmy now rolls over onto his back and, holding his cigarette in this exaggerated stilt-way, starts reading out.

He reads it in an American accent like 'I Love Lucy'.

*I followed him into the changing room and as he rammed his 10-inch black cock into my mouth, I gagged but then I found I liked it and I started . . ."*

He stops now, glances over at me. I'm so naked I grab the book off him. He's surprised I'm so violent. I grab the book and I start reading, practically calling it out at the top of my voice, practically singing:

*And I just got down on my knees there on that dirty floor and started worshipping his prick, with people just outside the door, on their way to work, but, oh, so help me God, the demon of sex was upon me and I couldn't, I just couldn't keep a control of myself!*

Everything's so silent all you can hear is our breathing, a charged duet, and I know I've got to go on reading.

I feel something dismal and confused and magnetised, I can't explain it and I look at Lemmy and Lemmy has this flushed

28

look and then I hear my voice and it stops me: *'I don't believe you, Lemmy Stephenson. I just don't believe you.'*

'What?' he says, all flat again. He rolls over onto his back and looks up at the ceiling, bored. Then he stubs his cigarette out real slow, he kills it.

'I don't believe you. Gene's not one of *them*. He can't be.'

'Why not?' He doesn't even look at me.

'You're making it up. Aren't you? Tell me. *I only want to know the truth,*' I say. Both of us know I'm lying and I know we're both thinking, *thinking* about this world we've just opened up.

'You made it all up!' I cry out, my voice all dry and full of hurt, and Lemmy looks at me suddenly like he really hates me and then he yawns very elaborate and long and slow like he's just heard the most boring thing in all existence and I'm it.

Lemmy acts like he's just suddenly been woken up from a snooze; he's such a good actor, Lemmy. He acts like he's surprised to see me there, with the sex book in my hand. In fact he acts like he's surprised he's even on planet Earth. He didn't plan it. 'Oh . . . sorry,' Lemmy says to me, fanning his fingers over his open mouth. 'Someone must have slipped some librium into my coffee. You were saying . . .?' and he looks at me, enigmatic.

'Nothing, Lemmy,' I say all defeated. 'Nothing.'

And then suddenly Lemmy leaps up and goes over to the window out of which I can see, just see, a little old woman in a fawn overcoat wheeling her shopping trolley behind her like she can't get away from it and she's been walking for days and days but the trolley is still following her, and won't go away and she's just about going crazy with exhaustion, *yet she can't stop.*

Lemmy stands behind the net curtains, and he screams in this sound so shrill it's like spun sound made sharp and stalactited so like a sliver of glass it enters the flesh, breaks off, can't get out, aims straight for the heart, arrow of hate, sliver of hurt, all scarlet and drenched. Lemmy just opens his mouth and screams out in this high wavering falsetto, outdoing Lucille Ball: 'I JES' CAN'T KEEP A CONTROL OF MYSELF, SO HELP ME GOD!'

I crack up and Oh Lemmy, I say, I'm laughing but I'm actually frightened, Oh Lemmy, you're such a scream. Such a scream. And I think. Lemmy. Don't kill yourself Lemmy.

I had no idea I was doing wrong. I loved Lemmy. It was only later I realised it was wrong. *Yet it was necessary.*

I learnt this too, later, after it happened. *All the things which I did which were so wrong were also necessary.*

*'A town without pity.'*

'OK' says Lemmy, who's gotten over being bored. He's suddenly a fired-up crackercaper, he's 20-tied-together-tomthumbs all splattering and battering the silence out of the air, beating it up as the crackers crack, leap, ignite. Tang of gunpowder laces the air.

I look into Lemmy's face, his long straight nose, his gilded hair. His eyes glitter, outlined in mascara. Lemmy examines his nails, carefully, as if for dirt, but I know he's really thinking.

I stand there, wondering what's coming next. I hope he doesn't notice I've got a pimple coming up, right in the crease by my nose. Lemmy is very critical of things like that. But Lemmy is looking right through me, like he's read me cover-to-cover, I'm Sandra Dee, or Bobby Darin, positively South Pacific point, corny as Kansas. *No I'm not, Lemmy, I silently say: test me.*

This is how it always begins, right from the start: *test me.*

Lemmy jumps up and does his Pete Sinclair imitation - you know, from 'Happen Inn, New Zealand's Own Go-Go Show'. The Chooks inside cages, with rockhard beehives and go-go boots. Pete Sinclair jumps onto the blackwhite screen, like he's a genie just dying to get out from inside. He's wearing his old old crooked smile and baked-on hairdo. He turns sideways, sort of Spanish, clacks his heels, claps his hands together twice, hard, like castanets and yells out, 'Let's go!' Clap! Clap! '*Let's go!*'

When Lemmy does it, it's like he lets you see the joke inside. And the joke is this: everything in New Zealand is so crummy, it's laughable. Once you see the joke you can't stop laughing. This is the trick Lemmy taught me.

So we decide to fan the breeze, as Lemmy says. We escape into town, on the trolley bus, looking for excitement of which, that day, there is none. Instead it is cool, wet, lead-grey. The sky is all laced down to earth by black powerlines, as if everyone in this town is frightened to let the sky get too high; it might show us up for how small we really are.

We have a cup of coffee in the mezzanine lounge in 246, watching people go up and down on the escalators, but still nothing's happening so Lemmy takes me down to this toilet in a carpark. He takes me in very casually and we have a cigarette and read all the messages and words on the walls. While I am reading them, Lemmy gets out this pen and, like he's done it before, writes right central and where it can't be missed, STICK YR STIFF DORK INTO MY HOT HOLE - a schoolboy'. Then he writes: 'I am all sexed up and ready'.

Underneath it Lemmy writes that very day, that very hour. I laugh, Oh Lemmy, I say, you're such a scream.

Lemmy goes deadpan: 'Let's go outside and watch the fun develop.'

We hide behind the concrete pillars and smoke away about 5-10 minutes of no-time, when time stops and waits for something next to happen, to push it along again.

While we're waiting, Lemmy goes back to his old point: *Why?*

'Why what?' I say to Lemmy, my heart sinking because I know what he's talking about.

'Why bother?' Lemmy says then, throwing away his cigarette, so I watch it roll over and over itself, disgorging ashes and splinters of fire and spark, till it dies. The wind then rocks it back and forth, gently, as if to show its emptiness.

He's talking School Cert.

'*What's the use?*' Lemmy says then, his unanswerable question.

What is the use? I don't know. I did once, I thought I did, then Lemmy showed me different. 'I haven't decided yet,' I say to Lemmy, stalling for time, trying to stop him, *lying*.

'I just gotta get outta this dump, Jamie,' Lemmy says, using my name which he hardly ever does – only when it's serious. '*If it's the last thing I ever do . . .*' and his voice dies off into silence in which there is no sound at all, only a distant car horn suffocating. I think about what he means. Yet I know what he means: it's like we're on gas and it's being turned down so low you can hardly breathe any more; you're slowly dying on your feet but you keep on walking. It's like there's all the air in the world in this place but no oxygen.

'Oh Lemmy, look at this,' I say, then I do an imitation of the Supremes singing 'Baby Love', with a mike and everything. I sing all falsetto. Lemmy looks at me, kind of smiles, a crooked curl of a smile, then he changes again, quickly. He forgets me. He puts his finger up to his lips.

'I think we got a live one.'

I lean out from behind the pillar very slowly.

A man in clinging Bermuda shorts gets out of a car slowly, looks both ways carefully, then, with an almost elaborate casualness, crosses the road and disappears into the toilet so quickly it's as if he's never been in the road at all.

I know Lemmy has got it wrong. Because this man is like any man you might see on the bus, he's not a pansyfairyqueerhomo, and just because of his ordinariness I feel my whole flesh burn with the words on the wall *plugholearsecock* and I look at Lemmy *feelspunkdork* and Lemmy looks through me; he has the same fever I can see.

But Lemmy waits for one second then beckons me from behind the pillar with his finger. It's very like a movie this: we silently move forward to the toilet door beyond which we can hear the slippery silvery sound of the water in the urinal cascading down and there's a kind of great silence, waiting.

I look at Lemmy as he listens. He is so tense his face has turned to metal: only his eyes flash over at me as he decides to enter, occupy this empty cell of silence.

He goes inside there for a moment, creeping in. I suddenly feel alone. I realise where I am. *What if someone who lives up the road sees me?* Then Lemmy tiptoes back, hides. Now his mouth opens wide, and Lemmy lets out his great screaming shriek from behind the wall.

I feel an intense rush of fear and excitement as Lemmy's scream echoes all over the concrete carpark, multiplies, comes together again, crashes and splinters apart. I don't know what to think, I am so excited by what Lemmy has just done.

The man torpedoes out of the toilet, quickly, not turning around, as if his face couldn't be seen, at all costs he must remain anonymous. I see now he is not so handsome, he is frightened. He gets into his car, a grey Morris Minor, registration number EY 6542. He accelerates away while I scream out, taking over from Lemmy: 'WierdoQueerPansy PoofterHomo! You Ought to Be Put Down! You Ought to Be Dead!'

*He kissed me on the lips till I came,* I think.

'Serves them right,' I say to Lemmy after we've run away and finished screaming and shrieking, when we've slowed down and we realise there is nowhere else to go; that is our excitement for the day.

'Serves him right, eh Lemmy,' I say, but Lemmy doesn't say anything, doesn't say a word, just walks along all silent and unknown. Then suddenly he looks at me and I am scared. *No Lemmy, no. Don't. Please Lemmy, don't laugh at me.*

This is how we met, in violence.

We were playing tiggy one day at school. You take the ball and spin it, and brand someone, so the ball, which is wet, heavy and harsh, hurts. In the game, you could do this to people and they wouldn't know till it hit them. Then everyone laughs. And everyone laughs nervous, so it won't hit them. Everyone is praying it'll be someone else. And when it hits whoever it is – someone with glasses, or fat, or thin – everyone laughs even louder, because it's not them.

This day, I'm dreaming, I'm dreaming about our head prefect who I can see. This prefect, I can't help myself, he's so handsome and each night I have this same dream: the school catches on fire and I rescue the head prefect and then alone, together, *amo amas amat.* Then I hear Lemmy, four foot nothing, fatboy with legs so fat they rub together at the knees, and he says very low, whispering in that flat voice I get to know so well, without emphasis, without any emotion: *Let's brand the beanpole.* Me. Five foot 10, aged 13.

I am fast, too fast: I am the champion sprinter in all the school. I am famous for fastness. So the ball skids past tearing open the air as it goes, hurtling past me, then into the creek.

I run now to get it, I am hot. Behind me I hear over the wet grass the heavy heartbeat poundbash of other footsteps rushing to get the ball so they can brand me again. I know now the ball will be wet: it will sting. But as I bend over the kikuyu forest, in among the stamens and tongues of green, I see this sandwich, just floating so innocent.

It has been luncheon sausage, and the bread, white, has turned into softsoft blotting paper, floating apart so it comes to pieces and gently nudges the turd floating beside it.

My fingers close around the sandwich, I pick it up real gentle and careful so it won't fall apart and then I balance the soggy grey mass cupped inside my palm. I feel tendrils of power rushing down my arm, chill, cold as death. Boys shy away, stand still, panting inout inout scarletblood danger. I hold it high now and then I find *fatboy* and he's looking at me now, without any expression, I see this in a quick glimpse, like a photo, then *beanpole* yells to *fatboy* so loud everyone can hear, urgent, as if to catch the real ball with which I'm going to brand him forever, TAKE THIS FATBOY!

The sandwich flies through the air, disintegrating as it whirls, catching in its path all the power from the other boys whose eyes watch entranced, chanting, singing, yelling in one rush of breath, an arrow of pleasure it's not them: BRAND HIM. BRAND FATBOY. BRAND FATBOY.

The sandwich splatters all across Fatboy's face. He stands there with it dripping and dropping, his face that frozen expressionless mask I get to know so well, when I know what it means. At the same time, his whole face, from his neck up, starts going deep bright red – *the stain.* Everyone laughs now, released, relieved it wasn't them that got hit. Everyone is secretly pleased too it is fatboy who has this cruel laugh.

But Lemmy is not finished. He picks off a piece of the sandwich and fishes out the scarlet skin of the luncheon sausage and, holding it between his fingers like it's a delicacy, he opens his mouth, looking at Ken Johnston who is lying on the grass laughing with tears forcing through his lids going heeeeehhhhheeehhheehhh, like he's punctured and all his fear is coming out. 'Fatboy got hit,' Ken says over and over again, so glad it's not him. Lemmy goes M . . . MMmmmm!, as if it's the Maggi soup ad on TV, and we all stop so still because, just for one second, *we believe it.*

Then Lemmy opens his mouth, drops the luncheon-sausage in, and we all go totally quiet watching him and he looks at all of us one by one as if he is remembering our faces for later retribution. And when we are all silent apart from Ken Johnston who is wheezing now, having an asthma attack of tears and nerves and joy, Lemmy finishes eating, licking his fingerpads delicately clean. And when he swallows I swear across the whole football fields under that dirtysheet sky, you can hear us all swallow hard and dry, as if we are trying to swallow a lump, a rock, sand, dirt.

When it is all gone, Lemmy just says, '*Tas-ty!*'

Then he walks away from us, on his own, his fat legs rubbing together at the knees.

A few days later we are sitting in Latin class. Lemmy, who usually sits down the back, quietly takes a seat right behind Ken Johnston. We're waiting for Mr Chisnall, our Latin teacher, to arrive.

Now Ken Johnston has this Brylcreemed swished-back hairdo he is very proud of. He has an old grey-yellow comb he slips out of his back pocket, sharp as a knife, which he then pulls luxuriantly through his hair, so we can appreciate the extra length. This comb always has a thin line of pus in it from grease and dandruff. Normally someone would have said something about it but the fact is Ken Johnston's father has the only swimming pool in our class and a two-storey house, and you could tell every time Ken pulled that comb through his Fabian hairdo he was just thinking about being the only boy in our class with a swimming pool *and who can he invite home for a swim.*

But Ken Johnston is pretty clever; he never actually says his father has a swimming pool. He doesn't have to. Every move he makes advertises it, and the way his hair is all sort of elaborately piled up on his head and swished back into a kind of duck's tail says it for him. Ken has a bike with turned-up handlebars, which he rides looknohands, and to see him you know all he's thinking about is how to get that beautiful Brylcreemed hairdo home in one piece so he can float it, all reflected, in his swimming pool.

Anyway, we're all waiting for Mr Chisnall to arrive, to bang his books down on the desk with an extra thump and for him to look at us fierce and angry, and begin. Mr Chisnall is a sports hero. He represented New Zealand in sprinting and it's always like he's straining at the start line, muscles tensed, waiting for the gun to go off. We're all making a lot of noise, filling in our freedom with waiting.

Suddenly I notice the others nudging one another and pointing down the front. I look. There is Lemmy looking very very serious and, while Ken is putting out on show his native

36

woods ruler and pencil sharpener in the shape of San Francisco Harbour Bridge, Lemmy is very very intently picking something off the back of Ken Johnston's black jersey. It is the way Lemmy is doing it that gradually gets everyone's attention.

He plucks a little piece off like it's gold, just on the tip of Ken Johnston's shoulder, just out of his sight. Lemmy then holds it up in the air, as if he's inspecting it: then suddenly, it turns into a flea, he drops it with a look of distaste on his face, blows it away from him, flicks at it as if it might jump back on him.

He starts off slow and concentrated but, bit by bit, he is finding so much of Ken's dandruff that, one by one, everyone in the class starts watching.

There is this pure corridor of silence, we all stand down one end and watch Lemmy touching, or rather *not* touching Ken, so delicate is his whisk. Then Ajax Murphy, who has thick pebble lenses and is just about as unpopular as Lemmy, starts off this hyena laughter; it's like he can't really control it.

Ken can hear this laughter and he turns around but Lemmy is faster. He's reading his Latin book very seriously, slowly turning the page. The moment Ken turns away, there is Lemmy back doing it, even more exaggerated and *bored*.

Ken starts going red, he can't turn around too quickly or his elaborate hairdo might sort of glide to the side, the fringe'd come unthatched. Besides, Ken is so cool he can't move quickly; cool people don't. So he just sits there wanting to die with this big cheese-eating grin on his face every time he turns around, *suddenly*, to find everyone just looking at him and laughing and laughing, and Lemmy sitting there so cool and still and flicking over a page, his lips even moving as he reads.

I looked at Lemmy whose face never changed once, though you could tell behind its whiteness beat this fierce rush, and I suddenly thought I want to know you, Lemmy Stephenson. I need to know you. *Lemmy please know me.*

'I usually wait till Mum's gone out then I go through her cupboard and use whatever eyeliner I like. I think it's really important to have *eyebrows*. Don't you?'

Lemmy looks at me. He has this way of looking which is to look all over your face like suddenly it has turned into a great big planet and he's a long way away on the moon gazing at every square inch of it through a telescope.

'You're a runner,' he says, more like an accusation. 'You're the fastest boy in the whole fourth form.'

I can't help it Lemmy, I want to say, but we are just getting to know each other, standing by the wire-mesh fence high above the swimming pool, Lemmy giving it a good hard vicious kick every so often, so it rattles.

In the background we can see the tall stooped figure of Mr Brakevich, our gym teacher, who Lemmy christened Mr Shitalot. Mr Shitalot likes to cane a lot; a kind of cloud of unhappiness envelops him so much that he looks out at everyone, not quite seeing them, but spraying them with hate. It was his job every year to make sure that any boy who didn't participate in sport took part in the school marathon, which was by way of punishment. You had to keep running till you dropped, over the school farm, up the extinct volcano, through the creek, avoiding the hidden boulders, with everyone waiting at the finishing tape to see how much pain you were in. Sport is important at our school. It builds character.

Like Mr Shitalot, who this very moment is pushing into the chill water the boys who are too slow getting in. He's really enjoying himself. You can tell because the creases in his face go white, and he bites his lip into a sort of grimace, as if he's laughing to himself inside all the time.

The biggest mistake Mr Shitalot ever made was sending his son to our school: he was a punching-bag within a week and he stayed that way till he ran away and was brought back. Then he got sent away to somewhere mysterious. But in that time Mr Shitalot's son changed. For life. Our school builds character, you see. It makes us into men, which is what sport is all about.

And this is how Lemmy and I first ended up being together.

We both had letters from our mothers saying we weren't allowed to swim. I had earaches and Lemmy had a complaint nobody was allowed to know about. Lemmy told me he was his mother. 'It makes things so much easier,' he says airily. 'You just have to make sure your writing shows confidence.'

I look at Lemmy and I can tell there's something strange about him when he talks about his mother. Or rather when he doesn't talk about his mother. It was like he didn't have one. But I knew he did.

'I hate running,' I say suddenly. 'I don't even know why I do it. Or rather I do, I s'pose. It's because,' I say bitterly, though this vein of bitterness is new to my voice, like I was just finding it by saying it, 'it's because, like, my mother and father were *so good at sport.*' I said the last words like they were one word, which they are in a way. Anyone who went to our grammar school knew that beinggoodatsport was a single attribute, like truth, or beauty, or knowledge.

Lemmy gave the fence an extra hard boot. Unlike me, he was wearing orthopedic-heavy shoes and socks, even though it is supposed to be summer. I reckon to myself that he wears them for extra protection. Getting home without being bashed up can sometimes be difficult.

The fence rattles in complaint.

'My father was almost an All Black,' I say, 'and my mother played basketball for Southland and. . .' It was like a catechism stretching back into my childhood.

'*Misses* Stephenson and Caughey!' drifts across the grass. It was Mr Shitalot, suddenly catching us in his spray of acid. The other boys' laughter follows in a curtain. We both straighten up, whipped. 'If you can spare us the time from your hen party, perhaps you can get on *picking up rubbish.* Quicksmart!'

'Yessir,' I call back, then feel Lemmy look at me again like I am the planet Earth and he is deep inside a crater on the moon, so distant.

I follow Lemmy away from the swimming pool, losing Mr Shitalot and the boys. Lemmy doesn't say anything. We just walk on. Then we are alone, on a playing field down by the school creek, pitted and pitched with volcanic rocks. Lemmy lies back like a beauty queen, stretching himself out comfortably.

'We'll empty one of the bins for our rubbish,' he tells me and yawns elaborately. 'Shitalot's such a mental retard he'll never notice.' He yawns again.

*I don't say a word.*

I lie back too, slowly, and watch a radiating sphere grow around the sun. The sky is very white, stretched tight like a drum. A single bird, very high in the sky, changes its direction and flies away from the flock. In the far distance we can hear the occasional roar of Mr Shitalot on his way, as Lemmy says, to his first heart attack ('and hopefully his last').

'I'm going to leave New Zealand just as soon as I can,' I say in a tight voice. I am looking up at the sun and thinking how it looks like a giant diamond. I glance at Lemmy, who seems ruby-purple, streaked with orange flares of light. I can't see him but I speak. 'I'm going to be a famous dress designer in Paris.' I tell him what I've told no other. 'I'm already doing designs after school for my first collection.'

Lemmy doesn't say a word.

'*Who wants to be a millionaire?*' I sing falsetto. '*I DO!*'

Lemmy lets out a croak.

In the distance Mr Shitalot's voice reaches a pitch of intensity approximating insanity.

'Do you know Archie Bumstead?' Lemmy says suddenly.

Before my eyes I see us all in the changing sheds, struggling out of our clothes, trying not to reveal ourselves. It is cold and wet. And there, on the far side of the shed, is Archie, standing completely naked, no towel, nothing; displaying for us all to see his thick long penis softly embedded in a luxurious nest of black pubic hair. Archie Bumstead, who

40

spent all his science lessons drawing pictures of bums, making them into a kind of targetboard, with circles moving concentrically inwards. I gulped. My throat is dry. The sky suddenly races with stars.

'Why?' I ask, trying to blank the screen out. It frightens me. I know it is wrong, very wrong. 'He's horrible.'

'He lives down the road from me.'

Silence.

'What,' I say very faintly, 'Lemmy, what are you going to do when you . . .'

'Grow up?' he offers darkly.

I flush scarlet. Lemmy is now sitting up. He has a stone in his hand and he throws it, sharply, at a cow which freezes, turns a startled eye on him then shambles away. The other animals awkwardly follow.

'Yes but,' I hurry on, 'what are you going to do when you leave school?'

Lemmy looks at me, surprised. He leaves a long pause in which we both stare at the flat horizon of small houses all crouched down under the sky, as if it is crushing them with its invisible weight. From over by the pool comes a frantic tugging whistle, frayed by the wind, flittering the sound apart till it fades, an echo inside its own emptiness.

'Nothing,' he says, as if it is a matter concluded long ago. 'Nothing,' he repeats in a lighter voice as he gets up and I struggle to follow him.

'Hey Jamie,' he says to me suddenly. It's the first time he's called me by my Christian name. I hum with pride, with happiness. All five foot 10 of me follows along happily behind his four foot nothing, tailing his every step. 'Hey, do you want to go into town this Friday night?'

'I can't,' I say automatically.

'Why not?'

'I'm not allowed.'

'*Ask.*'

I look at Lemmy and Lemmy looks at me.

'OK,' I say. 'I'll ask.'

Lemmy doesn't smile. But he suddenly yells out, like I told you he did, 'Let's GO!' and he smacks his hands together so hard a startled flock of sparrows lift up, zigzag in panic and speckle through the heavens. I laugh and laugh like something in me is broke and I say, 'That's right, eh, Lemmy? That's *right*.'

*'Ever since we met you had a hold on me.'*

When we walked into the sunroom, they could see it all over my face.

I could see AuntyJoy, UncleBill, MumnDad just stop everything they'd been doing up till that time and freeze in their armchairs, the only living thing in the room the smoke twirling out the end of their cigarettes and the little beads, inside their glasses of beer, racing to the surface. It was like time had stopped and they all just stared into my face together with one set of eyes and then I saw all their eyes – the *eyes* inside–turn to look at Lemmy.

'This . . . this is Lemmy,' I said to UncleBillAuntyJoy-MumDad.

Dad and UncleBill expect Lemmy to come into the room, to shake them by the hand. But Lemmy doesn't move. He doesn't even come into the room. He stands by the door. By me.

AuntyJoy, who is six foot three (UncleBill, five four), uncrosses her long legs and places her stilettos on the carpet as if for support. She taps the ash off the end of her cigarette and says to Lemmy, friendly-like, 'Hello Lenny, love.' I feel Mum wince at AuntyJoy's lower-class speech.

'It's Le-*mm*-y,' AuntyJoy,' I say in a low voice so the others can't hear. 'Not Lenny.

AuntyJoy pulls one of her 'Aren't I a mug' faces, rolling her eyes up to the smoky ceiling when Dad cuts through.

'That's a *funny* name. A very *funny* name.' You can tell he doesn't think it's funny.

UncleBill doesn't say a word. He doesn't need to. I can see by the way he's straining to look at Lemmy, he doesn't think he's exactly *normal*.

I turn to Lemmy and suddenly I see him as they might. To me, all night, he's very smart in his cut-down secondhand double-breasted herringbone tweed jacket and leather gloves. The powder on his face is barely discernible. His eyes darkly glitter. But to MumDadUncleBillAuntyJoy, to whom English *Vogue*'s Winter Styles are all still a mystery, Lemmy is danger.

I can see their eyes change suddenly and they're all looking at one another, quickly, darting some foreign intelligence between themselves like a bird which leaps and bows and stabs its bright bloody beak into the watery pools of all their eyes and suddenly the birds start to fly at me.

But I know like Lemmy now. I know how to make my eyes, my heart, into an iron plate where the birds can't go. I have learnt how to play a part.

I turn away and playing my new part which Lemmy taught me tonight I pretend to be the same person Jamie I was - and because I look like the same person I was up until I changed, *they believe it*.

I turn around and pretending to still be Jamie-the-good-boy I call out, 'I'll take Lemmy into my room and show him my records. Then I'll make you a cup of instant if you like.' And I look at Lemmy and Lemmy looks at me as I hear Mum say, 'That's a good boy, Jamie,' and we go into my room and shut the door tight before we break down into helpless crazy laughter because the play has begun.

### *'Cos you started something'*

This is what happened.

I met Lemmy outside the Civic and he was there already waiting. I saw him standing there, smoking a cigarette, watching intently in the way only Lemmy can watch. It's like he's searching for someone in the crowd. He suddenly saw me and looked a bit taken aback, *don't laugh Lemmy*. His eyes swept down to my new chiseltoes, up to Dad's corduroys I had altered to fit, to my school jacket I'd dyed brown last Sunday, to my hair which I'd washed, brushed one way, then brushed the other, to get the curl out. He threw his cigarette away then, as if he'd have to make the best of a bad job.

I was trying hard not to show him it was the first time I'd ever been into town on my own at night, and it was *Fridaynight*, you could feel it in the air, all the excitement and rush. It was like being near the top of a huge waterfall, maybe Niagara, and the river's rushing and you can hear the distant roar and suddenly it's all gushing so quick you can't stop moving, you're being swept along in the boygirl crowds past all the Hell's Angels lined up in leather, candypink bulbs flashing, oh flashflashing like my heart.

Lemmy led me, Lemmy led me out into the middle of Queen Street, right into the streaming traffic, where we stand, *together*, dodging death with the cars streaming by, red rinses flashing in my eyes. *Downtown downtown* I sing to myself in a fierce subdued whisper. Lemmy sings *I'm a mod, I'm a mod*. And I realise then, in this pure and crystal moment, as if everything around me has stopped, all traffic, all noise, and in this moment of perfect silence I realise I am thinking: I can be killed with Lemmy and *it would be perfect*. This knowledge is so overpowering that, when Lemmy lurches off after a car breaks open a gap, I don't hesitate to follow. I don't even look. Horns scream, brakes screech, a car skids, someone even calls out: 'Stupid kid! Why don't you look where you're going?'

But I know where I am going.

'I feel hungry,' Lemmy says, not even looking at me, not even noticing that, with crossing the road, at that moment, I have changed all my life. 'I wanna eat, honey.' Lemmy often talks American, all whiny and bored. We have both agreed Lucy is OK. It's like Liz Taylor is OK: Doris Day is death. Norma Holyoake is a signpost pointing to hell.

'But I don't have the money,' I say, feeling suddenly into my pocket to find the thick disc, a half-crown I have lifted from my father's tobacco-smelly trouser pocket.

Lemmy says, 'Money? Who needs money?'

And now we move into John Courts, past the glacial mirrors and make-up stands where the assistants' faces are echoed in mirrors so many times that it's only when a red mouth opens out, like a pink flower, into a yawn, you realise it's a person you're looking at, not a dummy.

'*Fourth floor* ladies' lingerie, *fifth floor* manchester doilies draperies linen supplies, *sixth floor* furniture lamps carpets annnnnnDDDD resttTTT-O-Rant!' a little dwarf chants as he flings back the metal door, like he's opening the gates to heaven itself.

Lemmy selects a cottage pie, a sausage roll, two ham and mustard sandwiches, a cream doughnut, a rum ball, a chocolate milkshake and a lemon pudding. There's hardly any room on his tray for his cup of coffee. His face shows no expression. He's too busy choosing a good table for us.

After we have gorged, Lemmy points out his favourite waitress to me. She's so old that her back is bent as if from the weight of carrying so many trays of dirty dishes out to the back kitchen. Her hair is dyed this really improbable fiery ginger, and her face is like those theatre curtains at the St James, a cascading concertina of folds, tucks, bulges and creases. The real point about her is that, aged approximately a thousand, she is keeping up with modern fashion by wearing a mini-skirt. She has hand-altered the hem of her smock to raise it. And her wobbly old legs with heavy kneecaps look obscenely bent, naked. Lemmy calls her the Duchess of Windsor.

As she walks by, Lemmy very carefully flicks a whole spoon of sugar onto the lino. When she walks back again, we're both looking down, eating very seriously, swallowing our crazy laughter. But we hear the Duchess's footsteps all crunchy. She looks around a little surprised, then, as she passes again, *spray*, another spoon, all over the floor.

Lemmy does this for quite a while, till everyone going by our table has to crunch past, like Fijians on broken glass.

Suddenly the Duchess comes over, very quick. She bends down frighteningly close.

'Why are you boys doing that?' she says, and the surprising thing is she isn't angry: it's just like she's trying to work us out. This is far worse than if she had been angry. I feel a terrible shame as I look at her close up. Now this is strange: Lemmy doesn't say a word. I look at him quickly, imploring him to help. But his face is stone, no expression: *nothing*. Except this slow flush creeping up his neck, over his chin, up his cheeks.

'I'm sorry,' I say. Then: 'It wasn't us. Truly.'

She looks right into me with her thousand-year-old eyes, the pupils faintly ringed with white. She is wearing false eyelashes.

'It's me that has to sweep it up,' she says then, and we both turn to look at the mess sprayed all across the floor.

'It wasn't us,' I lie with a sinking sense of humiliation so that my face, the sweat on my forehead, everything about me is telling her the truth. She just looks at my lie for long enough for me to look at it too, and wonder why something which had seemed so funny doesn't appear to be now.

She lets out a very long low sigh, as if now, suddenly, she realises there is no hope. She's exhausted by us, the sugar on the floor, the people at the tables, the dishes out the back: everything.

She leaves our bill behind.

There's a slight pause now. I am uncertain. Lemmy's eyes scale across my face: he hates me, I can tell.

He suddenly gets up, as if he doesn't know me any more. He turns his back and, going straight towards the queue, ignores me, as if he's never seen me in his life before. 'But Lemmy,' I say out loud, because I want to say, I haven't got enough money to pay. I'm holding the bill in my hand. It is three pounds 17 shillings and eightpence.

But Lemmy will not turn around.

Other people in the queue turn to look at me, because the tone of my voice is so plangent, like a guitar chord echoing off-key. They look into my face. I break into a coughing fit, to disguise what I was going to say. Lemmy never turns round for one second. He does not know me any longer.

We inch forward. It's like the Berlin Wall here: you get to a window with a small hole in it behind which sits Madame

Commandante, uniform a black shiny dress, a marcasite watch, swinging earrings. Madame Commandante examines your bill, stares into your face hard and intense, then she relents and punches on the till, the drawer shoots back like a gun going off in your face, and you pay for the privilege of being set free from her stare. She always seems furious for some reason - perhaps spending most of her life in a glass box.

Lemmy has magically joined himself onto a flustered-looking young mother with three kids, all of whom are whining about what they got to eat. The oldest wanted a banana milkshake and got a glass of milk, the youngest says she wants to be sick. The mother's begging her to wait. Lemmy's just standing by them looking bored and cross, like you might expect someone that age trapped with a public embarrassment like that.

I watch as they get to the Berlin Wall. The mother is so harassed that she spills her money onto the floor. The youngest girl, who's going to be sick, runs through, heading straight towards the china department - Royal Doulton section. The mother pays desperately, grabs her change, sets off after the little girl, and Lemmy moves with them, amoeba-like, for a moment, till he dissolves away among the china stands.

Now he looks back at me, eyes glinting, the other side of the Berlin Wall. *He waits for me, he waits for me.*

I know now what to do.

As if in a dream, I quietly meld with an elderly couple having a treat by coming into town on a Friday night ('then we had a light supper at John Courts'). They turn towards me, glance at me, and the old man, who has a pink face so clean it looks like it gets Janola-ed every morning, smiles at me from behind his glasses as if he might know me. I go bright red but I don't say anything, I am so tense with excitement because now I know what I must do: I must act as Jamie the good boy. This will be my protection. I smile back at him and he and his wife exchange a look which says 'and there's a nicely brought up boy'. I realise, with a harsh laugh echoing inside me, yes Jamie-the-good-boy has his uses.

Quietly, silently, smiling and bobbing my head, looking at this elderly couple covered in camel-hair, stinking of Remuera, I act

like I'm their boarding school son and as they pay I move
effortlessly through with them. They turn, a little startled to find
me still with them, and I flash them one final special smile and I
thrill as I see them softly taken in, thinking: do we know that boy,
perhaps he's the son of . . . ?

Then I see their faces change. They are looking at my
clothes. I quickly abandon them, and I find Lemmy by a
crockery stand. He smiles at me and says, '*How is the air up
there?*' and I say, '*Boo to you, I just don't care.*' And we laugh and I
think, *I only want to be with you.*

'*Being good isn't always easy.*'

After this Lemmy takes me into a shop and very carefully,
while the shopkeeper is attending to a customer, Lemmy slyly
picks up a packet of cigarettes and *quick*, up under his jacket it
goes, held gripped in his armpit. I goggle. Lemmy just looks
the same, sort of waiting impatiently when the shopkeeper
glances at him. Lemmy looks as always – *bored*. My heart bangs
away, I have never known such excitement. Then I realise
Lemmy is waiting for me to take some too. I can't stop myself.
I look at the shopkeeper then my hand of its own will moves
away from my body and I see it lift up a packet of Bold Gold
so sophisticated and smelling of swinginglondon and
twiggyandcarnabystreet and this gold bar attaches itself to me,
joins my flesh. It cuts in, hard.

Suddenly I get frightened. I think of what it might mean if
I'm caught; Jamie the good boy has to meet Jamie the bad
boy, everything would change. But already it is too late, I am
caught in the river again, whirling me along, too fast for me
to stop. I realise that now I am giddy with speed, *I can never
stop.*

The shopkeeper's face under fluorescents looks faintly sick,
with great big pools and bags under his eyes (overhead lighting
is no good, I memorise, practical as always, grabbing at details

– as if they'll save me). But it is like snatching at dry leaves as I whirl by, spinning aroundroundround, getting nearer and nearer the edge of the waterfall: the door.

'Oh *boys* ,' says the shopkeeper suddenly, moving round the counter. 'Hold on a minute.' But Lemmy keeps walking as if he can't hear, so I can't hear either, our ears are sealed over, till we hit the door, the dark, then we break into a run, joining our flesh onto the flash of speed we feel inside our veins. We run until we meld into boygirl.

I don't know what I've just done. I don't know what it means. I look down at Lemmy trying to work it all out. 'Here,' I say, and give him my cigarettes. But he already has his packet out and he's unconcernedly ripping aside the cellophane, as if it's so thin it just doesn't matter. The cellophane falls to the ground, blows away. I watch it and feel suddenly tired and sad. He pops open the top, offers me one. I look down at the cigarettes, then I look at him, then I look down at them.

'I don't smoke,' I say.

Lemmy just shrugs and lights up, and I watch him and he doesn't look at me. We move back under the pink flashing lights, swim through the river of looks, and I think how different we are now; my life has so suddenly changed and it's because of Lemmy. When we're on the other side, in the warm dark, I say, 'Oh Lemmy,' very casual-like, 'could I borrow a cigarette. Would you mind?'

Lemmy squares his herringbone tweed shoulders (as seen in English *Vogue*) and he shakes out a cigarette and offers it to me and I feel this shivery feeling all over me, right down to the bottom of my socks. I can feel the sweat pricking and I feel suddenly – oh – I'm being washed, showered all over with silver and I take the cigarette and Lemmy leans forward and lights it looking into my eyes quite curiously and the cigarette catches fire and I say, 'Thank you Lemmy. Thank you.'

So it happens Lemmynme are always together, fatboyandbeanpole; people see us so often, they forget even to laugh.

We walk home from school together, then when we get home we rush to the phone and talk to each other *for hours*: we talk about hairstyles, fashions, what's on TV, film stars; our parents, their friends. *This is important.*

We go to the pictures a lot. I mean what else is there to do in Auckland except sit in the dark and imagine living some place else? One night at the St James the film wasn't any good, it wasn't even funny; but Lemmy doesn't let that spoil his enjoyment in the sweet jaffa dark with the men and girls all glued together flesh touch-touching.

Lemmy sits there looking all around at them, then is silent. Then he starts laughing. He starts off very low and casual, like he's the only person in the audience who *really* gets the joke, and the couples aren't noticing under the wall of wash which flickers silver shade all over us. But Lemmy wants to let out his laugh so he laughs some more, even at things which aren't funny.

I start laughing too. We laugh in the dark like our laughs are coming from somewhere else, some other part of the plastery ornate theatre. Lemmy starts laughing more and more, like he can't control it and he's watching the funniest thing in the world.

And suddenly it *is* funny because up there on the big dream wall are all these stupid film stars acting and carrying on, opening car doors and looking at each other and patting their hairdos and *they* can't see the joke: they're locked out.

Now Lemmy in the plush lush dark has all the couples coming unglued. Lips leave lips as the air all around us fills with Lemmy's uncontrollable laughter, backed up, bit by bit, seat after seat, row by row, by other people who start off laughing *at* Lemmy's laugh but before long in the tight night everyone is laughing, the whole place is going mad, a sad man along from us sitting alone is laughing so hard he's in pain, he's crying and he's laughing and he's pleading *please, stop, please, stop* and the back doors have swung open as the usherettes swarm in, their torches strobing the dark, and Lemmy stops laughing, he just cuts it off with a razor, he nudges me sharp in the ribs and whispers Petesinclair, *Let's GO!*

His voice is so urgent that I cut off my own laughter and we run out of the dark, push open the back doors and leave all these people sitting in the dark laughing so hard some of them are crying. And the wonderful thing is: not one of them knows *they* are the joke.


'*I must go where my destiny leads me.*'


Lemmynme go straight down to 246's record bar and, feeling so good, shoplift two 45s, (me, Shirley Bassey's '*I Who Have Nothing*'; Lemmy, Julie Driscoll's '*Light My Fire*' ), except we say we 'bought', not 'shoplifted' because, you know, if you change the words, the meaning changes too, don't you feel?

Anyway we're standing down at Lemmy's bus-stop, I'm spending every last second with him, Lemmy's trying to get me to come out to his place to have some instant and listen to our new records. But I'm saying to Lemmy, I can't, I have to be home by 11 o'clock at the latest. Lemmy says it's only 9.30 now, he'll drive me home. But you don't have a licence, I say. So? he says.

But while Lemmy is persuading me and I'm hanging round, lingering still in the stardust of his glance, I can't help notice Lemmy is looking at this ugly man, about 30, short, muscular, drunk. He is so ugly, chills frill and flitter up and down my spine; I feel my back arch.

But Lemmy, he is so excited about what happened at the St James, he's not thinking. He keeps just looking at this man. *Lemmy*, I say, *Lemmy!* but he doesn't say anything, he just keeps looking so hard the man sort of wakes up; he lifts his head up from looking into a deep tunnel-pit in which all he can see is himself standing alone, at a bus-stop, on a girlboy Fridaynight.

And he suddenly starts looking at Lemmynme and of course he doesn't know we're the two who started everyone laughing at the St James and it's like he's confused about what he's seeing: because we are not boygirl but boyboy. Worse, he looks at us as if all he can see is a short fatboy four foot nothing and an Audrey Hepburn kind of boy.

Lemmy is already laughing at him. I laugh too, but I begin to regret wearing the waistcoat from my father's evening suit, my tasteful pale grey paisley tie, silver watch chain.

I get on Lemmy's bus; we are together. The man comes right down and sits opposite us. As the bus moves his legs bump into mine. I shift mine away, as if I'm burnt.

The bus is full. I don't even dare look at Lemmy but I see in the window Lemmy is looking ahead just blank and like he can't even be bothered registering what's going on.

'Well, suppose we share the joke then?' this man suddenly says right in my face. His breath is warm, beer-bloaty. His eyes burrow into my face.

I could just die. I dart a look at Lemmy but suddenly Lemmy's acting like he's not with me, he doesn't even know me. *Don't leave me on my own Lemmy* I cry but Lemmy does not move, even when the man says again, in a loud voice, so the whole bus can hear: '*What's the fucking joke then?*'

My eyes pass over his face, very quickly, a fantail dart, then I quickly shoot them away because I know I can never speak. Everyone on the bus is looking at us now, a few people are laughing. I hear someone call us an ugly name, a word which hurts.

At the end of the following century, Lemmy's arm, almost of its own accord, rises up to the cord, pulls it sharp. People are laughing at us, pointing at what we are wearing, but I say nothing. In silence now, under everyone's gaze, we get off the bus and it pulls away.

We walk along in the dark, silent.

I can't understand Lemmy not saying anything. I wait for him to speak, explain. But Lemmy does not speak.

## 'Half heaven, half heartache'

Not long after this Lemmy's father went up north to look at some land he had. Lemmy's father always had these bright schemes for making money and as time went on we just sat back waiting for them to turn to dust.

That day Mrs Wilson came along. Lemmy had told me about Mrs Wilson and how she was Lemmy's father's *special friend*. Lemmy had nothing against her personally, he just hated her. And Lemmy always had this way of honing in. He picked on one little thing and you might have noticed it and thought nothing of it but by the time Lemmy was finished that one thing was all you could see and the person in question was a hostage to this one detail.

So with Mrs Wilson all Lemmy said to me, deadpan, was: 'Neat the way she goes to so much trouble to dye her roots black, eh?' And sure enough, if you looked really closely – and Lemmy had this way of looking at everything from a great distance, through a telescope, so all the pores and dents came up in ultra close-up – you suddenly noticed in a very embarrassing way that Mrs Wilson's hair, which at first glance appeared very 'naturally blonde', actually had this thin black line peeping out, under the thatch, looking at you, staring you in the face.

Miss Clairol 1932 is what Lemmy called her. Often he'd say it in her presence, but vague, like it was a riddle, as he looked between Mr Stephenson and Miss Clairol: 'Now which twin wears the Toni?'

No wonder Mrs Wilson looked a little edgy every time Lemmy came close to her, and gazed right through her. She'd flush this very old faded pink and look at Lemmy's father, as if she *understood*.

Anyway, there we were, all four of us in Lemmy's father's rundown old Vauxhall, bright blue and blowsy, heading away from all this, up past all the caravans with the fridges sitting on a square of carpet, the sea fighting to get through all the lines of washing. I had a special costume on that day, 'suitable for those unexpected alfresco invitations to dine outdoors' (*Vogue*).

Where was Lemmy's mother, you ask? I asked myself that, but I knew more than to say it out loud.

I'd only ever seen her once, that night after the St James, when she came into the kitchen while we were heating up the jug for coffee. She was very short, like Lemmy, but dark and brooding like she carried this storm along with her, and when she saw some crumbs on the floor, she just fell on them, letting out this cry, like she was *killed* by them. I looked at Lemmy quick, I didn't know what to do. I was standing up ready to say Howdoyoudo, like you do to people's mothers, but Lemmy's mother hadn't heard of that game, I could tell. Lemmy just said, speaking to her slowly, 'Mum, this is Jamie, he's from school.'

It was like they were speaking code. Then her eyes, *Lemmy's eyes*, turned and focused on me and looked all over me, from my shoes up to my hair. I got very embarrassed and the words howdoyoudo suddenly seemed very stupid.

She looked embarrassed too and almost ashamed. ''ello,' she said in a small hurried voice. Then she was gone. It was as if she was hot on the trail of more crumbs. For once Lemmy didn't say anything to me and I knew not to say anything to him. Later on, just when I was about to catch the bus home, I said it was nice to meet your mother. Lemmy looked away. I said, 'She's not from here, is she? And he said, covering it over quick, because it is a flaw, a blemish, a terrible thing not to be like we all are, born here: 'No, Dad met her in the war. She's from Italy.' 'Italy?' I say and feel sorry for Lemmy. And he says as if he just wishes I'd stop talking about it, 'Hey, do you want to see my postcards I found at the tip of Mamie Van Doren? She's got the cutest colour hairdo.' And I say yes. After that we never talk about it ever again. It's what Lemmy wants.

As we left the houses behind, Lemmynme scrunched down as far as we could in the back seat so we didn't have to look out the windows at all that boring scenery of hills and sea and stuff. We compared favourite TV programmes ('The Avengers' versus 'Get Smart', no competition) and in between, when we got bored, we just sang, me doing Dusty's bits while Lemmy did the back-up chorus.

Every so often Lemmy's dad would turn around and say to us in this really peeved voice, like he didn't like what he was hearing, 'Will you boys shut up for a minute? I want to catch the 2.45 at Avondale.' He'd start trying to dial up the races on the conked-out old car radio that he was so proud of. Lemmynme'd sit there trying not to burst out laughing, thinking what hopeless horse he'd backed now and how far back down the track it'd be and if it'd reach the glue factory by the time we reached Warkworth.

Miss Clairol 1932 sat beside him, looking straight ahead. She was acting out the bit in the Sunday movies where the heroine, *the love interest* (another Lemmy term for her), sees the problem, can't do anything about it but *understands*. So that we had an excuse to let out our laugh Lemmy did the Chicks' instant pudding ad, crowing out, Whisk Up A Treat! Just the thought of them two in their boots and sprayed hair and everything was enough to crack us up.

'*Lemmy*,' Lemmy's dad'd say, as he tried to get the races and only got this scratchy scrawling static sound instead, '*I'm warning you boy*. I'm only giving you one warning.'

Lemmy's answer was to give the back of the love interest's seat one hard vicious kick, *but as if by accident*. We'd watch this red flush creep up the back of her neck but for Lemmy's father's sake she pretended nothing was happening, she *understood*. That sent us off deeper into laughter and Lemmy only had to mention the word *chook* and we just about wept at the ugliness of everything outside the window as we went through all those one-horse towns which get the movies even after we do in Auckland, most of them with not even a dairy open or anything, and only a spare mongoloid swinging on a farm gate.

'This is not Carnaby Street,' I whisper to Lemmy as we pull into this dirt patch covered in thistle, toitoi and gorse. Mr Stephenson, a socialist, can only see gold: all it needed was a change of government, he said, and the industrial project across the harbour would leap ahead. Mr Stephenson was always full of pipedreams, like working in a socialist bookshop where everybody shares the profits. Translated, this means, he ends up selling sex books out of a dairy in a busy no-name street. Everyone knows it's no use having dreams in this dump.

Well, Lemmynme wouldn't get out, we just sat in the car eating a whole packet of spearmints followed by caramels, feet up on the back of the front seat while Mr Stephenson and the love interest walked all over the dirt patch, first of all vaguely, then from side to side, as if by walking around it they were getting closer to *feeling* its true value.

In the end the love interest and the eyebag went away together and had a cigarette and talked quietly. Then the eyebag came back and pulled open the car door and let in all this cold air and asked, Why didn't we get out and stretch our legs?

Lemmy said we didn't want to; we were listening to the Top Twenty.

The eyebag said we could listen to the Top Twenty any time.

'Not Dusty, we can't,' says Lemmy then, sharp and intense.

I nod.

Mr Stephenson looks from Lemmy to me, from me to Lemmy and back again. It's like he's never seen boys like us before, like we're a new invention or something. I pick imaginary lint off my knobbly tweed trousers.

He lets out this breath which goes on for a long time, as if it's coming from a long time back, maybe from when he first met Mrs Stephenson in Italy, when she was a laughing dark-eyed beauty, sort of a pint-sized Sophia Loren maybe: before Lemmy had even been invented.

Now the eyebag is looking straight at me. I am embarrassed, I suddenly feel naked.

'I've been listening to you two all the way up,' he says then, leaning right into the car so I am embarrassed by his personal odour – I mean, *hasn't he heard of Old Spice*? 'I've been listening to you two, and all the time you two boys have been going on about how nothing – *nothing in New Zealand* – is good enough for you two. *Everything's a joke!*' He is lost for words. He gestures towards the blue peeling sky, the clouds, the hillscape. 'Isn't there anything you boys like?'

Silence.

I look just beyond Mr Stephenson's right shoulder, concentrating on space. Lemmy has taught me this trick. It helps you to appear very blank.

'You boys are in for a real shock when you grow up,' he says then, in a voice which has no anger in it, only a vague undertow of sadness mingled with bitterness.

Lemmynme sneak a look at each other, then, in simultaneous action, like the Chicks, raise our eyes up to the car roof.

After Lemmy's dad takes his eyebags away, I let out a long sigh. *I mean*, what does he mean? A shock? What exactly does he think this place is?


*'In the middle of nowhere'*


'*Why bother?*' Lemmy takes up his favourite theme, rolling over onto his back, looking up at the sky.

We're at school and it's a warmwool day, this day, the clouds are all light puffs running across the sky, chasing themselves. Even the earth is breathing. I rub my body into the grass and don't say anything. A worm slithers succulently round a blade of grass, its rings all concertina-ing in as it disappears. I am hot, sweating.

'*Dontyouevenknowyourleftfromyourright*' comes out in one long screamed sentence.

We're lying on a grass bank low enough for nobody to see us.

Lemmy has got me out of military service by getting me into the medical unit where all we do is wind bandages and smoke cigarettes as, natch, there are no casualties (unless you count, as Lemmy says straight-faced, everyone out there on the field).

I hear Lemmy let out this hollow laugh. 'Which twin wears the Toni?' he murmurs. Lemmy and I are only at school because I've persuaded him we have to turn up sometimes. We write each other's exeat notes about once a week now, go off on daytrips, things like that. Last week we took the train up to Wellsford, this hell-hole tinpot town at the end of the line. Lemmy shoplifted up one side of the street while I did the other. It was a competition to see who got the most. I did, by one can of hairspray. We only take important things like deodorants, hairsprays, cigarettes, bath perfumes: *things that'll come in useful*. On the way back we sort of went mad and sprayed each other with the shaving foam and perfume and everything then threw it all out the windows. It was fun.

'*Why?*' says Lemmy, his voice almost dramatic. Because things are changing in our lives now. Things are getting different.

This is what has happened.

I told you how I was the fastest boy in all the fourth form. This is not a small thing, at this school. It sort of protected me, being an Audrey Hepburn kind of boy, from being bashed up. But things went really wrong when I fell out of favour with our French teacher.

It was after the word went round that Freckles'll bum you for free, and some boys said that made him into a homo, and then everyone argued because, up till that time, nobody had connected bumming, which was just boys having fun with each other's bums, with being a homo. That connection had not been made. But someone in our class said the connection was there, pure and simple, and it was wrong.

I can remember this moment, very clearly.

We were all standing outside the gym, waiting for Shitalot to start his performance; he was late for some reason. It was a cool day, it was about to rain. And the word rippled up and down the line we were in, about Freckles Friggs being a homo. And our

French class was next. And Ken Johnston, in front of everyone, asked me if I was a homo. I said *No!* because of course I am not. But it frightened me, because I am still not sure what being a homo *means*, apart from being in *Truth* and having to commit suicide in the bath with blood running everywhere in ribbons from your wrists so someone you love finds you and is haunted for life.

I am confused, really confused. I mean, I feel this sort of hot uncontrollable feeling overtake me at the sight of the hairylegs, hairychests – *hair anywhere* – it just makes me feel I can't hardly breathe at all, yet suddenly my whole body's breathing for me, it's like my whole fleshy form is just this one big breath shimmering soundlessly, almost crying with the want of it, the fear of it. I just don't understand.

I even look at a library in town covered with virginia creeper and when the leaves fall off I sort of look at the way all the whiskery veins connect and feel their hairy tendrils out from a central knobbly root and this strikes me dumb because it's so like that little tickle, tiny twists of hair, lying softly against eachother as they weave themselves a rope-ladder up over that long taut muscle all the sports boys have, at the back of their thighs: I keep seeing the hairs riding up, climbing up under the black serge, at the very back of their shorts.

*Yet. Yet.* When I found I had hair *down there*, I did the strangest thing, I can't even explain it to myself, except I had to do it, I was driven to it (this is what I mean by wrong but *necessary*). I got home early from school, went into the bathroom and got Dad's razor and, alone in the white room, sun shining in the opaque window, I lathered up some soap and pulled my trousers down. I looked down at that thing, sitting there, all very carefully snuggled up, innocent . . . and carefully, very carefully, I razored all the hair away. Then I carefully washed out Dad's razor. *This is the truth.* I don't want it to happen to me. I don't.

Our French teacher, Freckles Frigg, is a small wrinkled man who, Lemmy pointed out to me, likes to get the boys lined up writing on the blackboard then he walks up and down with a ruler, whacking it smackily on his palm while he looks with glistening eye at the boys' rumps. He gives free French lessons to promising pupils, *at home*. They even get to stay the weekend.

And he liked me because, as he said, I wasn't rough like the other boys. I had a nice soft voice.

Normally at French I sat down the front, being almost his pet. But this time, as we came in, I ran down the back, me with my shaved *downthere*, being called a homo, I ran down the back, just *dying*, and when Freckles asked me, of all the boys who were cowering down the very end of the class, rubbing their hands all over their legs and in between them, breathless with excitement, with the thought of the danger of it, why I wasn't sitting up the front as usual, I said I just wouldn't ever sit up the front again, not me. I would just die if I had to.

It somehow didn't matter too much about being the best runner in the whole fourth form after that.

Each time in French, Freckles got me to read out loud and my voice would falter and the boys would laugh and then Freckles would say, Listen boys to how *soft* Caughey's voice is and suddenly, as if for the first time, everyone heard how *soft* my voice was and now everyone wanted to hear my voice, as if it had never been heard before, and each time I spoke they would scream and laugh and imitate it as if it was the funniest thing in the world. I began to realise I could never raise my voice again.

Lemmy was the only person I could talk with, after that.

'So why bother?' says Lemmy now, lying on his back, blowing a cigarette ring while, out in the sun, all the casualties carrying heavy rifles around on their shoulders get yelled at.

I know what he's talking about. Because Alan Blender, the biggest boy in our class, has come to me and asked me - rather, told me, as if it was a big favour - that I was going to be allowed to be the last runner in the fourth form relay at the end-of-year school sports. I could represent our class. What it really meant was, if they were lagging behind in the other three parts, they could rely on my speed to get them out of trouble. 'Being so fast. Eh, Caugheyboy,' says Alan Blender as he runs his hand up my back, then punches me companionably.

'Why bother even turning up?' Lemmy says this in a voice which has so little emphasis in it I suddenly realise how easy it might be, *not* to turn up. It's as if it doesn't mean anything at all, any more.

I lie there, not touching Lemmy: *we never touch.* I think about it all and as I think about it I just start laughing. This laugh sort of forces its way up my chest, like a big bubble of air coming up from the deep ocean floor, it rises upwards towards the surface and it pops.

'But where'll we go?' I say tentatively, not letting Lemmy know I've suddenly crossed that bridge too, almost too quickly, I'm in such a hurry to get away from Blender and Johnston and all their voices always asking to hear my voice so they can laugh. Yet now they seem as far away – no, *further* – than their voices carrying in the slight soft wind.

Down below Ajax Murphy is being wrapped in bandages then dipped slowly into the school creek. We do not listen to his muffled screams.

'Go?' says Lemmy, as if there is a question. He looks me in the eyes. 'Why don't we just stick around and watch the fun develop?'

We both laugh then, as if gasping for air, we really need the air to breathe, but suddenly it's as if we're laughing so hard we can't get the air into our bodies.

It didn't matter even being bashed up after that. I decided then if I was going to be hated I might as well give them something to hate me for. And it was worth it for that moment, sitting beside Lemmy up in the back of the school grandstand, watching them run that race and get to where I was meant to be: and I just wasn't there. I thought to myself: I'll never be there again. I'll be with Lemmy. And I was glad.

*'Now I need a place to hide away.'*

After this Lemmynme really started not turning up at school, it was like this sickness got into us and we wanted to just keep moving to get rid of it, keep walking and talking and not doing very much at all. It was then Lemmy used to take me into toilets and we would read everything on the walls and I started to learn one or two things. We would shoplift and maybe sit on the beach and smoke cigarettes and talk about what we might do in the future. Lemmy thought he might go to Swinging London. I wasn't sure.

There were all sorts of parts of Auckland being demolished at that time for the motorway and we spent days just sitting inside these very old houses, sometimes smashing them up and laughing, other times just talking about film stars and sex and things. But while we didn't talk about it too much, ticking behind all this, like a huge bomb about to go off, was School Cert, its sound growing louder and louder the more we chose not to listen to it. Because Lemmy had already told me, he wasn't going to sit it. And when he said that he just looked at me and went silent, like he was waiting for me to speak.

*'He's no rebel to me'*

'Why?' I say. '*Why* ?'
'Because Dad doesn't like him.'
'Why not?' I say very quiet.
'Because,' says Mum, and she's floundering suddenly, switching her eyes away from my face which is searching hers for clues, for knowledge. '*Because*,' she says finally, like it's been decided between the two of them, 'because he's not a good influence.'
Mum and I are standing in the front room, that is how important it is. Out our front window you can see the reef, the

dump, the city, then, behind it all, rising like a green-black moon, Rangitoto.

A trolley whistles down the road. First of all an eerie sound, almost a presentiment: then the bus, the pub bus, full of men drunk enough to come home cheerful, till they open the screendoor. Mum and I watch little lights and fires fight and flare at the end of the trolley poles, like birds trying to escape as they are dragged along. Dad is on that bus. Dad, the disappointed almost All Black.

'Mum, he's not a bad influence,' I say softly. 'He's just not.'

'No James,' says Mum in this sort of firm voice which says it is going to be law and it hurts her but it has to be. 'Lemmy's a bad influence on you and we' – *we*, I thought, I've never heard that before – 'we don't want you to see him.'

'But he's my *friend*, Mum.'

'You've got other friends.'

I think of them. Alan. Kevin. Lionel. They all faded away into complete nothingness when I got to know Lemmy. Besides, Lemmy doesn't like me having other friends. He gets *critical*.

'But Lemmy's my *special friend*, Mum,' I say looking at her, not moving, after a pause. We can hear Dad's footsteps up the side of the house, the special, almost blind, bang of the flyscreen as it closes behind him.

'That's what we don't like. We don't, James. We don't think he's having a good influence on you.'

But I'd die without Lemmy, Mum, I want to say. I'd die.

*There isn't a mountain too high. There isn't a valley too deep.*

But I say nothing. Dad is home. The vegetables are overcooked.


*'Anyone who had a heart'*


'You mean there's not even a *dairy* down there?'

We are on the way out to Rangitoto Island. It is now three weeks two days, four hours before School Cert but Lemmy wants to go on a trip to an extinct volcano which sits out in the harbour, not a living soul on it. I know it is a challenge, I have to accept. *Test me.*

I am wearing an interesting outfit, 'suitable for country rambles': tweed trousers with a soft nubbly weave, a suede emerald-green jerkin, with a softly rolled polo neck, a small silver chain on my wrist. But the *coup de grace* is my new shoes.

I was so excited when I got these shoes I could hardly sleep. I kept waking up all through the night, thinking it was a dream I had them: then the sweet smell of soft leather and newness would greet me, I would reach out to touch them, just softly. The tissue paper would crinkle crisply, singing its song of 'justbought', while below, waiting to slip onto my feet, wings of happiness to uplift me, speed me along to all those places I dream of going to, chariots of dream: my new chiseltoe suede shoes.

Lemmy says nothing. He looks at me, eyes sceptically sweeping up and down my person, as if he can't believe he has to be seen out in public with me. He hunches over his cigarette, bitterly almost, as if he can hear the silence which is growing all around us, which comes from us not talking about School Cert: that is the thing we can never talk about, and suddenly it is as if we can't find anything else to talk about either. Fashion, movies, film stars: they have all fallen away from us as the boat leaves Auckland, and the city, the town, becomes a small toy behind us, just little buildings and cars growing smaller by the second. I wonder if I will be seasick. The waves glow green and silken.

Ahead lies Rangitoto, vast, still, uninhabited.

'I just can't believe it,' I murmur to myself. All I have brought along is a can of lacquer and an apple. 'It sounds so *uncivilised.*' I wonder secretly to myself what on earth we will do there. There is no shoplifting to do. No movies. Nothing, I think as I gaze at all the horrible green so uniform and dense and unchanging: a jungle.

Lemmy doesn't say anything: he is wearing jeans. I look at him and think of how I can entertain him: Lemmy is getting moody these days, it's like he's listening to that silence growing around us too much.

'I'm not supposed to be seeing you Lemmy,' I say then, as if he can see it's a joke, because I am with him. Lemmynme, forever together. Beanpole and fatboy.

'Why not?'

Lemmy says this flat, while his eyes run over and over the greendeadflatness of the volcano. It's like he's hardly even interested. I don't like Lemmy when he's like this. He frightens me a little. It's like he can't even see I'm on his side. It's like he sees *me* as the enemy.

'You're a bad influence,' I say to him, laughing mouthdry.

'Oh.'

It is like this has happened to Lemmy before. He turns a little away from me and I can see his face is a mask, shutting me out. I look beyond him to the wharf, over by a mangrove swamp. It is a grey day so pale that the sky is a hot iron sheet on the tops of our skulls, descending, the sun a blind orb, pupil covered over with a skim of skin. Stink humid.

I can feel my fashionable emerald-green jerkin cutting up under my armpits. It was my mother's, I have not cut it down properly to size. *But it looks good.* I have also powdered my face just faintly, so I look more *English.* Then a ghastly thing happens: my porkpie hat just lifts up off my head and flies out, onto the waves. And Lemmy *laughs.*

'*Lemmy!*' I cry, hurt. But then I have to laugh too, flushing a painful red which creeps up my skin from the inside sole of my foot, right inside my suede chiseltoes.

Other people, ordinary New Zealanders dressed in sensible shoes and walking boots, look at me like I am from outer space. They are interested in Lemmynme, *very.* They look at us like we're a sideshow. Normally Lemmnyme'd laugh right back at them, Lemmy picking and pointing out how the fat woman has a bra-strap just about bursting up on her shoulder, held by a safety pin; how her kid just missed being a mongoloid by a half-second. But today, *listening to the silence,* Lemmy just edges away from me.

I sit on the boat, grasping the thick peeled paint of the railing. I watch the crown of my hat bob away from me, moving further and further away: my heart somehow turns to lead, sinks, plummets. But I say nothing, my own laugh frozen on my lips.

There is no dairy. There is nothing but gnarled old trees like arthritic hands curled round and trying to pick up something. Even the tide is out: there is mud, pick-picking sounds and this ugly scoria of dried-up old explosion which hardly allows anything to grow on it. Already it is warmer. I wish I had a mirror to check my make-up. There is only the green water pleated into little waves, which withdraw, a soft sneer in every move.

Around us the families organise themselves into troops. The Dads give orders and lead them off.

'Rangitoto,' says one, wearing most *unfortunate* walking boots and reading from a pamphlet, 'was once a Maori burial ground, home to parrots, a look-out during war. It is particularly inhospitable, because of its lack of soil, absence of water, and harshness of scoria.'

Lemmy says to me: 'Let them take off. With a bit of luck we'll find them, half-fried to death in the interior.'

The father folds away the pamphlet and blows a metal whistle.

Lemmy watches them go: 'Hawkmeat,' he yells at them.

A lone kid cries as they blend into bilge green.

I can see Lemmy is thinking of what I have said to him about being a bad influence. He's not even seeing I see it's a joke. He is not looking at me. Or if he does, it's as if I have changed into a mirror which he doesn't want to look into. As if he no longer likes what he sees.

Oh Lemmy, I think. *Don't.*

We begin to walk off, following these ugly tracks sort of carved into petrified lava which convicts have been forced to make, under the lash, under the sun which beats down now as if it has never stopped. Suddenly it seems like the face of a too-hot iron, pushed right up close to you. I push my sleeves back, gently, so they won't wrinkle. Lemmy is walking too fast. I hurry to catch up. But the track is uneven: there are all these little snares and catches just to wrench at my chiseltoes. I look down: already a soft white-clay powder is dusting the ends of them.

'Don't go so fast,' I say to Lemmy, pleading even while I'm asking.

Lemmy doesn't answer. He doesn't slow down either.

I realise I'll just have to look down at my feet all the time, making sure my suede shoes aren't damaged. I can't look at the countryside, the 'views', anything. In fact, in front of me turns into this extremely long monotonous movie in which the only image is a clay-grey stretch of ground interrupted every so often with this stumpy semi-mongoloid piece of twig which looks about 3,000 years old and yet it's only grown two inches: it hates you for putting your foot onto it. In this movie, the front of my chiseltoes zigzag, hastily finding a smooth place to fall as I hurry to keep up with Lemmy.

Lemmy is wearing old sandshoes, so ugly.

'*What's the race?*' I call out.

'Lemmy!'

It is heating up as we climb, in fact it is quite steep. When I interrupt the most boring movie on Earth to glance around I see only an uninterrupted vista. The convict roads snake away into nothingness. There is nothing on this island, except a cone which rises up, seemingly the same from every side, which only makes it more of a nightmare. I mean: how do you know where you are?

'*Anyone who ever loved,*' I sing to myself in a tight bitter voice.

Lemmy is just far enough away from me to pretend he can't hear.

'*Anyone who ever dreamed*'

'Lemmy,' I say. I raise my eyes up and feel, like an attack, my feet catch on one of those abrasive little snags which maliciously wait to trap my new shoes. 'What's the hurry, Lemmy?'

A small rivulet runs down my face, disgorging through the powder, dragging it down and round into a crease by my neck. The polo neck grabs up at my throat, rubbing against my soft skin, sandpaper. My eyes smart. The sheeny sky wavers for a moment.

Lemmy doesn't even answer. He keeps on walking.


*'Without you I'd die dear'*


I do not want to be left alone here. I stop for a moment, to catch my breath. Far down below now, across the sheet of water, I see the small whiteness of Auckland. It looks like a whole lot of crushed shells littering a hillside. For the first time ever I long to be back there. But the sea stretches between us, a cruel mirror.

'Lemmy,' I call, 'Lemmy!'

I want to reach out and grab hold of his back, to hold him still, to keep him from moving remorselessly away from me. But I don't dare. 'Lemmy,' I say. 'Can't I have . . . can I have a smoke?'

Lemmy doesn't stop walking. It's as if he hasn't even heard. Then he slows down and stops so abruptly I practically walk into his back, I am walking now on such automatic scramble.

Lemmy turns, his eyes scald as they pass in a beam all over me. I do not look my best: I am sweating, scarlet, almost panting. But we have stopped moving upwards, at least for a second.

I look down. My suede shoes, 'black as a summernight', are now clouded over. And a small wire of pain is begining to announce itself, growing at the back of my heel, where they rub up and down, cruelly. This is strange, I have never noticed this before. But my feet, inside the suede, are starting to burn, pumping with heat. White light dazzles.

It is so eerily still. There are no birds, no people. In the far distance, I can hear a family calling to one another. You could get lost here, I think with a small freeze of fear.

'Please,' I say. 'I'd love a cigarette.'

Lemmy fumbles in his pockets and brings a packet out slowly. But he doesn't offer them to me, pulling the lid back like he normally does, offering them like in a cigarette advertisement.

He throws the packet at me, hard, with real force. It hits me on the neck but I scrabble to catch it before it falls onto the ground, boldgold forever tarnished. Just before it reaches the petrified lava, I catch it. My fingers are shaking. Tears sting my eyes: tears or heat, I can no longer tell.

'*Who can I turn to*'

I look at Lemmy's face, which has no expression whatsoever; just this blank masked look, as if he won't even let me see what he's thinking, *feeling* . . .

'They think they can separate us. That's what *they* say,' I say, lighting my cigarette with a small, scratchy flare and drawing in deep. I breathe out, like Lemmy does, through my nose, very sophisticated, *hard,* and I laugh. But my laugh comes out funny, off-key, thin. It betrays me, reveals me. Now it is the silence again, the big and noisy silence, knowing, growing around us, accentuated by the hideous emptiness of that island.

'That's what *they* think,' I say, brushing the sweat off my face, holding my polo neck open so the air can get in. But the air is sticky, hot.

Lemmy doesn't answer.

'It doesn't mean a thing,' I say, dropping the lit match onto the ground so it lies there, burns on the rock for a moment, then, getting no sustenance, flutters, withers, dies. 'It won't mean a thing. When I ring you up, I'll just put on a voice. You do the same for me. They won't even notice.'

'Really Lemmy,' I say again, when he says nothing but slowly moves away from me and climbs onto a boulder of dead lava, which he stands on, looking right over my head, as if he can see something far away. I look up at Lemmy outlined against white, cut into it, backed by it, harsh, and I think with a shock: *Lemmy's getting thinner.* He's lost weight quickly, he's no longer straightening his hair, it's starting to grow curly and long, wild.

Lemmy's *changing*, I think. He no longer looks like one of the Small Faces, he looks more like David Hemmings or maybe even Terence Stamp. My heart sinks. It's like he's almost changed in front of me, but so gradually I haven't even noticed. I'm so busy studying for School C, I hardly notice anything. I feel fear.

What will we be if we're no longer fatboy and beanpole, Lemmynme forever together. *Who will I be?* Maybe he's even seeing someone else.

'What do you think, Lemmy?' I say, slowly rising up so that, as I grow taller, all around me everything is suddenly this beautiful orange-red as blood sweeps down through my head, my lids, everything. 'We'll both just pretend we're someone else, eh? That won't be difficult.'

But Lemmy says nothing, apart from a very casual, flat, 'Whatever.'

Lemmy has never said *whatever* before.

And slowly, all around me, the beautiful fiery reds fade away and I am left with a dark empty moonscape, the silence going from horizon to horizon. Lemmy has his back to me, walking away, growing smaller and smaller.


*'Something beautiful's dying.'*


I follow behind Lemmy; my shoes are now definitely hurting and each footstep is a rinse of pain, a raw scraping at the back of my heels. Inside the suede, my feet pump hot angry blood, like bombs of defeat which might go off.

'Lemmy,' I call out.

He doesn't answer.

I stop.

I call out across the petrified lava, 'I can't just be *nothing!*'

Lemmy keeps walking.

'I mightn't get to be a dress designer in Paris. *I mightn't be an opera singer!*'

No answer.

I look around this moonscape: we are the only people alive in it.

'. . . I don't want to end up in a factory,' I yell out.

Lemmy finally turns round. He looks at me.

'I'd die, Lemmy,' I say in a small close voice, because he's not that far from me. Yet he seems so distant.

'It'd . . . kill me,' I say. '*They'd* kill me.'
He doesn't answer me. His feet do.
'Get lost,' he yells. 'Why don't you?'

'It's *such* a climb, eh Lemmy?' I say to him, between gasps. 'Sort of like Auckland's Eiffel Tower, eh?'

We are sitting on top of the world, on a World War II observation bunker which was built to see the Japs come into our harbour and kill us all, except it never happened. Graffiti covers it and a family sits, their legs over the edge. They even smile at us, palely, as we emerge from the undergrowth, almost staggering. Lemmy surprises me: he speaks to them. Normally this is a contract he refuses.

We sit in silence for a long while, just looking at the world we have lived in all our lives, without ever seeing it, as it were, from the outside. It almost surprises me, it looks so pretty. There are harbours and small eruptions and flares of landscape with the odd distant domes of volcanoes under the sky. It is both tiny, detailed, and immense at the same time. It soothes me.

The family move off, down another path.

I wait, almost breathless, for Lemmy to begin. I look down at my shoes. I take them off. My feet inside throb like my heart. I know now it is useless to talk of film stars, movies, fashions. Even the Chooks lie faded and pale, old props from a senseless play.

Then Lemmy speaks. He does not look at me; he turns away, as if to hide his face.

'Glen Miller,' he says after a long while, as if the word has been forced out of right inside him.

I pause. I do not know this game. 'Glen Miller?' I go.

'On the radiogram.'

'Oh no,' I breathe out then, a long long breath, as long as the time we've known each other, since we first met.

' "Moonlight Serenade"?' I murmur to him, hardly daring to say the words.

Lemmy barely nods. His face is turned totally away from me, hidden.

I look at the back of his neck. It says nothing. Except I notice, again, how his hair is growing long, changing, changing forever. Mine is still so curl-less, rigid with hairspray. I pick up my stupid can of lacquer, I throw it away into the scrub.

We watch as it arches into the air, glitters static, is lost. A single, very small bird flutters up into the air, then dives back into the green.

I don't know quite what to say. You see, the last time Lemmy's mother stuck her head in the gas oven she'd been listening to 'Moonlight Serenade'. Lemmy'd found her with the record still playing, the arm going back to the beginning whenever it finished. It was music she'd known when she first met Lemmy's Dad in Italy: before he got eyebags and Miss Clairol, and ended up selling sex books in some no-name street. Perhaps it was what she thought life in New Zealand might be like: a Moonlight Serenade.

'Pills,' Lemmy says in this flat emotionless voice.

'Oh Lemmy,' I say, 'I'm sorry, so sorry.' Then: 'Is she OK?'

Lemmy just shrugs, gets to his feet and starts singing hard and angry, in imitation Yank, yelling out at the world lying there silent and distant and unhearing at our feet:

*'I like to be in America!
Everyone free in America!'*

He turns and looks at me for a second and I can tell that he hates me.

'She's in the bin.'

Then he starts walking off, like he wants to leave me behind forever.

I quickly stand up. I glance around again at the world down there, a last glimpse. It has changed in that second from being a landscape which all fits together, a brief puzzle which makes sense, into a series of discarded shapes, without sense: or something which makes sense only in its senselessness. Why does it never change? I hurry to follow Lemmy. He moves remorselessly ahead, too quickly, my heart misses a beat. He is taking another way down. He disappears into the scrub. I know now he is trying to get away from me. I hurry to follow.

The sun is a high cynical eye which gazes down on two small figures as they move across a dead landscape, along the roads trapped convicts have made. And one of them, Lemmy, spits out his song, in falsetto: 'Everybody *free* in America!'

'No Lemmy,' I say. 'No. That's the wrong way.'
Two threads in the stone road wind away into nothingness. Heat hums, stings.
'We'll miss the boat,' I say, firm.
'Will we?' he says in this flat voice, like he couldn't care if we did.
'Oh Lemmy,' I say. 'Come on, this is the way. I'm sure of it.'
But he says nothing. In fact he does a surprising thing: he picks up a stone and throws it at me. Hard.
It hits me.
'Oh Lemmy,' I don't even laugh now. 'What are you doing that for?'
He throws another.
A trickle of blood burns down my face.
'You bloody bugger,' I say, copying my parents. 'Stop that.'
But he doesn't. He throws another stone.
He walks off on one path.
And I walk off on mine.
I watch him grow smaller. And as he does, I sing to myself,

*'If you see me walkin' down the street*
*and I start to cry*
*each time we meet*
*walk on by*
*don't stop!*
*walk on by.'*

After a few hours of agony I finally see, up ahead, Lemmy,

sitting silent and still, smoking, as he watches me limp towards him. He doesn't say anything but as I get near, he looks at me and says, 'Go beanpole,' and I sort of don't say anything but crease down and sit on this excruciating piece of lava which bites into me.

Lemmy takes me to a cool chill pool under some trees and I bathe my feet, savouring each moment. Lemmy waits for my feet to dry, then he tells me he's found some fun. It is a bach with a louvre window left open.

'They must be expecting us,' says Lemmy.

'Oh Lemmy,' I say. I am tired still, I am exhausted and uncertain. But Lemmy climbs in and is silent so long in there I know I have to go in, I have to join him, if we are to be Lemmynme forever together.

I crawl in and there is Lemmy standing there, looking around very interested. It is someone's bach, with old Crown Lynn cups on a painted wood table, and a bath mirror hanging off a dressing-table, and wooden furniture.

Lemmy breaks open the still. He goes over to a cup and, picking it up, looking at me all the time, just loosens his fingers around it so it falls down to the concrete floor. It smashes.

He looks at me, in the dark, eyes glittering.

'Silly me,' he says, and does one of his yawns. I let out this laugh, weird, tortured, thin. And Lemmy watches and waits. I feel a kind of sickness in my stomach, a terrible fear. He is asking me to finally kill Jamie the goodboy, to assassinate him forever. To join him.

I tremble all over. As I move my chiseltoes rub against my heel, a mat of torn flesh, dribbling blood. Lemmy watches me, dares me to prove we are not forever together, beanpole and fatboy.

I go over to the washstand and pick up a dinner plate.

I am in a dreamtrance as I kiss goodboy goodbye forever. My eyes glaze shut as my fingers grow stiff: the chill porcelain brushes past my flesh and I watch as the plate hurtles away from me, growing smaller for a long time till it suddenly fractures, shatters, and is still. It lies there, broken yet still in its old shape. *Goodboy goodbye.*

'Silly me,' I say, '. . . so clumsy.'

I have hardly finished speaking when, in a quick symphony sealing out soundlessness, Lemmy picks up another cup, it smashes. I do likewise. He reaches for the glasses. *Fuckycuntcockdork*, he says and smashes one. *Cuntyfuckshit* I say and smash the window. Soon Lemmynme are moving so fast breaking so much all we do is scream this crazy laughter and let out all the words we've read on walls and kept inside us, forever cutting, slashing, killing: *smashfuckycuntcockdorkqueercuntpoofterhomo* we scream, laughing so crazy, emptying it all out, everywhere around us.

Finally it is over, all is still, we are exhausted. We look at each other. And quickly now, quietly, we open the door and walk away down to the wharf where the families await and silently now, like two good boys in heavy disguise, we wait with beating hearts for the boat to come and take us back to a place we know.

As we get on and the boat leaves our eyes lock and we both think: we will never be able to tell anyone what we have done. Neither of us says anything of what has happened on the island as we get back to Auckland. It is our guilty secret, one we will always share together.

As we say goodbye, we can't meet each other's eyes. I am frightened, terrified, the police will want us now, we are on the wanted list. And everyone will then find out Jamie the goodboy is dead. It will be Jamie the badboy and just like in that bach I will have to live up to it, smashing and screaming till I am broke too.

What was in me to do that thing, I ask myself. What? But there is no answer. I have acted now. And it was necessary, that is what is so terrible. We have acted and it was necessary.

Just before we say goodbye, Lemmy turns to me and says with a faint smile, 'See you,' and I say with a dry mouth, 'See you next weekend, eh?' And Lemmy just smiles at me and says, like, cool, without any expression, 'Maybe.' Maybe.

And he walks away.

*'These are the eyes that watched him walk away.'*

When I rang after that Mr Stephenson'd answer the phone, if anyone answered at all, and he'd always say, 'Lenny's not here,' and I'd say, 'Oh that's all right, I'll call back later.' And sometimes I did but the phone just rang. I'd listen to those beeps and as each one sounded I thought it was like watching lorries speeding along on a long lone road going somewhere and you were stuck in one particular place, like one of those dumps we saw up north, and you knew in your heart of hearts, you were never going anywhere *ever again*.

So I stayed in my room and listened again and again to Dusty's 'Colouring Book' which seemed to soothe some part of me while I worked away desperately getting nearer and nearer to School Cert and Mum'd bang on my bedroom door and say, What's going on in there, and I'd yell back so angrily I wanted to cry, *Nothing*, can't I have some privacy, is that too much to ask?

*'This is the room I sleep in*
*and walk in and weep in and*
*hide in, nobody,*
*nobody sees,*
*oh call it lonely please.'*

And the phone never rang.

*'I only want to be with you.'*

It happened after this, but not in direct sequence. That is the strange thing of setting this confession down, to make sense of what was *necessary* in it. It all connects up like it was always meant to be but, when Lemmynme lived it, none of it made sense, none of it apart from him knowing me and me knowing him, that was the total sense of it. And that was necessary.

But after all this and School Cert, which Lemmy never sat and I did, he got new friends and I became sort of an embarrassment to him. It was like, with his new friends, he didn't want to know an Audrey Hepburn kind of boy any longer. Then this thing happened.

Lemmy slit his wrists.

I hadn't seen him for quite some time, he'd even left school.

I rang up his father. It's Andrew speaking I say in my imitation-Andrew voice which I know never fooled anybody, I mean, *anyone who's ever loved could look at me and know*, and he said Lemmy's in the bin, not those words, Lemmy's at Kingseat he says, like it was my fault too, just hinting at it, and my voice said, now no longer pretending to be Andrew, whoever he was, but Jamie, Oh, why's he out there Mr Stephenson, in the bin I don't say, why's my lemmy in the bin, *without you I'd die dear*, I think, and Lemmy's dad says then, like he accepts me as Lemmy's *mate*, which I am most definitely *not*, he tried to kill himself and I think oh Lemmy why didn't you call me, why didn't you tell me, *you don't have to walk alone.*

I went out to see him. I'd never been into a bin before. I was frightened but I was strong too, I knew I had to see him.

It was different from what I imagined and suddenly there he was, thin Lemmy now, with long straggly hair hardly even looked after, like it no longer mattered. He wasn't expecting to see me, I could tell that.

Hi, he said to me and I could hear this little echo in my head saying Let's go . . . but it just died, very faint like a pin falling in space, falling, now, forever, end over end, glinting as it fell into darkness. I am in this darkness, this space of unknowingness. But Lemmy looked at me like he didn't hear it and Oh hi Jamie he says and he looked like he wasn't *un*pleased to see me but he also didn't look pleased. I thought *yes my life seems dead and so unreal, there's nothing left to feel* but it was as if Lemmy couldn't hear that: it was like he was listening to some other sound now.

It was quiet there.

We went and sat away from everyone else on a park bench and I got out the cigarettes I'd bought and gave them to him. He looked at them then up at my face. For the first time he seemed to recognise me. A faint smile flickered across his face, making him seem like Lemmy. He shook one out, put it into his mouth, then hesitated. It was like we were suddenly strangers, we didn't know each other and had to make it up, to get to know each other again, introducing ourselves. *I close my eyes and count to 10*, I think, *and I open them and you're still there.*

And Lemmy says I cut my wrists and I close my eyes because I see the razor and I can't stand the thought of losing Lemmy, of being alive without Lemmy, alone without him, I just wouldn't be able to live, no. But I don't say that.

We sit awhile in silence and let the silence breathe its way all over us and Lemmy takes in a breath, sharp, and he looks at me and says Jamie?

I say Yes Lemmy?

And Lemmy pauses then, he takes in another breath and looks at me right into my eyes deep into my soul.

Jamie, he says. I'm one of *them.*

I can hardly breathe.

Oh Lemmy, I say with this sick laugh which dies in the air and crumples to the ground, I watch it at my feet. Oh Lemmy you're having me on. Of course you're not.

If you are, I am, I think to myself in a flash. *It is not possible.*

I am, he says. I am one of *them.*

I don't dare move or breathe or even look at Lemmy, I keep very quiet.

We both look straight ahead.

Then my hand sort of falls down, of its own accord, like in an accident and just *grazes* past Lemmy's. For one moment he goes to take his hand away, I can feel it, but, instead, he just lets it lie there. He relaxes.

Have you heard Dusty's latest? I say, in a strange voice.

Lemmy doesn't say a word.

It's called, 'I Only Want To Be With You', I say.

Then Lemmy says again,

*I'm one of* them, *Jamie.*

And I say nothing.

We sit together for a long while in the silence not knowing what more to say to each other, whether it's the end, or only the beginning. Then I say, Lemmy, like, would you like to hear how Dusty's song goes, and he nods very slow and I stand in front of him and I sing:

# ENCOUNTER

HE WAS WALKING along Karangahape Road neither slowly nor quickly, with the almost directionless pace of one who has no appointments, no commitments - no one even waiting at the other end, to hear how entirely tedious his day had been, looking for work.

Occasionally he glimpsed the fact that his pursuit of suitable employment - the emphasis was on the word *suitable* - was in itself an end. It provided a structure for his days: he could expand excitingly in an interview and amaze his interlocutor with the range of his past experience: law clerk, stevedore, lighting cameraman, callboy. Yet perhaps it was this very range which finally unnerved the recipient of so much variety. The question almost inevitably arose: how could someone so talented, so accomplished in the English language be so finally unemployable? It was as if there were something a little wrong *architecturally:* like a fantastically ornate Victorian cupola perched precariously on the corrugated-iron roof of a crude concrete *fale.*

That day Henry Lawson looked more Polynesian than Italian. Henry's looks varied greatly according to which racial side sought genetic mastery. When he went out to the pub or nightclub, hair trimmed, clothes neat and chic as possible on a non-existent income, he could pass in dubious lighting as a European of around 30, possibly of Italian ancestry. This pleased Henry, who had a romantic disposition. Besides, who in New Zealand wanted to claim Polynesian ancestry when it was so often seen as a demerit?

Yet, when Henry grew moody, or blue, or black, his looks underwent a subtle weatherchange: his face became puffy, his clothes less a costume carefully attended to. To any stranger who saw him at these moments - and this was one of them - there was no doubt that he, Henry Lawson, was not an Italian who happened to find himself stranded in this *infinitely tedious village:* he was that discount thing, an Islander on K Road. His

Boston-Apostolic genes lay submerged like a frail lost boat on the bottom of the pellucid Pacific.

He was lost, he was lonely. If only he'd bump into one of his many friends, strike a pearl in the net of his vast social acquaintance. Perhaps there was a good-looking man to cruise, leading to an encounter which would dissipate an hour or two – or hopefully several *nights*. He liked to think he was a good lover, or at the very least an entertaining one.

Yet there was no one.

Why was it, Henry asked himself almost hysterically, there were some days when the streets were made of handsome invitations, lingering looks, whereas on others, as today, the world seemed peopled by leftover rejects from a Gormenghast movie, to which one seemed fated, unwillingly, to belong? He let out a grim cackle to himself: he enjoyed the melodramatic bleakness of this thought. With a flourish, he helped himself to his last cigarette. Then caught the bearer of an angry yellow hairdo turning to him, staring at him edgily, as if he, Henry Lawson, almost a Polynesian *princess*, were just another of the resident weirdos who plied their tragic trade along Karangahape boulevard.

The very *idea* of it! He felt like turning round and shrieking at her, with almost Judy Garland-like bravura: 'I was *ruined* in my youth!'

So was she, so was she, cried the wind.

As if in confirmation of his inner mood, he saw, presented against a brilliantly backlit cyclorama of cloud, a single figure poised on the very apex of Hopetoun Street bridge. This image of suicide seemed to him almost an hallucination. He gazed at it momentarily then rebuffed the enticement: it was some mere *amateur in existence,* gazing down through the chasms of interweaving motorway.

Too entirely *tedious.*

The only person ahead was a fat Polynesian carrying himself home from work. He had a physique, or, as Henry would say sharply, the *shipwrecked* remains of one. Probably heading for the pub, Henry thought tartly, to drown his sorrows in a glass.

81

At this thought, like a desire too long suppressed, Henry began to long for the absolution of a good drunk. He remembered the small amount of gin which remained in the bottle back in his room: enough to at least blur the outlines of the present, to allow himself to focus inwards on that sense of self-knowledge - absurd, wronged, ironic - which allowed him to live.

Henry let his eyes rest, theoretically at least, upon the man getting closer to him by the moment. The man's slightly softening form was cloaked in dusty blue overalls which, sexually, casually, were lowered round his hips, as if he were too tired, too exhausted to himself make the connection.

Henry's lovers nearly always turned out to be blue-eyed blonds, as if he were seeking, wordlessly, some lost part of himself. Yet automatically now, cruising on auto-pilot, Henry flirtatiously checked out the Polynesian man's face.

He was possibly 45, light brown Polynesian skin yellowed to ricepaper by tiredness and dust. He carried a quietly absorbed air of exhaustion along with him: a man whose physical strength was his one asset. Yet as they drew closer and closer, Henry felt his heart spurt into action.

The features were undeniable, though blurred by age and tiredness: there was no doubt: *it was him*. Henry felt an infinitely powerful electric current of memory start through his body. His eyes clung to the stranger's face. He felt the present and the past activate. And he felt in that one moment of recognition a crumpling of his soul even as he cried out in protest, like the voice of someone far distant, and falling: 'I was *ruined* in my youth.'

The day was hot as it nearly always was on the island, a pleasant lingering warmth which caressed the coconut trees, sent the waves flopping against the coral reefs: made the flies buzz around the tins of bullybeef cut open in his grandmother's large kitchen. It was Henry's job each day to ring the heavy ship's bell which hung, pendulous as an enormous flower, on the open porch.

This ringing of the bell gave Henry his importance. He was, after all, only 10, yet even as a 10-year-old he was clearly the heir to the master, the favoured grandson. He was the oldest male of the oldest male, gathered back into the grandfather's nest so he could learn the requirements of his chiefly status. Well, now his grandfather was dead. He had, as it were, drifted out to sea in search of his Boston ancestry and never returned. His grandmother, vast, 23 stone, commanding as a mobile effigy, was industrious in plying her financially rewarding trade of copra and tomatoes. She ruled her tiny plantation like a replica of the distant queen-empress.

Henry's daily ringing of the bell was, in part, to summon the workers to food. Yet each sharp strong clang sent a further message to the sweat-stained youths and men that it was he, Henry Lawson, son of Josiah, son of Jeremiah, who would one day pay them: it was he, Henry Lawson, who would oversee their lives. And he knew it.

That day, he let the tintinnabulation settle, then die, absorbed in the heat, suffocated by the more persistent drone of surf, cackle of palm tree. He watched the glistening torsos of the men as they moved towards the crude tin shelter which served as a wash-room. His eyes narrowed on one young man in particular, a youth of perfect form and symmetry who glided along slightly apart from the other men, as if enclosed in his own dreamworld which sealed him off from their rough jokes, their sexual jests to which he reacted a little late, as if awakening from another world which moved ceaselessly, colourfully, *persuasively,* in front of him as he moved, hypnotised, along.

Henry felt for this youth a passionate absorption which was so powerful he could only follow behind it, drugged as a sleep-walker, intent, spying and enthralled, needing to fill his eyes every waking moment he could with the vision of Tere, as he moved in his sweet dream behind his plough across the earth.

Henry followed Tere with his eyes as he went into the compound. Each man had a kind of stable-like area to call his own, a cot. Henry picked up his small plastic jet so expensively sent from New Zealand (and the only one among all the children on the island). He moved in counterpoise, seemingly, to Tere's motion, following silently behind him. He walked into Tere's area and stood there, jet in hand, playing it along his palm.

Tere was slumped on his cot, legs apart so Henry saw in the soft dark the lolling shape of his sex which he stared at fixedly, hungrily absorbing its petal-like details, its flowering pendant shape.

A little unnerved by Henry's gaze, Tere shifted his powerful legs to one side and gazed down at Henry. They looked at each other for a moment in silence - during which Henry heard very clearly the rise and fall of Tere's even breathing so that his own breathing fell into accord with it and they breathed together in a frightening duet.

Henry felt an overpowering longing to reach out and touch this *mirage*, to break the union, but at that second one of the other men walked down the narrow passage, and, seeing Henry ahead, called out to him good-naturedly, 'Greetings to the Little Capitaine!'

Henry looked at the elderly man with a heavy, serious gaze which made him feel uneasy. He did not like to be stared at so silently by a mere child. But in an instant the mere child had gone.

The impressions were jostled and juxtaposed confusingly. Henry had recently learnt of a strange form of behaviour which fascinated him. The local boys - some his own age, some older - had taken him on raids on neighbouring plantations. During these informal sallies, Tuaivi, the leader, led them silently on a warrior mission whose point was to watch fat Mr Hastings and fatter Mrs Kelston wrestling together in the undergrowth, sweating and grunting, both of them, Henry thought, trying to find something which was locked underneath them: yet they were both clamped together so tightly neither could reach it.

Their desperation, the animal cries of Mrs Kelston and the answering grunts of Mr Hastings, drew Henry into their vortex. Then Mrs Kelston's face, drained of blood, sweating, suddenly focused on the ring of watching faces. She let out a cry of fright, of ruptured modesty. Mr Hastings jerked painfully back, apart. In that moment Henry saw his purple, distended cock, angry as an exclamation mark, glistening and moist. Mrs Kelston was on her feet, pulling her lavalava up, running away. Mr Hastings, entangled by his pants, could only bellow. Tuaivi had led the boys away cacophonous with laughter which echoed and re-echoed throughout the village, mocking and hilarious.

They all ran away, fleeing with the knowledge they had just gained, drugged.

Afterwards Henry thought seriously about the purple distended cock and gazed down secretly at his own tiny cockleshell which showed no propensity to stiffen. He touched it softly, roughly pulling it out. The sensation was immediate. He looked down at himself thoughtfully. And above his head, as if the very sky had changed into a silver screen, the heavens became filled with images of Tere, multiplied and remultiplied: and gradually Henry grew languorous.

The following afternoon, when the light was bright and intense as a dream, he followed Tere's shadow into the compound. He had been thinking all night, all morning of what he wanted to do.

Henry held his jet tightly in his hand as he looked at the glistening gilded flesh of Tere as he lay back, spent from labour. He looked silently at the pillowing breast muscles as they planed down towards the large flowering nipples. Above this profusion of taut flesh Tere's face looked down at him, brow furrowed slightly. His eyes had just opened. He had been dreaming about Nane, a girl in the village.

Tere looked a long distance down at the small boy who gazed longingly at him. Without saying a word, Henry reached out his hand and, placing it lightly, uncertainly, even caressingly, he ran his fingertips up Tere's ankle, speckled with mud, to the smooth agate of his calf muscle. Tere let out a small laugh, and his face for a moment became animated. Henry looked intently into Tere's face, with its perfectly symmetrical features, the dark black eyes now gazing down like the sky itself into his own eyes.

Henry slid his hand up further, slowly, looking all the while at Tere. Now Tere's face clouded over. But his hand was almost, now, it was, actually, touching Tere's cock. Tere scissored back. He looked down at Henry, frowning.

'What do you want?' he asked, almost whispering. His voice was thick from sleep.

'I want to feel you.'

There was silence for a moment.

'You cannot touch me there.'

'*Why* ?'

'It is not right.'

'*Why* ?'

'Mr Samuels says so.'

Henry's small fingers crept closer.

'*Why?*'

'Because the Bible says so.'

'*Why?*'

His fingers moved now into a caress.

'Because that is what God has decided.'

Henry's answer was to look at him uncomprehendingly and reach his hand out again. This time he went straight for Tere's cock and held on tight. Tere grimaced.

'Go easy! Stop!' he cried out.

One of the men walked by and they fell silent. Tere was now flushing and sweating. To Henry he looked more beautiful than ever, caged, animal.

'I want to feel,' Henry said again in a firm voice he had heard his grandmother use. '*I want,*' he said, tersely. And he did.

But as he reached out, Tere effortlessly leant down and swept his hand away. Tere held his hand suspended, so they both looked at it, for one moment, as if it had a separate life, like a crab. It was very hot. The iron roof pinged like a gun. Tere twisted Henry's arm then, painfully. He brought his face close to Henry's.

'Go away and play with your jet. That is what little boys should be doing.' He said it not unkindly and immediately released him.

Henry took his arm back with as much dignity as he could muster. He continued looking at Tere intently. He felt a kind of sadness. 'You must do as I say,' he said very softly.

Tere had to lean forward. Now their faces were very close, Henry could count the number of eyelashes around Tere's eyes, he felt. Tere's warm, pungent breathing fanned softly onto his cheeks

'You must do as I say,' Henry said very clearly, 'otherwise I will tell the old Breadfruit' - the men's name for his grandmother - 'that you . . . forced me.

Henry said the last piece very slowly so that Tere could fully understand it. They both knew of the palagi mission woman who told how she had been forced by a local man and how the man was sent away to prison in New Zealand.

Tere's face went a pale grey as he looked down at his small master. His face receded as he fell into thought. Then his beautiful large eyes slowly moved back to Henry's as Henry said to him in a matter-of-fact voice, as if it had been evident all along, 'You must do as I say.'

His grandmother had gone to the other side of the island, on one of her tours of ritualistic enactment. Her presence was so powerful that, as soon as she moved around the palms at the bottom of the road, in her sedate old Austin, the whole place seemed to change mood. The workers out on the kumara patch sang to themselves, stopped to have a smoke. Inside the house, Poko, the kitchen woman, a vague relation of his grandmother, would sing old American songs like 'Rum and Coca Cola' and listen to the radio from New Zealand

Henry felt all these changes happening around him uneasily. He knew it placed him in a weak position. Maliciously Poko would flick the end of her broom on his backside, saying to him slightingly the 'maggot' must make room for 'the meat'.

Henry rather dreaded these days because, when he went to ring the bell, the clang no longer seemed to have its old authority. The workers weren't even really working, so how could two sharp tolls signal an end to what had not properly begun? They all looked through him on these days, too, as if he didn't really exist, whereas when his grandmother was around, several of the older men made some attempt to humour him, and call him 'the Little Capitaine' in honour of his grandfather.

Now he felt the flick of dust in his face, and he didn't quite like the timbre of the laughter from the men as Poko put down the food for them. He felt almost, at these times, that he himself might end up on the table, dressed and slit open as they all leant forward to take out of his insides the delicate, pink bits.

So he made himself scarce on those days his grandmother went away on business.

This afternoon, the whole plantation was silent. Henry came down from the palm where he was hiding, spying on Tere who alone had kept on working, moving along in straight methodical strips, ploughing. Henry went back towards the house.

First of all he thought everyone had run away, it was so quiet. Then he saw fat Poko polishing the glass in the windows. She had a big white cloth and she was rubbing against the glass, but not industriously: rather she was doing it languorously, in slow, small caresses.

He observed her silently. She did not see him through the window. He moved silently along a little further. She was bent over, leaning towards the glass and he could see a strange thing: there was Mr Hastings standing behind her, bumping into her rhythmically. Each time Poko cleaned, she bumped forward towards the glass. Henry looked at her face, which was trance-like and sweating, her eyes slightly glazed. She had her mouth open a little and she seemed to be gasping, or was it smiling?

He tiptoed very very quietly across the chill concrete, skirting the noisy mats. Now he was inside the house he could see them side on. He could see Mr Hastings was joined to the back of Poko, her skirts were thrown up and his trousers were down. They moved together in their strange dance.

'What are you doing?'

They both looked startled for a moment. Then Mr Hastings' rhythm speeded up urgently, as if they were both caught in an undulation which, once begun, must now continue on to its end or neither would ever rest in peace again. All the while Poko tried to reach him with her duster, trying to shoo him away.

'Pffffftttt! Pffffssssttt!' she hissed at him angrily.

But Henry stood out of range and silently watched.

The following day Henry waited for Tere to come into the compound. He heard slow footsteps, then Tere stood in front of him. Henry made room for Tere, who sank down silently beside him. Henry quickly, as if there was no time to lose, placed his hands on Tere's cock. He felt its coldness, the way it was pulled up into itself, like a snail unwilling to come out of its shell. He stroked it kindly, then looked up at Tere's face.

Tere lay with his face turned towards him, but his eyes were firmly closed.

Henry ordered him to open his eyes.

Then he squirmed down towards Tere's musky smelling legs. Tere was so inert, so still. He placed his own soft body beside the crisp wiry hairs of Tere's legs. With hand, with palm, with tongue, he now set about coaxing Tere's cock into life so he too could experience the strange dance, the magnetism, he had seen with Poko and Mr Hastings. But no matter what he did, Tere was gripped so tight that Henry could not make his cock come to life.

It was now the third day of their rendezvous. Henry had begun to feel a little annoyance, a sharp dissatisfaction with his beautifully proportioned lover. He no longer sat up a tree gazing with longing at the ploughboy. The day before they had almost been discovered. Tere had himself caught hold of Henry and held him close, shielding him from one of the old men walking down the passage. Both their hearts crashed in unison and Henry, clamped tight to Tere's chest, almost suffocated under his weight, had felt an exquisite pleasure. But then Tere had lain back again, passive and immobile, a fabulous fountain of flesh which refused to yield its music. Henry had pulled Tere's penis then, painfully, flicking it from side to side with his fingers, like it was some useless toy. It had not been good.

So this day Henry went to Tere feeling full of purpose, power. Tere already lay there, silent, brooding. Henry came closer. Outside he could hear the men laughing. By now it seemed all the men knew and were calling Tere strange names and all their buried dislike of Henry's grandmother was now breaking against Tere in waves. A kind of deep sadness had come over Tere, his beautiful bronzed flesh now seemed yellowed, almost jaundiced. He lay there, still.

Henry began his games.

But today there was no response. There was simply nothing. He persisted. He felt so angry, it was like the day before when his jet refused to go any more. He had picked it up and smashed it against the wall. It hadn't mattered that he was later whipped. The satisfaction of seeing it break was too great. But today, as he felt the clammy, chill flesh of Tere, he had a strangely adult feeling, almost like disgust. Then he heard a strange sound, like a sigh, a moan. In one long movement, Tere turned his face to the wall and began, like a small boy, as if he were Henry's age instead of seven years his senior, to weep.

Henry looked at him silently for a while, amazed.

But Tere's tears did not cease. In fact they increased, and he began sobbing soundlessly, like a girl, like a small boy humiliated, lost.

Henry did not know what to do. 'You are useless,' he said to Tere finally, looking once again upon his nakedness.

In the end Henry got up and walked away.

And that was the end of it.

Henry's face was now only a few feet away from Tere's in

Karangahape Road; they were moving closer and closer together and Henry felt a moment of panic that Tere, an aged Tere now, beaten down by work and probably a grandfather already, a son in prison most likely, daughters in the church, might shift his gaze and suddenly recognise him. Henry's sense of humiliation at this possibility was so profound that for that one instant he wanted to cry out to Tere, poor Tere, with his thickened waist, downcast face, to forgive him, to grant him the sweet absolution of accepting that he was only a child, he had hardly known what he was doing.

Then the thought came that Tere would see Henry as he was now, not well-dressed, unemployed, completely unsuited to the world of the palagi around him. Tere might ask after his grandmother, all 23 stone of her now as thoroughly vanished as their ownership of the estate, now turned into a runway for stinking jets, his grandmother's very grave urinated on nightly by tanked-up tourists uncertain of even where they were on the globe. All these contradictory thoughts and feelings - to reach out, to touch, to perhaps make him his lover again for one night, to salve, to heal, to beg forgiveness - all these feelings flashed through Henry's mind as they moved closer and, oh, infinitely, almost within kissing distance, apart.

At that moment Tere lifted his gaze from the asphalt and his beautiful brown eyes, deep as the earth, black as the Pacific night, passed over Henry's face as it would over any stranger's. Perhaps there was for one second an intelligence that this stranger was looking at him so intently: but Tere was tired, and men with strange looks were common on Karangahape boulevard.

At home, in his room, Henry poured himself a stiff gin, filling his glass with water from the tap. He thought about those things he had not considered in over 20 years. In truth he had forgotten Tere completely, his body as it were buried beneath other bodies of more or less beautiful men who were all a form of Tere, although most were more willing, certainly more rapturous. He thought of the lost world of his grandmother, the child he had been, and he began to do something he hardly ever did because he despised it as weakness: he wept.

And as he cried Tere's face came to him silently as it had been on that final day, sweat-sequined, tear-rivered. And as the tears coursed down Henry's cheeks, he had the sudden sensation that they were Tere's tears coming out of his eyes and that, after all – after all that time – they had perhaps truly for the first time come together: they were one.

# OUTING

'WHY IS FATE always so fucking inscrutable?' queried Perrin McDougal as Eric knelt at his feet, guiding his dead toes into his shoes.

'I suspect,' said Eric rather too tartly, because he hadn't actually thought he'd be acting as nursemaid, 'it means, that way, the old fraud is never quite caught out.'

They were in Perrin's exquisitely muted bedroom, with its frosty Viennese chandelier reflected in perpetuity in the floor-to-ceiling mirror. This now returned an image of themselves, ironically, in poses of almost biblical simplicity. Though Eric thought he caught a faint ammoniacal pong from Perrin's socks. 'Isn't it time, darling, these putrescent articles were, well,' Eric tried to sound noncommittal, '*substituted* for something more savoury?'

They used the telegraphese of old friends, accentuated by the frequently sharp, sometimes hilarious, even acid appendage of '*dear.*' Though in the present situation, with Perrin so ill, the *dears* had taken on a warmer, more amber hue.

'Can you find me my walking-stick?'

Perrin had phoned up that afternoon and commanded Eric - the tone was properly regal and brooked no contradiction - to take him off to the Remuera Garden Centre. Eric thought ironically - though fondly too, because in the contradiction lay the quintessence of his character - that here was Eric almost certainly going to be absent in the flooding spring yet he, Perrin, was planning a lavish bouquet for his 'spring' garden.

'What I see,' Perrin had announced over the phone in that way that had the faint edge of the visionary to it, 'is a mixture of marigolds, blue violas and delphiniums. Don't you remember . . .?'

Eric didn't, but it didn't matter.

'Don't you remember how Aunt Priscilla down in Te Awamutu always had a daphne bush by her front steps and the way it always used to *invite* you - yes, *invite* is the right word -'

Perrin kept his legal precision intact, a careful weapon against the unknown, 'so that as you ascended the stairs into her hall, the scent was *incroyable!*'

Perrin now rose to his feet unsteadily. His once fleshy form had been stripped by the disease to a frightening gauntness. His stylish garments – once bought in Melbourne or 'inexpensively' run up in distant Bangkok – clothed his skeleton in a simulacrum of 'health'. To the outside world – that crowd of on-lookers who instantly became extras in the cinema reel of Perrin's declining life – he probably looked only frail, possibly suffering from cancer.

Eric clung to these illusions as he handed Perrin his elegant malacca cane. He was still getting used to the shock of being seen with Perrin in public.

He had told himself as he drove over to Perrin's Epsom bungalow (a clever pastiche of Frank Lloyd Wright, via his Napier disciple, Louis Hay) that the public gaze simply didn't matter, that it was more important to simply help Perrin, that this accompanying him a little along the road was the very least he could do. But the truth was he had gone into a state of near shock when he thought he'd left his sunglasses behind.

He realised when his fingers touched bakelite – they connected with the impact of a lodestone – that he was sweating uncomfortably, not even watching the road. His heart was banging away, in a mocking Judas dance.

'Give us your arm, dear.' Perrin now stood at the brow of his front steps whose very sweep and height had once signalled power. Now they simply spoke danger: Perrin's grasp of Eric's arm was surprisingly tight. Eric registered Perrin's fraility as he leant into him.

He watched the almost random – yet hesitant, hesitant – fall of Perrin's numbed feet.

Suddenly Perrin lurched to a halt. 'This!' he cried in a voice full of emotion.

*Shit*, thought Eric, stopping back his alarm, *the bugger's going to cry.*

'This is where I want to have a whole *flowery mecca*,' Perrin waved his wand towards a dug circle of dirt. Even though he was facing financial ruin he'd hired a student to create a new flowerbed. 'When people come to see me, I want them - to - feel *welcomed*.' The last in a breathless rush. Then Perrin took off suddenly, as if blown along on the coat-tails of his inspiration. Eric hurriedly shadowed his movement, getting ready to catch, hold, balance. But Perrin had miraculously connected with gravity.

'The scent of marigolds!' he cried out in something like rage.

'This is the whole fucking trouble,' Eric said to himself in an aggrieved way. You can never tell with Perrin what tangent he's going to hare off on next. He thought of the long somnolent telephone conversations they had each night while Perrin waited for his sleeping pills to take effect. Eric would sit in his armchair, armed with a glass of gin, half watching the televisual fantasy of reality while Perrin's voice purred away in his ear - sometimes thin as cellophane, occasionally close as a voice in a dream: his needs, emotional, physical, his dreams; his plans for the future. To sell the house and go to Venice. A week later to offer the house to people with the disease. Another week and he is planning to repaint the hall a Polynesian shade of blue. 'Sea-blue, just that shade of light at dusk - the moment before the sun sinks.'

Shit, and I'm only one of his friends, Eric often said to himself. Not even his oldest. What about his *family*? But Perrin's family in faraway Te Awamutu were in disarray. They were busy tending to their own emotional wounds: they would leave Perrin alone to attend to his actual torment.

Yet, if Eric were honest with himself - and he occasionally was, by dint of necessity rather than pleasure (he was old enough now to realise that honesty, though cruel, was the best policy in the end) - Eric's truth was, silently and subtly, he himself had come almost to depend on Perrin's presence: his closeness. The fact of the matter was Perrin's reality had become the ballast in Eric's somewhat unsteady life.

Ahead of them, as if a testimony, lay Eric's blue, shockingly dented Renault.

Eric's boyfriend was 14 years younger than him. He was a student of architecture who had never heard, thankfully, of aversion therapy as a 'cure' for homosexuality. He could not imagine a city in which there were no bars, saunas or nightclubs. Matthew, handsome, athletic like a basketball player, with an engaging sweep of hair that never quite managed to stay down, had pranged Eric's car in fury one night because, as he yelled out for the whole street to hear, 'You care more about Perrin's dying than *loving* me.'

It was unfair, it was emotional blackmail: it was true.

Eric needed Matthew, his beautiful boyfriend, for the warmth of his flesh, the passion of his kisses: the way he connected him back to life. In the middle of the night he could reach out and let his hand just roll down Matthew's flank and find that softly sweating crease in his knee. This soothed away the phantoms which hid in the dark: Matthew's body was so tangibly real.

Yet for Eric his experiences with Perrin - Perrin sick, Perrin dying - were almost like a pre-vision into the future, a kind of warding off of evil spells so that he would at least know the path of the disease if it should ever strike near him. This was his private truth. And Perrin, who never for one moment doubted Eric's presence by his side, communicated the full phalanx of his illness to him so that Eric's daily equanimity was conditioned by Perrin's. They moved in uneasy duality, two friends linked like horses on a circus merry-go-round, ceaselessly rising and falling together till that final moment when one horse would rise alone.

'Now my funeral,' Perrin took up as the car moved along the streets.

This is what is so odd, thought Eric, as he drove along. When he was with Perrin it was as if that became the centre of reality in the world. Even driving along it was as if the streets of Epsom outside, with their casual realities - a father pushing his babycart into the drycleaners, a woman ducking into the wineshop in broad daylight - became like a moving cyclorama which streamed past them: Eric and Perrin were at the storm-centre, stilled.

'For my funeral,' Perrin was saying in the matter-of-fact, 'now take note of this' voice he used for the important formality of his funeral. He was planning it as he had planned his famous dinner parties, with the exquisite silver, linen and flowers acting as courtiers, nervously anticipating the throwing back of the gilded doors, the regal entrance of the food. Now the unpalatable truth was that Perrin's body would be the main course: and Eric, as a friend who had come forward - and for who came forward and who fell back there were no rules - was to act as courtier, arbiter of Perrin's final feast.

'I only want flowers picked from people's gardens. I don't want *one - one!*' Perrin tapped the floor with his stick vehemently, 'of those embalmed creations dreamt up by florists! And fruit should be whatever is freshest in the shops. Vegetables of the season - organic. And definitely kai moana. That shop in K Road, you know the one. Only the freshest. Can I rely on you for that?'

'You can rely on me for that.'

A slight pause. Eric turned and looked at his old friend. 'Your Celestial Highness,' he said.

Perrin smiled but did not laugh.

Going through the Domain, they were suddenly accompanied by a flock of graceful runners. Eric slowed down in appreciation. There was one man, sweating in the silent chiaroscuro of sport which echoes so closely the fury of sex. They both watched him silently.

Suddenly Perrin wound down his window. 'You beautiful man!' he yelled out in the voice of a healthy male. 'You're the most beautiful flower in the whole fucking Domain today!'

Eric blessed the presence of his sunglasses while inwardly shrieking.

Fortunately the runner turned towards them and, in his endorphin bliss, showered an appreciative smile at them. The other men pulled away. They passed in a blur of sequined sweat on muscular flesh, with frolicsome cocks beating to and fro like agitated metronomes inside their tiny shorts.

Swiftly the runners became manikins in the rear vision mirror.

'Thanks, darling,' said Perrin in a small voice of exhaustion. 'I really appreciated that.'

Eric felt a surge of exhilaration as he moved closely behind Perrin through the gates of the garden centre. Already queues were forming, with well-heeled Aucklanders guarding trundlers full of merchandise. Eric realised he hadn't felt so good – dangerous would be the wrong word to use – since the very early days of Gay Liberation, when to hold hands in public with another man was a consummate – if inevitably provocative – act.

Now time had shifted the emphasis somewhat – but Eric felt a shiver of pride at Perrin who, once so socially nuanced and named, could now lurch – almost like a toddler in reverse, Eric thought with a saving sense of hilarity. He was completely oblivious to the reactions of people around him. Indeed, as he stopped to pass a cheery word with the middle-aged housewife acting as a trundler-guard, he was actively engaging everyone in his act of dying.

Behind his shades, Eric was aware of people staring. They looked on silently, hit by the stilled impact of thought.

'Perrin!' Eric called out, because it suddenly seemed imperative to keep up contact, 'it's marigolds you're looking for, isn't it?'

He moved over to Perrin and, in a movement he himself had not contemplated, hooked his arm through Perrin's frail, bird-like bones and clung on. That was the mystery: it was he who was clinging to Perrin, not the other way round. But Perrin was off, putting all his suddenly furious energy into pushing the cart along. He was calling out the names of the plants as he went, voice full of glee: 'Pittosporum! Helleborus! Antirrhinum! Cotoneaster!'

Now people *were* staring.

But Perrin was unstoppable. It was as if he were gathering in energy from the presence of so many plant forms which, embedded in earth, nourished, watered and weeded, would continue the chain of life: just as his dust would one day, soon, oh soon, too soon, be added to the earth, composting.

Eric felt an uneasy yet piercing sense of happiness, a lyrical rapture in which he conceived the reality of how much he loved Perrin: of how Perrin was, at that very moment, leading him on a voyage of discovery so that they were, as in the dream, two circus horses together rising, leaping wonderfully high, almost far enough above the world, so that for one moment it was as if Perrin and he were experiencing in advance that exhilarating blast of freedom as they surged away from the globe on which all of life was contained, and beyond which there lay nothing – at least nothing known.

The plants were loaded into the boot. Eric had, at the last moment, tried to modulate Perrin's buying frenzy but, as if in testimony to his mood-swing, Perrin had impetuously bought too much, ordered Eric to shut up, and had sailed past the cash register issuing a cheque which Eric felt sure, with a lowering degree of certainty, would bounce. But Perrin, like a small child now, exhausted, almost turning nasty, threatened to throw a tantrum in front of the entire queue. 'I must have what I want,' he had cried. 'You don't *understand*. I *must!*'

And now, thankfully safe inside the car, Eric began breathing a little easier. He shook off his sunglasses, which now weighed heavy on his nose. He felt the beginning pincers of a headache. Perrin was saying to him that he wanted – he *needed* – to take Eric's car for a drive. He needed to be on his own. He could drive still. Did Eric doubt him? Why was Eric always doubting him?

'Trust me,' said Perrin in a small voice, like a caress.

Eric looked at his old friend. How much longer would he have him with him, to trust, not to trust, to doubt – to be astonished by. He did not know. So, doubting everything, doubting his own instincts to be firm, to say no, Eric allowed himself to be dropped off outside a mutual friend's townhouse, a refugee, and, standing on the pavement, about to go in, he watched Perrin drive away in his car, faltering out into the middle of the road, hugging the centre line. And seeing Perrin move off, odd, slow and cumbersome, trying so hard to control his own fate, Eric watched his dear love, his friend, turn the corner, with as much grace as possible, attempting to execute his own exit.

# BUM TO YOU, CHUM

## PART I

*Mrs Hazard gathered her children close
about her for the long night of terrible
vigil. Through the window they could see
the fearful glare, and to keep the children in
good heart, they prayed and sang hymns.*
The Story of the Great Tarawera
Eruption, 1886

### 1

ALTHOUGH IT WAS only half past 10 at night, the streets
were deserted. Only from hotels - booze barns out of which
chaotically drunk people staggered, as if from some conflict -
came sounds of life.

International hotels, looking out upon the sulphurous pools,
darkened lake, were facades of light - and emptiness. Upon the
brooding water, three black swans bobbed.

It was as if some terrible disease had struck or civilian
evacuation had taken place.

As he drove into the town, the landscape appeared more LA
than Sulphur City: more deliberately anonymous than almost any
other part of the island. Yet this was a town which celebrated -
lived off - its own special locality.

A wisp of steam slid in front of his carlights, expired upon the
asphalt. He breathed in: yes, it was the sulphurous smell of the
world-famous city.

So it was that by the invisible and intangible - by an act of
memory and association - he realised he had reached his
destination.

He chose a particularly anonymous motel, neither Spanish hacienda, nor Italian Riviera nor Miami deco. It simply had two cypresses trimmed into an inanimate state, a soothing blandness.

He got out of his car and stretched. He took out his luggage. It was simple. An overnight bag, as of one used to travel, and a worn business satchel.

He rang a bell, a door opened.

The owner of the Sharima, a Mr Lapidus, came down the staircase wiping his lips with a paper napkin. He had been interrupted from his family dinner. The waiting man could hear a television playing upstairs, the momentary lap and pause of fragmentary conversations. He felt a brief and acid longing.

Mr Lapidus, as he came down the stairs, looked at his customer. It was the off-season, it was late. The man looked in his mid-30s, tired perhaps from the long trip: from Auckland, by the style of his clothes. His shoes, he noted, were those of a man used to an indoor occupation. He was tall, with a large, beakish nose, yellowy-blond hair and red knuckles. No wedding ring.

Lapidus noted the car was from a budget rental firm. Its mudguards were splattered with mud, as if it had been driven at high speeds, even dangerously, through the rain and night.

'Weather should clear up tomorrow,' Lapidus said with professional optimism.

'That's good,' the man replied vaguely, as if weather did not enter into his plans.

'Down here on business?' Lapidus was going to say, but something about the silence of the man stopped him.

Giving him a small carton of milk, that token of New Zealand hospitality, both familiar and somehow intrusive, he left.

## 2

Lights flared around the room. It was totally anonymous, as if any aspect of personality was a risk factor and had been hygienically expunged. The dreams which had passed through this room had left no signs: only a slight wearing of the wallpaper round the light-switch at the end of the bed.

Nick Burns was strangely soothed by this lack of context. He put his bags down, investigated what would be his home for several days. Noticing it had an outside door which communicated with the street, Nick judged it perfect for his purposes.

He took three photos from his satchel and leant them up against the wall. Beside them he placed a rectangular black book: a photo album. On its cover were two words: *Happy Memories.*

He went over to his bag, took out a bottle of gin, poured himself a long drink, plashed some tap water into it. Then he went over to the television, turned it on, turned the sound down.

He looked at the words on the front of the album. He laughed.

After a while - and there was an air of inevitability about it - he went over and picked up the three loose photos.

One was of a suburban scene, outside a back door. There was a small boy, scarf wrapped round his ears, sitting beside a tall, mannish-looking woman smoking a cigarette. There was also an elderly woman, looking directly at the camera, quizzically. She wore black.

Nick was the child in the photo and the elderly woman was his grandmother. He looked at this photo for a while, then glanced from the woman with a cigarette to the next photo. This was a cheap studio portrait of a woman in her mid-30s, looking directly at the camera. The photo was touched up to the point that the woman's personality - even face - was difficult to read. On the back was written, in errant calligraphy, 'Stardust Studios - Hinemoa Street'.

The last photo, over which he lingered longest, yet, ironically, treated with less care, as if the person in it did not belong to him, was of a child frowning as she looked into the camera. The girl was wearing her Sunday best, and looked unhappy. On the back was written: 'Thelma Mae, aged three. For Mrs Ngere.' The photo looked as if it had been taken in the 1940s, possibly in a rural location.

Nick lay down on the bed. There was a dating game on television. He drank his gin. After a while he masturbated, though without any great enthusiasm.

He fell asleep.

He woke up before dawn. Someone out in the street was walking by, laughing and talking. He thought he heard the person say, 'Crumbed cup cakes' – or was it crumpled cup cakes?

He looked about the room, uncertain where he was. Then he saw the gin bottle, the photos, the album. He lay there and, perhaps because he was least prepared for it, was suddenly attacked by memory.

She was lying in the hospital, dead. She had been put in a room empty of other people. As he came in he had the unnatural feeling that he was, perhaps, disturbing her. The room had all the confining sense of silence of a church: outside he heard the receding conversation of people as they moved along – a conversation about crumbed cup cakes or crumpled cup cakes, he could not decipher which.

He had suddenly felt diminished back into being the boy he once was in relation to her. As he took a few hesitant steps towards her, he seemed to experience his entire life, not in a flood of pictures or images, but in a sensation of changed size and perspective: as if in his motion towards her dead body, he was growing smaller till he was a child again. Yet oddly enough, by the time he arrived at her bedside and looked down at her, he knew from his height he was an adult again and, what was more, a thing unthought of as a child, her survivor.

He had gazed down at her face, with the prominent nose forcing all the features towards it, as if it were some mountain landscape which ran away into rivers of shadow and sudden chasms round her eyes. They were half-closed, so there was the odd sensation of a barely glistening pupil, almost cynically watching him. He gazed down into the immense semicircles incised into the flesh by her mouth. Her false teeth had been put in, so she was at least not denied some form of dignity in death; yet her lips were parted, as if in a last, desperate intake of breath.

His indelible impression was of pain.

She looked as if she had been caught in an immense wind-tunnel which, carrying her up into the sky, had created a force of such velocity that, as she spun away, she had felt only fear. Yet, too, a kind of passivity underlay her expression: a sense of dismal foreboding that this was what she had, all along, expected – though she may have entertained notions to the contrary. That, the woman lying there dead implied, with a shrug, was life.

He had wanted to cry. He had wanted to beg her forgiveness. For a while he almost succeeded in willing tears up his chest. But finally he became aware that his body would not allow him to cry – to mark her death, as he felt, correctly. In fact he was absurdly tense: each footstep outside the door seemed to hesitate and he had a distinct feeling of being an impostor, even a fraud, incapable of emotion.

'Forgive me,' he had whispered as he turned his back and walked away.

As he lay there now, in that anonymous room, he was surprised to feel his cheeks were wet. He realised he was crying, and gradually, in an almost formal musical progression, his crying turned to weeping, his weeping to sobbing, his sobbing into a dry barking of grief.

He cried out to her.

There was no answer.

He fell into profound blackness.

*Please leave your room as a member of
your own family would like to find it.*
Motel Guide

'I've got this terrible flu, I'm sorry,' Nick Burns was saying as he
stood in his room, cleanly shaven. Morning light cast a pale
effulgence across the motel carpet. 'I reckon I won't be back at
work for at least a couple of days.'

He caught his face in the mirror: it was vividly alive, his
disparate features - the greenish eyes, sallow cheeks, blond hair -
for one moment cohering into an image of energy. Carefully he
lowered the tone of his voice, to imitate illness. 'Yes, it's a real
drag, I'm sorry.'

He listened to his boss, in the newspaper proofreading room,
complain. Then he hung up.

Now he dialled, transfer charge, another number. It was an
answer-phone. 'This is the answer-phone of Alistair Nielson
and Nicholas Burns and we're not *available* right at the moment
but if you'd like to leave a message that would be *great*.' In the
background he could hear Strauss's *Der Rosenkavalier*, one of
those silvery duets where two women, one dressed as a man,
address each other in perfect harmony. He waited impatiently
for the beep. 'Look honey,' he said then, quickly, 'I know you'll
be pissed off me going away without telling you but. But I'm
OK. I'm all right. I'll be back, OK? I'm not with some hot
hunk having groovy sex. *Unfortunately*,' he added, then laughed.
Then in another tone. 'Don't worry. I'm OK.' He paused for a
moment. He could hear the reel turning at the other end of
the phone. 'Ciao.'

Now he stood there, uncertainly.

It was a wan day outside the net curtains, as if the light had
been strained, diluted to an essential colourlessness. A flail of rain
fell, caught in the sun, was dispelled. Mr Lapidus walked past
his kitchen window, wearing a towel hat, whistling.

Nick looked down at the phone number he had been carrying with him all week. It was a local number. Even though it was written down, he knew it off by heart. Yet now it was the actual moment – when he should ring – he prevaricated.

He went and opened a pack of cigarettes, Camels – lit one, breathed in. He had given up for eight years. Now, since that day, the day he had found out, he had been driven back, restarted. He smoked half his cigarette, then, almost against his own volition, poured himself a small – well, a medium – gin, which he drank neat.

Lapidus walked back past the window, still whistling.

Nick found himself standing at the phone, the beeps sounding inside his own head as if they were phosphorescent bullets arcing through his night.


4


The phone was lifted with that clumsiness peculiar to the old and very young. 'Yes love,' the woman replied when he asked if she were Lulu Short.

'I'm a . . . a relative of Tizz Freeman,' he said carefully. Unwittingly, his voice had fallen a note.

He felt out and dragged on his glass of gin. Some invisible act of faith occurred in the interim.

'Ooooooh Tizz the old darlin'.' Lulu Short's voice took off like a sleigh glissando down a slope of sentiment. 'I was only thinkin' of her just the other day. Funny isn't it how things happen.' A slight pause. 'It's a terrible thing to outlive all your friends.' A slightly longer pause. Then her voice, keener, younger, sharper. 'So what are you doing in this neck of the woods?'

'Just . . . passing through,' he lied.

'You want to come and see me, right?'

'Yes. Yes, please,' he said. 'I would like that.'

'Can't see you today. Maybe tomorrow. Are you still here tomorrow?'

She was shouting down the phone, like someone deaf, or used to a lifetime of bad connections.

'Yes. Tomorrow. That would be lovely. That would be great.' He despised himself briefly, listening to the metallic clink of his own charm. She started to give the kind of elaborate directions which assume someone lacks something as rudimentary as a map. He knew her address. He knew the directions. He had studied a map. Yet carefully he left enough time to allow her to think he was writing them all down.

'I look forward to seeing you tomorrow,' he said, then put down the phone.

'What's that?' she yelled back. 'What are you saying? *What's that?*'

Nick Burns, alone in his motel – no one on earth knowing exactly where he was, what he was doing there, even, when he thought about it now, who he was – did an impromptu fandango, clapped his hands together and let out a yell of vindication.

Then he cut over to the photos, picked up the studio portrait of the woman, yelled at her heavily retouched face: 'See! *See! SEE!*'

She looked back at him, lips stretched in an enigmatic smile.


5


*Clara Hazard walked towards the door as the ceiling collapsed.*


Now, in the motel, he moved towards that photo of his grandmother, himself and the mannish woman as if it were a talisman. He picked the photo up and, in the brimming light, angled it so it caught the glare outside. The image swam and sank and resurfaced, glittering and viscous, as if it had just come from the developing liquid and he was looking at it for the very first time.

It was a small snap, no more than three inches by two, curled slightly by heat into a convex shape, black and white.

Uncle Stan, the man his aunt was living with when they lived next door, had taken the photograph. His only presence in it was a long shadow which stretched towards Auntie Tizz, his grandmother and himself, engulfing his grandmother's feet in shade.

He was nine years old and they were sitting outside his grandmother's back door, having a cup of tea in the autumn sun. He had a bad earache from swimming and Gran had tied a scarf round his head: he also lacked some teeth.

Auntie Tizz sat beside him, a hand lightly placed on his shoulder. She was formally dressed, for her, in a dirndl skirt which he remembered was corn yellow with red piping, figured all over with small Mexican hats and miniature cacti. She wore a cardigan which he recalled then, with an almost painful feeling of loss, was pea-green. In her hand, the dangling point, as if an inevitable punctuation of her exclamatory personality, a smoking cigarette.

Was Aunty Tizz's arm, so lightly resting on his pullovered shoulder, claiming relationship by proxy? Was there some deeper ambiguity in her gaze, or some shared secret from which he had been excluded, up until this moment, when he was finally alone and could ask no one but himself?

He looked at himself in the photo and saw his almost triumphant smile: the absorption of any single child surrounded by adults who gaze upon that child as if towards the central point of a compass. He felt a surge of rage at his innocence. To him then it was simply a case of having adults around, to comment anxiously on the progress of his terrible earache. Yet now it was as if, in his earache, he had unconsciously sought a state of mind which only allowed him to hear the adults' limpid talk at a distance, muffled, ambiguous, capable of a thousand readings. He had had no awareness. He was too greedily intent upon extracting all their love.

His grandmother alone did not look towards the camera. She looked out towards the edge of the frame, as if something else had caught her eye or her mind was intent upon another, unsettling, thought. It suddenly seemed to Nick as he craned down into the snap, so her face rose towards him, then segmented apart into prisms, that her face was as inscrutable as a mask, hiding rather than revealing: a tacit confession of her awareness that this image-making of a 'family' was false.

Now he read the entire image with deep mistrust, looking from Gran to Auntie Tizz, reading into their gaze towards the camera, and hence towards him now, as a 34-year-old man, an implication in the weird fictions which surrounded him at that time so invisibly. For a moment his separation, his *exclusion* from the truth, seemed unbearable. He wanted to rip the photo up.

Outside the motel window, as if recalling Nick to the dimensions of the real world, the imperatives of the present, Mr Lapidus walked by. He was carrying a plastic bucket, a mop. He glanced in through the net curtains. Nick realised the motel had settled down into a quotidian silence. In Lapidus's glance was the imputation - silent yet barbed - that there was something vaguely unhealthy about a guest who stayed indoors, in a famous tourist town, mid-morning.

Nick laid aside the photo. He threw back his gin. Cleaned up the room. Flushed tissues down the toilet. Poured himself, at the last moment, another drink. After all, he told himself as he stood there, poised on the brink of his mission, he himself was on a kind of holiday. A holiday from himself, perhaps: from Nick Vaughan Burns, aged 34 years, unmarried, night proofreader at the *Herald,* homosexual, brought up by his paternal grandmother (now deceased).

He had, knowingly, only ever had a grandmother. Yet through her and her memories he had inherited a whole family. For his grandmother, short, stout, whiskery of chin, face innocent of make-up, wearing black to the day of her death -

good grandmother, fine grandmother, *lying grandmother* – had passed on to him a whole series of phantoms, figments of grandfathers, great-grandfathers. So, even if he had grown up knowing his life was cauterised by the absence of his parents – who, he was told, had been killed instantly, painlessly, again according to his grandmother, whose word to him had the force of biblical injunction (*like the words of Michael Savage*) – he still knew he had forebears. He knew that his grandfather had had a small musical store in Symonds Street (now demolished and replaced by an outdoorium selling plastic garden furniture and kiddypools); that his grandfather and his brother had gained a monopoly on piano-tuning for the entire western suburbs of the city in the 1900s; that he, Nick, had inherited his great-uncle's colouring and size, his great-uncle Grey who had died on some piece of French soil in the 'Great War', his great-uncle like his mother and father, people who mysteriously went away and never returned: except in talk, in thought, in memory, that act of miraculous recall, which his grandmother possessed, like a magician, like a sooth-sayer, like an ancient priestess through whom the ghosts of the past returned to enter his own psyche.

So he, Nick Burns, inconsequential kid, lacking two known parents, with only a grandmother who was palpably from another age, he yet knew (as in those time-lapse photos in which layered images imprint all the actions up to that point) that inside himself was not merely his spindly physical shape, his dry freckled face and blistery elbows and stubbed toes, he was also his grandfather who had made his piano-tuning shop into a successful business, his great-uncle who had died in a distant war, his grandmother too. But not his parents, not his mother and father who were always absent, burnt out, expunged from the family tale: his father who was a disgrace, who had fought with his grandmother, who 'took up with a racing crowd, of ne'er-do-wells, drinkers and drifters, happier in a pub than in God's house', his father who had been sent to Grammar, who made the First XV, whose only survival in his grandmother's house was an ugly carved wooden owl which she touched at certain times of pathos, with an almost overpowering sadness.

His father had been a wharfie before his sudden death, at a crossroads with his young wife: his abrupt summons to a stern and unforgiving God who had, according to Nick's child's mind, exterminated him for having caused his beloved grandmother such pain. His dead grandmother, of whom he could never ask a question, except, as now, in dreams, in moments of torment, of sudden uncertainty. And she could never answer beyond what he, tentatively, trusting only in his knowledge of them, his love for them, could – like a manikin, a wooden doll upon the knee of memory – supply.

He grabbed the gin, tipped back the glass so the silver liquid flooded down the glass towards him, a miniature tidal storm of fury against his grandmother who never drank – except once, on that memorable day, she had told him, to celebrate the defeat of the hated Japs, the barbarous Japs, the infidel: that night she had allowed herself to have a glass of sherry for which a sly neighbour substituted scotch, from which she suffered, a wowser's revenge, a furious headache – the stamp of the foot of an angry god, as she heard it. For inside the wooden and tin bungalow he shared with his grandmother, there were many and angry gods, with laws and rules and songs and sermons. Now he, Nick, dragged into his insides that burning intoxicating fluid, his aunt's, *his mother's* favourite tipple – and now his own.

He wanted, not to get drunk, not to be drunk, but simply for his consciousness to be loosened out of the tight lasso that held his mind in bondage. He walked out the door quickly.

Mr Lapidus was waiting, clean towel in hand, ready to remove the old sins, make clean. 'Looks like it should be sunny by this afternoon,' said this arbiter of heaven.

Nick walked away. 'Can you tell me where I can find Hell's Gate?' he called back.

## 6

*Hell's Gate, I think, is the most damnable*
*place I have ever visited, and I would*
*willingly have paid 10 pounds not to have*
*seen it.*
                                    Bernard Shaw.

He was sitting on a small emerald sward, intercut with a floral
pattern. It was a shimmering memory of colonialism,
perfectly held, imprisoned.

The knock-knock of bowl on bowl pickpocked the air,
imploding. In the distance the surreal turrets of a Tudor
palace: a bathhouse, a place to wash away the sins of the flesh,
the aches. Nearby a forgotten king-emperor, staring with the
wooden eyes of an avenging hei tiki towards a swamp. Drifts
of steam, wisps, silent ghosts emitting from the fissures in the
earth: for this was the town where the brittle skin of earth
had fractured, emitting, now, vapours, thermal wonders:
turning it into a site of worship for those who seek to
imprison the miraculous in photograghs, and videos, and
memory.

The gin was wearing off.

He was hidden behind his sunglasses, passing himself off as
an alienated tourist, 'a man alone', holding in his hand his
papers of identification: a map of the town, information
pamphlets, his wallet, cigarettes.

He lit a cigarette and looked down. He saw his aunt's hand
there, holding the cigarette in the famous calligraphy of
moviedom. He was unaware, till that precise moment, that
that was where he had learnt the elegant art of holding a
cigarette: a quietly faggish way, owing as much, he suspected,
to Noel Coward as to the vamps of the silver screen. He
realised, looking down at his own hand, that he was seeing
not only his own fingers, roughened and red-knuckled, but

his aunt's hand, holding a cigarette in that special way of hers, as if it were a flag of personality, useful for moments of emphasis, accusation, enigmatic utterances during which, like a silent pouring, the blue furbelows and curlicues of smoke would eddy and layer, as beautiful as any sea-anemone opening in a celestial lake: small Chinese rivers which would flow and flash away, then suddenly, finding a draught, move swiftly, seeping and slithering towards the outside air where they evaporated, leaving behind the enigmatically smiling genie, memory.

'Got a match?'

He looked at a businessman in a crisp white shirt, stockbroker's tie, dark suit. He had a faintly red face, chipped front teeth and he was smiling.

Gardens are always cruising grounds, small parks, plots of desire.

The man looked intensely into Nick's eyes, and smiled at the same time, a shared joke, an existential appeal to undercut the idiocy of desire.

'Sure,' Nick said, lighting the stranger's cigarette, though as the man's hand - wearing a wedding ring, he noticed - rose up to catch, *touch,* steady his own, Nick's hand withdrew.

The man understood. His eyes instantly did a survey of the sward. 'Quiet here today,' he said, converting Nick into a fellow cruiser.

Nick shrugged.

'Down here for long?'

'A few days. On business.'

The man's hand was discreetly working away inside his pockets. Nick glanced down to see the thick tube of an erection, then away. He felt disconnected, yet somehow responsible. He waited a moment, but the man took his presence as concurrence. His hand worked faster.

'Well, I'm off,' Nick said, suddenly rising.

The businessman did not change tempo. 'OK buddy, see you,' he said thickly, not looking at Nick, his eyes searching a distant figure, statue of life on the lawn.

As he walked away Nick thought of her funeral, drably held at the crematorium. He had met a hired cleric a few minutes before. When the priest asked Nick if there were details he could give him, in order to flesh out the service with a little of her personality, Nick had laughed out loud: 'Nothing you could mention in a church!'

He had felt embarrassed then, because he did not seem to be acting 'appropriately'. He had thought to himself quickly: what was singular in her life? She had been a wardsmaid, a cafeteria worker, a hotel maid, even a cinema usher at the Civic. She had married a man years younger than herself and lived with him till he died. She was hard-working and paid her bills on time. This was not the stuff of eulogies. And he knew nothing at all of her earlier life, apart from a few random stories which never exactly cohered. Hers was, by and large, the biography of an unknown woman.

The cleric had nodded, anxious to squeeze her funeral in on time so the whole day's schedule did not go awry. You would be surprised, he said to Nick, comfortingly, the number of families who cannot summon up a eulogy because of all the conflicting emotions of the grief process.

Anger/loss/pain/acceptance flashing by like windows on a train.

So, during her service, Nick had waited, tensely, while the minister led up to her name - Mary Fresia Freeman - 'or Tizz, as she was more popularly known'. The minister had left a tiny pause before her name, so he could have time to glance down, yet not in the space where her name fell, so the mourners would not witness that ultimate sign of anonymity, a funeral with a small slot left for the individual's name. Yet this cleric's act did not fool any of Aunty Tizz's few caustic mourners (himself, Alistair his lover, a nurse, a neighbour). At the time Nick had thought, that is the story of Aunty Tizz's life: that brief pause, that swift elision, a prelude to the larger anonymity which awaits her.

Nick went into the town. It had an eerie likeness to all arid civilisations everywhere: a frontier town for a wilderness no longer visible, except inside the lean faces, distant eyes of the men and women as they sauntered out of the dole offices or the betting shops, the dour-smelling pubs.

He watched a large car drive down the centre of the road. Inside was a brave with a tattooed arm, like an extra fin of masculinity, leaning out the driver's window; his girlfriend was sitting in the middle of the front seat, adhering her form to his, obliterated. The car did an abrupt wheelie, tyres screeching. The girl inside did not interrupt her chewing of gum for a beat. In her face, the cool of a small-town siren. She has seen all the marvels the world can present. Even in this town, which once possessed the 'Eighth Wonder of the World', the Pink and White Terraces.

Finding himself in Hinemoa Street, *site of Stardust Studios*, he walked along the thin schism of memory, hoping to come across some connection to his past. Instead he came to the remains of a cinema. Its main foyer was now blocked up with budget chairs. Only the thick plate glass and exaggerated swirls of plasterwork told him that here was once a cinema.

Nick, interested in ruins and remains of illusion, was about to move on when he saw the words 'Stardust Studios', in an art-deco logo, written along the wooden top of what was once a glass display case. The windows had long been smashed. Inside were pinned several Xeroxed notices. 'Lost, Thursday 19 March,' Nick read, 'rottweiller pup arnsers to Pig. Reward.' Beside it was pinned another notice, written in demotic capitals.

SEND NO MONEY. SEND COPIES TO PEOPLE YOU THINK NEED GOOD LUCK. DONT SEND MONEY AS FAITH HAS NO PRICE. DO NOT KEEP THIS LETTER. IT MUST LEAVE YOUR HANDS IN 96 HR. A RAF

OFFICER RECIEVED $470,000. JOE ELLIOT RECIEVED
$40,000 AND LOST IT BECAUSE . . .'

Nick took it down and put it in his pocket. 'Faith has no price.'

Nick put his sunglasses back on. He walked past the Hair
Planet, the Shoppinge Basket, a Farmers Co-op. He felt
suddenly out of place, as if he were somehow cut out and
placed upon another scene, like some uneasy back projection
wherein an actor continues to perform a scripted scene
while behind him, moving in slightly eerie syncopation, a
documentary street scene is projected, with passers-by - non-
actors - entering doors, walking along holding their shopping,
with only occasional sly glances towards the camera indicating
that they are aware they are participants, accomplices in an act
of illusion.

Small-town life.

Nick passed two Japanese honeymooners staring down at a
map then glancing down separate streets. They looked up at
him expectantly, yet he had no better idea than they, perhaps,
of their situation, let alone their destination.

He smiled at them. The woman smiled back.

Beside them, an elderly Japanese man was filming, on
video, a completely ordinary three-storey building. Tojo's
soldier, now in mufti, moved the camera up and down
diligently.

Nick went into a coffee bar to have a cup of tea.

9

The White Horse Inn was a misnomer: it was a simple
concrete-block building with mock colonial furniture, a
spinning wheel, and a copper bed-pan. Watercolours of
English landscapes, which Nick recognised as representing
local views, were for sale.

He sat alone.

At another table a heavily made-up middle-aged woman, marooned in her jewellery, sat so still she seemed to be tranquillised: on her face a look of worn sadness. Her eyes were fixed on a gargantuan Maori woman with a small child banging her spoon, again and again, on the side of a teapot. The Maori woman made no move to stop the child. The air was charged with the light negativity, or restrained depression, which passes for everyday life.

Nick quickly looked away.

He thought of the undertaker who had wanted to know details of his aunt's death certificate for her funeral. A curiously young-old man who was used to essaying meaningful silences and soulful looks, the undertaker wanted to know where Tizz Freeman was born, who her parents were, what they did.

Now, sitting in the White Horse Inn, Nick's reply came back to him with a clarity so crystalline its edges cut and bled.

'I'm not really a relative,' Nick had explained, with a small smile on his face. 'I just sort of grew up with her. She was our next-door neighbour, so I don't really know much about her background at all.' The undertaker had clicked his ballpoint conclusively, in a small sound segment of disappointment. The gaps grew larger on his page.

'I know she came from Sulphur City,' Nick had said quickly, 'as she liked to call it.' He had smiled at the memory. She had always used the term with a special ironic imprint, a subdued savagery in her tone. *Sul*-phur City. She brought to it a smell of provincial magic acts, ones which, however, might reveal after the flash of titanium a dead and very old rabbit. Sulphurous hades, stale and befumed. A version of hell.

He had been surprised when the undertaker, who suddenly gave the appearance of having had another occupation quite recently, said he would check back through records. 'Your aunty', he said then, 'was 74 according to hospital records.'

To Nick, 'Aunty Tizz' had given out her age as 65 right up to the last: as if to admit some small detail was to risk withdrawing a tiny quoin which yet upheld the whole arch of her fictive existence. At the time, he had quickly put down the disparity in ages to the normal camouflage a woman of her period used when she was wed to a man many years younger than herself (Uncle Stan was five years younger by her fictive age, nine years by her actual age).

Nine years, he had realised, was an enormous fictional gap to bridge. He suddenly saw how exhausted she must have become by the constant pretence, and how, as she got older, her cheerful vivacity came to seem more and more like the tricks of an old actress who must rely on certain turns of phrase, well-known glances, even an animated countenance to cover a deep tiredness: perhaps an exhaustion with the whole charade.

Why had she never told the truth to Nick? It haunted him. There were many moments, which he speedily reviewed in his head, when she could have done so.

He thought of the drives as he took her up to the hospital for her 'treatments'. He would be trying to steer the car as smoothly as possible, so as not cause her any extra pain with bumps and sudden stops. Desperately he would ransack his brain for topics of conversation which were general, and easy. Yet she was holding on so tensely to her sense of self preservation that it was hard to connect on any rational level. But they had achieved some sort of peace in those moments, as she gazed out at the city she had lived in for so long. 'Hasn't it got big?' she would say, as if she were seeing it for the first - or possibly last - time. Nothing more profound.

It was on one of these trips, which in his mind now changed into an endless sequence of perpetual motion, of never arriving, of eternal transit, when she had looked at him, groggy with painkillers, and said, almost with surprise, 'You're a good kid, Nicky.'

He had felt one of the most intense pleasures of his life. For she was saluting him for the fact that he was with her at this last, and loneliest, moment in her life. And they were, both of them, surprised that the links they had both supposed so tenuous had survived. Did she pause, at that moment, on the brink of going on?

Perhaps she was too tired, too near the edge of final embarkation, to cross back over the bridge to what was inevitably going to be an intensely difficult emotional scene. Besides, she had by this time entered a strange gloaming world of fantasy in which Nick was almost an interloper. Hence the surprise on her face as she looked at Nick, calling him 'a good kid': she was actually surprised that this seemingly mature man, beside her, was related to the nervy, edgy child she had known.

And when he had taken her back to the private hospital, and was helping her up the two steps which she mounted with as much difficulty as a small mountain, and one of those depressingly vivacious nurses bounced out, asking her how her day had been, Aunty Tizz surprised him by saying to the nurse that he, 'her nephew', had taken her on a lovely ride all around the city, ending up at one of the best hotels for afternoon tea. They had even had a 'spot', as she and Uncle Stan used to call a drink, thus summoning up in his mind as a child a whole sporty world in which debonair couples stood together at fashionable bars, tossing back 'spots' while they exchanged witty repartee.

Now it was the nurse's turn to suffer Aunty Tizz's well-developed fictional skills. She had spoken with such authority and, indeed, against such real evidence of pain, the nurse was driven to continue the charade, asking for details of what they had eaten and what they had seen. Aunty Tizz abruptly ended by announcing Nick was taking her to Australia the following week, on a luxury cruise-ship. He had promised. A state cabin was booked.

At this point the nurse's eyes met Nick's, checking on reality. Aunty Tizz, sensing she was losing her audience, suddenly spurned Nick's arm and set off, tragically, attempting to walk alone to her hospital room where, without any comforting photos of Uncle Stan or other simulacra of family, she waited to be put to bed. There she would sit, silently and grimly mounting her watch against the angel of death.

She had told every nurse that Nick had a wife and child down in Wellington. Just as she confused all known dates and places, she had confused a time in Nick's life when he had left Gran's house, making a bid for independence to realise, clumsily and in private, his own sexuality as far as physically possible from the city in which they had all lived. Aunty Tizz had clearly rationalised this as 'having got a girl into trouble'. She persisted in this fiction even though she knew very well that Nick was gay, lived with Alistair and that her clumsy attempt to appropriate him to heterosexuality annoyed him. Yet as she entered more and more her gloaming world, she would ask Nick about his 'wife in Wellington'. It reached a point, in what had become almost a form of verbal ping-pong, in a hybrid hospital room which offered no clues for conversation, where he simply answered 'Fine', which despatched this fiction from their conversation.

Why had she not talked to him of the single thing which must have been obsessing her?

The last time he had seen her alive, she had been sitting almost bolt upright, back pushed into the iron bedstead. Nick had come unexpectedly and unannounced, so he caught her unaware. She was sitting there, her eyes almost bulging out of their sockets, staring straight ahead towards something which was clearly visible to her, yet not to him.

This vision was obviously so unearthly that he stopped still by the door. Her breathing was coming in harsh, ripping sounds, like lunch-paper rattling. There was terror imprinted all across her face. Nick had thought her face appeared like that horse which is being attacked by a lion in the famous Stubbs painting: what claws, what teeth savagely sank in, he could now guess.

'Aunty Tizz,' he had said softly as he walked across the pool of light which eddied across the polished linoleum, so he seemed half suspended in light, blindness. 'Aunty Tizz, it's me, Nicky,' he murmured as he got closer, smiling apologetically. 'It's me, Nicky.'

The fearsome orbs of her eyes, with the whites clearly visible all round the pupil, slowly turned towards him as she judged whether he was an hallucination, an angel of retribution, or mercy. For a second her eyes burnt into his, over his body, then with a very definite adjustment, as if the present now lay exposed and irradiated before her very glance, turned to dust and ashes, she simply lifted her gaze and continued to stare into the far-distant future – or *immediate* future – on which she preferred to concentrate.

She never spoke to him after that. The most she would do was lower her head, momentarily, to indicate she was aware he was present, or leaving her. Yet her gaze forward was so rapt, so intense, it was as if she could not for one moment risk taking her eyes off what lay ahead. It was as if she was already careering down a steep and slippery slope in an out-of-control sleigh whose safe transit she must try to engineer at all costs: yet everything around her was passing with such terrifying speed that all she could do was stare ahead, even the flesh on her face seemingly pulled back by the force of her momentum while she fought to pull breath into her body and her eyes bulged at the sight of the terrifying precipice ahead.

This vision burnt before Nick now, phosphorescent.

Just at that moment, he realised the middle-aged woman opposite was looking at him with heavy significance. He followed her gaze towards his cigarette. She was frowning at him, her whole face pursed in an expression of dislike – but it went beyond dislike, it carried within it a whole puritanical ethos: it carried the freight of her unhappiness.

She rose and came towards him. 'Can't you read?' she said.

The Maori woman opposite sat back and watched, entertained.

'Yes,' Nick said, 'I can read.'

The woman then swept across his gaze a newspaper which held, imprisoned, an image of the Minister of Health announcing the latest punitive measures against smokers. 'It's not fair on the non-smoker,' she said, angrily.

Nick got up and walked out.

Behind him, the woman called out. 'It's not only yourself you're giving cancer to. It's us – it's everyone here – the innocent!' Her voice rose up in a scale of impotence.

'Oh, bum to *you*, chum!' Nick yelled back at her, suddenly angry.

People out in the street looked at him, expressions withheld.

Nick threw his cigarette away. He had given up smoking before. It meant nothing. It meant everything. It meant nothing. Life was like that.

He walked away angry. Hideous little hick town, he said to himself. Nowheresville. It was like being caught in a prayer-meeting of the damned.

Then he heard his aunt's voice. 'You're a good kid, Nicky,' she said.

This slim sentence was all he had. 'You're a good kid, Nicky.' Goodbye.


PART 2


1


A tale told him by Aunty Tizz.

She had come to the city, she knew hardly anyone. She was a maid in a hotel, with a room up under the eaves. A man asked her out. They had no money. It was the Depression.

They caught a tram out to the zoo. Aunty Tizz had on her one good outfit, a white dress. They were enjoying themselves, just relaxing, when they got to the chimpanzees' cage. Here, her beau did a serendipitous rendition of how he saw the animals. Aunty Tizz laughed: perhaps she was laughing at the pleasure of her new man as much as at his wit. Unfortunately, a chimpanzee did not like this invidious human comparison. He shat into his paw then turned and showered it, forcefully, all over, not the man, but Aunty Tizz laughing geisha-like in her white dress. Aunty Tizz retires from this little film of memory, covered in chimpanzee shit.

Nick now heard her laugh, philosophical, a smoker's corrosive laugh, chesty, breaking apart into a hacking cough which then turns into a moment of anxiety – all illusion stripped aside as Aunty Tizz struggles to get her breath, clear her throat, while Uncle Stan sits forward, 'Tizz, you all right, pet?'

She would nod, not trusting speech: this conscript from Hollywood for whom to smoke was to be sophisticated and freed from all the small-town tyrannies of home and hearth.

Now Aunty Tizz has regained her speech, after a libation of beer, swilled down to soothe the ache, the burn in the back of her throat. She laughs at herself, at time, at pretense.

'*Bum to you chum!*' is her inevitable finishing line.

'*Bum to you chum*! cried out at bosses, toity shop assistants, bus drivers who take off too quickly, sending her spinning down the aisle in her wedgies. His grandmother, when she heard it, would wince at the vulgarity: she who never swore, never used any words which directly described sexual or anatomical functions. Aunty Tizz meanwhile remained obdurate and unrepentant. As she etched on huge Bette Davis lips in the mirror, watched by Nick, as the vast arc faltered just at that point where her relatively narrow lips were being transformed into the lush lie of cinema marquees, 'Oh bum!' she would say as she reached for some toilet paper to kiss between her lips while Nick, willing acolyte in illusion, rushed to get the toilet paper before her and gave it to her with tremblingly intense hands while she suddenly looked down at him, a little surprised, wrenched to a halt as if in recognition of him, of what he was, would become – years before he himself could articulate it.

This too was an intelligence, perhaps, that these three adults had passed in silent semaphore above his head: Uncle Stan, alone, and Gran, silently seeking to protect him 'from himself', or what they would see as 'his fate'. Kind Uncle Stan, who never called him 'sissy', and Gran, who never articulated her worry but who would later pray conspicuously to a God who could not hear her prayers on this subject.

It was beyond his aural range.

2

*ti'zzy* *n.* *(slang)* state of nervous
agitation *(in a tizzy, all of a tizzy)*
[20th c.; origin unknown.]

His first view of Aunty Tizz. Framed, as it were, by Gran and
her husband's hairbrush.

It was a venerable wooden brush, silver-backed, one of a pair
which Gran said her husband would hold in both hands to
flatten out any natural curl in his hair. There was only one
remaining brush. Nick's vagrant father had taken off with the
other. 'The only part of his inheritance he ever got,' Gran had
told Nick wistfully, thinking perhaps of the wider inheritance
he had had so summarily taken from him at that crossroads.

Gran was standing behind him, in the bathroom mirror,
dressed as always in black, her old breasts rising and falling with
an unreasonable passion as she flattened down his wet hair,
brushing abstractedly, angrily, her face closed and buried back
in some thought which had no relationship - he thought then -
to the child held tightly in her grip.

Nick had snaked away, crying out, 'Gran!', because she was
not a cruel woman, unless you counted the unconscious cruelty
of the pious.

Gran had looked down at Nick, red-faced and suddenly
felled by shame. He saw her eyes come into focus on him and
fill with tears. Nick had never seen his grandmother cry. She
prided herself on the toughness of her stock. She carried her
wounds in silence. But now the tears trembled and for one
terrible moment looked as if they might disgrace her, pouring
over her lids and down her cheeks.

Nick watched her internal battle. With an angrily jaunty
gesture, Gran wiped the back of her hand quickly across her
face, as if to banish the incriminating signs of emotion. Then
she did a very strange thing for her: she appealed to him

directly with an odd, distorted smile, a weird laugh which sought to ingratiate herself with him, as if to trivialise or nullify her over-emotional state. Nick had never known her to appeal to him, a child of eight, so abjectly before.

Gran said then: 'We are having two people round for a cup of tea. They might be moving in *through the wall*.' 'Through the wall' was the flat next door, in the bungalow where Gran and he lived.

The following day Gran enlarged on her theme: she spoke to him casually, as they sat together having dinner (timed always for 5.15 p.m., set out by the back door which lay open almost into winter 'for healthy breezes'). 'They're called Mr and Mrs Freeman. Mr Freeman works for the Electricity Department.' This delivered in a flat voice, stripped of all context.

Nick kept his own counsel.

But that night he saw Gran move the wooden owl, minutely adjusting its place on the mantelpiece, then stand very still, looking not so much at it as into it, as if seeking to ask it some mute question, or perhaps allay some ghost in her own mind. Even as a child he understood, and accepted, that he was witnessing some primitive act of magic.

When the time came for the arrival of Mr and Mrs Freeman – Nick and his grandmother never normally had visitors – he was crouched in readiness, mimicking a thousand radio serials, ready for crime, for a kind of criminality he was completely unaware was actually taking place. He hid under a native fuschia in the front yard and imagined he was invisible.

Mr and Mrs Freeman arrived in a shiny red Austin of England, with pale *crème de café* highlights.

In the harsh February sunlight, the chrome glittered and dazzled as the Austin of England did a graceful semicircle and came to a smooth, seemingly inevitable, halt by their front gate.

His first view of Aunty Tizz.

She is pulling in desperately on a cigarette, as if she is trying to get every bit of elevation the nicotine can offer: then, a pause as the smoke is held down: suddenly, through her immense nostrils comes an angry flare of smoke, enormous as cannon fire. She leans forward, as if having made an abrupt decision. She stubs her cigarette out, out, *out* with a passion which is almost operatic.

Now she turns her face full on to Nick, as her eyes, heavily hooded, made-up, flick over his head towards the windows of Gran's house. Her glance is quick, secretive: an initial surveillance. Nick looks at her thin lips, painted, the strange turban knotted on top of her head so she seemed, through the grey glass of the car window, at once tribalised, as if belonging to some strange unknown cult of woman, and yet quite naked, as if hair were some excessive frivolity she had long ago dismissed.

Now the man moved to the car door behind which the woman waited, like an actor behind a curtain, intent upon her cue. The man wore a brown pin-striped suit and two-tone shoes, something Nick had never seen before outside of the movies. Opening the door, he had something of the nervousness of aides-de-camp Nick had glimpsed in Movietone reels of the Queen's first tour.

Now the man peeled aside the door and at that moment, as the woman unfolded her legs, came the first surprise - she was wearing trousers! Then, as she placed her wedgie sandals on the scoria, she emerged from the car in an act of magic he would remember all his life: as she got out of the car and stood up, she appeared to grow and grow in height while beside her, in a seemingly parallel yet diminishing motion, the man grew smaller and smaller until, the transformation complete, he was revealed as almost comically short while she stood alone, gigantically tall, her own proud standard.

Nervously now, the woman adjusted her top in light fluttering movements, then the little man spoke a single word to her, a command, and she immediately obliged. In doing so, she moved back a little behind him, as if he, despite his size, could control her height and in that gestrue of power add to his own stature.

They moved past Nick in silence, the only sound the crunch of gravel crucified under the woman's shoes which he could see, gathering up clues like a detective, were odd, cork-cut wedgies into which her enormous feet were plunged and entrapped, to be carried indoors as a form of pagan sacrifice. Both of them emitted an intense nervousness, casually cloaked by the few words they murmured between themselves, as if to encourage each other that they would pass the stern test that awaited them behind his grandmother's door.

Yet, as soon as the strange man and woman – as odd as bit players in some vaudeville act, in Nick's world which was so lacking in *theatre* – mounted the two concrete steps, the front door fell open and there was his grandmother, formal in her black shantung, wearing her rare pair of formal shoes so old they were actually pre-war.

Did he imagine some glances exchanged over his head so he could not decipher their patterning? Did he sense a mystery which was playing all about him, and indeed centred, with an almost ferocious force, upon him? He had to answer, humiliatingly: no more than the way all life was a mysterious set of injunctions and laws – and these were new players.

The woman introduced the man and Nick watched as the man reached eagerly across the space, as if to signal a long-awaited honour, and offered his hand. Nick could see, even from his distance, that Gran did not like such forwardness: she hesitated. A few indistinct words from the tall woman were followed by her laugh – the first time Nick ever heard Aunty Tizz's laughter. It was truncated by the sharp click of the door.

After a brief period, Gran came and whistled for Nick. It was her own private whistle, a long trill which rose up suddenly and lyrically at its end, so it sounded like some obscure Australian bird she had heard, with prescient ears, distorted by distance, across the Tasman. That she could whistle at all was one of Gran's accomplishments from growing up with her brother. To Nick her whistle had its message: hurry up, I'm waiting; or take your time, dinner is five minutes away. At that moment it had never seemed more precious, more private, underscoring both their intimacy, and the intrusion, and *exclusion*, of the two strangers.

Nick's first reaction, however, was surprise. He had never seen Gran's front room with the blackouts down. She had kept them over the windows ever since the war, telling Nick with all the wisdom of the old that they saved the upholstery from fading. Everything, to his eyes, now had a sudden nakedness: you could see clearly the mould on the ceiling, the stalactites of watermarks where the roof had leaked last winter.

He saw all this, however, in a flash because the moment he entered the room, pushed along by Gran, he had had a terrible fright of shyness which so overwhelmed him he could not move, he had lost command of his limbs. He stood protectively close to Gran, whose smell of oatmeal soap and oldness guided him as he looked down at the autumnal sprays of leaves woven into the carpet. He could see Gran's old shoes, brushed up for the occasion, standing at right angles. For one second he had the hallucination that Gran had discovered his secret game: to creep into the front room and rob it of its somnolence by leaping from floral spray to floral spray, avoiding the pale beige background. But now Gran abandoned him, moving away to sit down.

'Say hello to Mr and Mrs Freeman, Nicholas,' Gran said tersely. 'Don't forget your manners.'

Mrs Freeman was sitting in a fawn moquette armchair, her long legs folded one over the other, so her top leg, as if to its own errant music, rhythmically joggled up and down.

Gran now sat a vast distance away from him, protectively beside the teawagon.

'G'day sonny,' said Mr Freeman, who, when Nick turned to look at him, was holding out his hand. It was a small, even dainty hand on which he could see a small emerald glitter. Nick looked quickly at Gran for information. Formally, ancient as an empress in some court dealing with possibly dangerous but certainly powerful emissaries, she gravely lowered her head.

Nick went forward.

'And this,' she said, as if such frivolity must lead on, be connected as in a criminal web, 'is *Mrs*' - was there a slight irony, a sense of heavy underlining, a tightening of the lips, or were all three so enwebbed in their trick upon him that none of the players could afford to give the game away? He looked

129

back down the years now, and did not know. He would never know. 'This is *Mrs* Freeman.'

'Call me Aunty Tizz,' the woman said. Her voice was lower in range than Gran's, more gravelly, a smoker's voice: but it also had a kind of sing-songy quality to it, as if everything she said was in quotes, or a joke, if only you could understand it.

Again Nick glanced nervously at Gran. She gave no advice: scalding tea began to descend into a porcelain cup.

The woman was still smiling at him, yet, unlike the man, Nick had a sense that she did not deeply care whether he liked her or not. Intoxicatingly, she left it up to him to see whether they would be friends. He could not ignore so frank and adult a declaration.

Holding his gaze with an almost flippant sense of power, she then said - brazenly it seemed to him now, because she was flaunting a connection he was not even aware of at that moment, though the other two people in the room were possibly tensed before her next remarks - 'Aunty Tizz,' she said in nonsensical incantation which yet played keys all over his heart. 'I'm all in a tizz, a bottle of fizz. That's what you can call me. *Yep!*'

Mr Freeman let out a laugh which rolled over itself, like bubbles inside a kettle as they fumed up the spout. It was as if something had been settled.

Nick looked at these two strange people. Aunty Tizz had said 'a bottler fizz', not differentiating between 'bottle of' and 'fizz'. Immediately he sensed how different the world of this woman was from that of his grandmother, who, along with cleanliness, God and Michael Savage, believed in clear and plain English utterance. The woman called Aunty Tizz, however, promised other delights, more louche, slacker, more carefree.

At this point Uncle Stan motioned Nick forward and showed him his cufflinks. He took them off and put them into Nick's hands. Nick gazed down at them. They were small - cheap he now knew, for he wore them - cufflinks of gilt and enamel. Their subject matter was an encapsulation of the universe which governed Uncle Stan and Aunty Tizz's life: a pack of cards, a bottle of champagne, a horse, a cancan dancer.

Nick had that day gazed down at them, aware they made up some intricate code which, at that moment, he had decided he must at all costs crack.

But Gran said to him firmly: 'Have a good look at them, Grey,' – she used his nickname, the name of her brother who died in South Africa, thus imaginatively reclaiming him: it was her idea that Nick looked exactly like him, not at all like his father – 'then give them back. It's about time you were out in the fresh air.'

Fresh air. Fetid air.

There was no question in Gran's voice. His time with the adults was over. He slowly returned the magic totems to the strange man who immediately, confusingly, made them disappear from his palm, then pulled them out from his ear. Nick took one final glance at *Aunty Tizz I'm all in a tizz a bottle of fizz*. But she simply looked past him, as if he had failed to be an object of sustaining interest.

Penitent as some envoy from an unknown and possibly barbaric tribe, he backed out across the carpet and found, with relief, there was still the known world outside their back door.

## 3

Now, in the motel room, he got up off his bed and went to the sink to get himself a glass of water. Outside, in the early night, he heard the sound of tyres screeching before, in waves of returning quiet, the absorbent sea of silence, of a small town gathered and ganging up and smothering its eruption.

Nick went over to the photo of the woman taken in the 1930s. It was to this photo he had turned, almost on automatic, driven towards it desperately, when he was haunted by her words, written on a piece of Croxley, given to Nick by her lawyer: '*I have lived a lie all my life.*' He had always believed it was a photo of 'Kay Francis Wilson', his mother. As a boy he had begged his grandmother for a photo of his mother and she, after a week's silence, had procured it. In that week Nick had cried, had tantrums, wet his bed, got sick. His elderly grandmother, no doubt wondering what she had taken on, handed the photo to him without comment.

As an adult, now, he was attacked by the thought that his grandmother – driven by a necessity as powerful as his own – had perhaps just gone to a junkshop and bought one of those unclaimed photos which sit, forlorn and unnamed, in boxes all over the world.

At that moment a vision of his grandmother suddenly appeared to him, in one of those moments of such astonishing closeness it is as if the person has reappeared, their closeness being almost in proportion to the ache of their physical absence. His grandmother was there, volatile as a movie image, violently alive. She was indignant at the suggestion she would lie to him.

He saw again Gran's face, miraculously alive, innocent of make-up except a little powder on the tip of her too broad nose, her bushy unplucked eyebrows and indeed the stray grey hairs which marked her pursed upper lip. He had come to love those hairs as the quintessence of his grandmother's personality, maddeningly annoying in their dogmatic assertion, expressing her refusal to conceal. Just as Aunty Tizz was a woman who expressed her personality through the camouflage of make-up – indeed, if you accidentally saw Aunty Tizz without lipstick, powder and paint you got a shock, a feeling of something almost indecent, as her skin, untouched by the sun but sullied by so many years of unnatural applications, gave off the eerie luminescence of people who live by night, shunning daylight: Aunty Tizz's huge Bette Davis lips were as much a trademark of her addiction to cinema as her hennaed hair pulled back into a chignon – so Gran, by contrast, never wore make-up: she was as honest in her presentation of her appearance as Tizz was, at least imaginatively (though the show was so easy to penetrate it could hardly be called so), dishonest.

This image of Gran now faded away, abandoning Nick. He knew Gran would never have settled for the subterfuge of a stranger's photograph.

He looked down at the face again. Slowly then, as if hearing the distant sound of an object dropped down an immensely long tunnel, like a silver coin ringing down a darkened wishing-well, he began to sense correspondences. He looked at the mouth again: he looked at the teeth.

The woman in the photograph had the smallest tip of what were clearly - if you strained your eyes - false teeth. Aunty Tizz had always had, from time immemorial, false teeth. It was one of the clues she would throw off, nonchalantly, about her past. This one she did with an almost celebratory dash, as if to illustrate her wanton frivolity, though in fact it was meant to celebrate her modernity.

Instantly he became convinced that the woman in the photo was the woman he had always known as Aunty Tizz. She was simply plumper and dressed quite differently from anything he had ever seen her in. She had a softer, even maternal look, her very plumpness and changed situation offering a disguise, a vision of a personality from another world. Yet in fact, once you accepted that the woman in the photograph was Aunty Tizz, all sorts of correspondences, hitherto overlooked, now emerged. And, as if following in sequence, like those paintings he had done as a child when he simply applied a wash of water to a page and a coloured image rose towards him, as he looked at the photo he realised he was looking down at his mother.

He gazed back up at the mirror in shock and saw, as in an overlay, the image of her face embedded in his own: the noses suddenly melded together, the whole facial frame. This eerie duality existed for one intense moment during which, unwittingly, he moved closer and closer to the mirror, inspecting his face - *her* face - all over as if it were the very first time he had seen his large nose, hazel eyes, tow-coloured hair: as if, in a way, he had had some remarkable facial surgery and now, after months, *years*, of being bound in bandages, he was being privileged to look on a stranger's face which from then on he would claim as his own.

Yet she was gone.

## PART 3

*'I need, I want, I met.'*

Nick went out to eat. It was a warm evening, a thin line of flamingo pink silk lining crushed mauve rain clouds. Sulphur City had settled into silence.

Nick chose a McDonald's along the road, as anonymous as an airport transit lounge. It was the eternal stasis of a fast-food restaurant anywhere. Customers occupied the building like transients, passers-by.

Nick first waited for his self-consciousness to subside, and gradually saw, to his side, one of those touching, vaguely sad couples, a middle-aged son sitting with his mother, eating food off their trays as if they were on a long, even an eternal, flight. The son, preternaturally aged so he almost matched his mother, seemed more like a husband than a son, like the vanished husband whose place he had taken.

Nick watched as the man reached out with a serviette and wiped, unselfconsciously, a dribble of mayonnaise from his mother's whiskery chin. She sat there, still, a child obedient to the odd asymmetry of her situation. Husband and wife, mother and son, tick of the clock.

Behind them, a child's birthday party was in progress. One of the mothers was bending over in genuflection to her desire to capture the moment for immortality, or at any rate grandparents: she held an Instamatic which engulfed the entire surroundings in blue fire, immolation of the moment.

What will happen to that photo? Nick wondered. Fire, divorce: lack of interest?

As he ate he watched one of the women, a young mother like many of his friends. She had two sons and one, the older, was holding court while the younger, snaking and slithering in his mother's arms, directed all his attention towards her, constantly pushing his body into hers, pummelling her breasts with his tiny fists even while he arched his back up to fountain out his love for her, demanding kisses, caresses which his mother, exhausted by the demands of her role, returned to him with a haunted, distracted gaze.

Now the children, half-crazed with sugar and salt, were running Redskin about the restaurant. The middle-aged son looked through them while his elderly mother, with crafty eyes, helped herself to a chip off his plate.

Nick ate his food ravenously, barely chewing it so that when he left he felt a vague nausea of indigestion. He always associated McDonald's with unhappiness.

Outside, the children were running amok in plastic.

As Nick began to walk back to his unit - his cell - a sudden nausea at his own company overcame him. The silence which awaited him, the introspection, suddenly appeared daunting, like a self-imposed sentence. He began to walk more slowly, taking in the busy street around him.

It was warm, the pink light had been replaced by a violet dark which now poured its glittering skeins and cloak over the small town. Tin caught fire, trees turned emerald. A church spire, becomingly, was its own metaphor. It was those few prescient moments before heavy rain.

Nick could hear, in the distance, the chant of a Maori concert party start up in an international hotel: the primal thump of haka upon polished parquet.

He passed a public toilet to his left. Outside it, harbinger of activity, a mud-plashed ute was parked. Red lights, white lights from cars dazzled as they strobed by.

Without giving himself a moment to hesitate, his body began walking him towards the door. He wanted a momentary escape, an exit from his fog of loneliness, of unknowing.

The spontaneity of his decision shook him alive: unhooked him momentarily from all the dragging fabric of his past. He was *acting,* alone, unknown, no longer son of Tizz: as he moved towards that dark place, centre of anonymous encounters, he was presenting himself as simply who he physically was - a male, flesh - in that wonderfully void slate, 'the stranger', the man passing through, the man-from-out-of-town.

Besides, he felt a hunger, which went beyond food, for touch, for the warmth of flesh, for the sudden inconsistencies of another human.

It is not true that grief and loss make a person isolated and alone. They send you like a rocket towards other people, simply for the sense of life, its banalities, tonalities, to be confirmed. How many children are conceived in the shadow of dying? And did dying itself, so many gay men dying, mean that there was no need for what, in essence, sex was?

A need for warmth, for touch, for flesh.

Now Nick moved, magnetically, towards another man, a zone of flesh.

Inside, the momentary darkness blinded him. Then Nick saw a young carpenter-type. He was blond-haired and like any young father with a toddler in a hardware store. Now he stood on his own, blessed by an endearingly ordinary handsomeness. His faded red Stubbie shorts were round his thighs, he was squeezing his cock, which was hard. He looked at Nick, laying out *his* flag of need.

Outside the traffic passed, lights splaying up and down the walls.

There was a sense of fission, a fountain, of being alive. Nick went into a cubicle and while the stranger frottaged him with one hand, and pulled himself off with the other, Nick read the messages on the wall *I need I want I met*. He pulled out his cock. The young man felt all around nicely, as a good lover would, and Nick felt a kind of relief seep through his body, unleash itself like a drug, that magical moment when the relief starts happening. He half-closed his eyes, he let out a groan, a moan. The stranger relaxed too and they hung together, touching, looking into each other's faces and eyes until they both, spontaneously - more enduring than a sexual spasm - broke out grinning at the situation.

Soon the young father came, squirted out onto the floor and, probably running late, patted Nick's arse nicely. They smiled again, hello, farewell, and he left. The stranger had a pink cap with a front brim which he had kept on, business-like, throughout.

After a decent interval Nick emerged, feeling cleansed, full of self-possession and even wildly happy.

Outside, in heavy drops, warm on his face, the pickpockplat of rain. He walked in a hot storm back to his room.

2

*'Happy Memories'*

Back in the motel, he was suddenly attacked by a need to talk to Alistair.

He got the answerphone. 'Hi,' he said, 'It's me. Everything's still. . . OK. I'm OK. I hope you're OK. I'm working things out . . .'

He ran out of things to say. He wanted to say: why aren't you there when I need you? Yet it was all so unfair. Alistair, who worked as a landscape gardener, had been so supportive when his aunt was dying. He had cooked for him, fed him, loved him: held him together, with those wiry arms of his. Yet he was not there now, at that moment, and it seemed such a betrayal.

'Ciao baby,' Nick whispered as he put the phone down.

He had not told Alistair what he was doing down there. He could not precisely articulate it to himself, it was just a sense of self-protectiveness, of nakedness maybe, a raw time in his life when he wanted to be as alone as possible, to find out – not exactly about himself – but about who he had come from, who he might be. He was naked, skinned, skint.

Next door he heard a quick burst of laughter, muffled, then a man's voice, clearly drunk, breaking into giggles. A woman's voice, soprano, took over and together, like two brooks babbling along, the sounds of twinned laughter came through the wall to him.

*Happy Memories.*

He opened the album. It was a cheap one, probably bought from a corner stationer's in the 1950s. It had 20 black pages, bound together by a thick black cord.

He had found it in his aunt's unit when he had gone over there that afternoon, after the news – '*I have lived a lie all my life*' – to find any evidence, any scrap, any clue which would tell him a little about his aunt's – or, as it was, his mother's – real life.

Already he had reviewed in his own mind, feverishly, like a video in fast-forward, all his images of and dealings with his aunt – his uncle – his grandmother. He had tried to snatch any sense of this hidden truth which, now he knew it, appeared so clear, even banal in its everyday presence. But what he wanted to do, after he had received the one-line letter from her lawyer, was to go out to her flat, to ransack it for evidence: perhaps a confession of *why*. Yet, like collaborators in a lost war, there was no evidence – nothing. Apart from an album named so ironically.

He could remember so clearly his mood when he had found it.

He was standing in her silent lounge, plants still growing, ash in the tray from her last cigarette. He had realised suddenly that everything about him signalled, not her past or her presence, but something more potent to him: an eternity of absence.

As he stood there, he had a distinct sense of the room watching him. It was as if the room were complete in every detail: it was he who was incomplete, requiring a totality which he might find hidden in any room.

Looking about him, he felt the spirit of his mother in every piece of furniture, as if everything was saturated in her smells, the miasma of her quandaries, the weight of her cruelly widowed gaze. All this enveloped him in a gauzy texture which silently sucked him in the door so that, as it clicked gently behind him, there was a kind of inevitability in that click, a sense of a fullstop.

He had gone into her kitchen. There was the table Uncle Stan had laminated in the Formica which echoed crumpled satin. The thousand empty miniature bottles still ranged along the pelmet. A cuckoo clock stood silent.

The sense of invading a set was overpowering. He had opened some cupboards. He saw the dinner service Aunty Tizz had used when Gran made one of her rare state visits through the wall for a meal. *Why why why*, his mind cried out.

Yet the answer he got was not to that question. It hung on every piece of furniture or item, no matter how small, in her flat. It is as if in death a personality falls apart and is shattered, attaching itself to any of the hundred thousand small objects which the dead person may have touched. And each one becomes pregnant with an intensity, a sense of belonging which goes back to the person who has just vanished.

So, when someone dies, the urge is either to keep everything or, in an equally excessive reaction, to throw all the evidence out. 'Starting afresh.' Which, he suddenly realised with the force of a revelation, was what his mother had probably done when she began her life as *Mrs Stanley Freeman*.

He saw then the way all the furnishings dated from one period, the late 1950s. He had never seen this as deliberate before, but now he understood how it formed a seamless carapace which effectively excluded anyone from knowing about what had gone before. The past had been deleted.

This enraged him: the room appeared fraudulent, deliberately opaque. Yet in some part of him, his homosexual part, he knew already what would drive someone to adopt another persona, to become 'another person'. The answer lay, not so much within the room, as in what had gone out the window.

Yet an unreasonable anger burnt through him. He had gone straight into her bedroom, over to her wardrobe and abruptly snapped a drawer out. But as soon as the drawer lay open in front of him, his mood, so equivocal and disturbed by everything around him, somersaulted.

The arrangement of the drawer was so complete he hesitated to touch anything. He had the terrible realisation that the apparently incidental arrangement of the drawer, the very eloquence of its casualness, was now as physically close as he would ever be again to the woman who had been his mother. And he felt so close to the moment in which his mother had just shut it that it was as if in one action she had pushed it to and, on the other side of time itself – a wall which cut him off from her as she was excluded from him – he was now pulling it open and looking down, hand going into the drawer, beginning to move towards objects which attracted him, as if by some mysterious pulse or magnetic field so that his hand, roving as a water diviner's stick, passed speedily over the ruffled handkerchiefs, the pieces of cheap jewellery (the wooden bowl brooch with its brightly painted fruit, the large pearl disc earrings) down to the bottom of the narrow drawer, picking up, then discarding a bowling pin brooch which had belonged to his grandmother, a few coronation coins in dented black plastic, an old tin thimble, dented and grey, with the words *SS Raumati* stamped on the side.

*This was not what he was looking for.*

He ached for something to help it all make sense. A direct letter, addressed to him, in which his aunt – his mother who denied herself to him – might explain her past life, the pressures which had led her to deny something so profoundly basic as a mother's relationship to her child. A relationship not so much denied as placed in that curious void of fiction: that she was an 'aunt', not his mother, and that she was not even a real aunt, but simply a woman who lived next door, familiar, friendly, distant.

She had never touched him, she had never stroked him. If anything, it was Uncle Stan, so profoundly childless during the post-war baby boom, who had claimed Nick by proxy; perhaps it was he, Nick had reasoned, who wanted to reclaim Nick as Tizz's child. Yet by that stage the die had been cast, and none of them could avoid playing out their fiction.

But he wanted evidence, he wanted some actual explanation to feed his ache, his fiery furnace of *wanting to know*. He had done research, quickly, quickly, and found out how women in that period, when having illegitimate children, were practically forced to part with them. They were given the choice of either keeping the baby after they had given birth, or simply letting it go, without ever seeing their child. 'It is better that way': tidier, cleaner.

It was a mystery Nick longed to, *needed* to, solve. Every part of his life, since he had found out, had faded into obscurity: his job, his lover, his present.

So he had found himself ransacking his mother's flat, searching for the reason.

He had glimpsed his face in a mirror. He was shocked. He had the appearance of a thief who, deliberately withholding any attachment to the personal effects around him, continues on in his work, single-minded, focused.

At last, when he was giving up, almost nauseated with all her scents and memories, he had found the photo album at the bottom of her wardrobe. It was under a pile of old *Woman's Weeklys*. Inside its back cover was a document. It made a point of identity, a thread from which everything unravelled: her marriage certificate to Stanley Freeman.

Wrapped inside the certificate were the three photos which Nick now had on the mantle in the motel room.

From the wedding certificate he learnt that his mother had been married before, to a Maori named Ngere, from whom she was divorced; that she had not married his birth father, Gran's son. Therefore Nick was what was once called a bastard: he was illegitimate. And Lulu Short, cinema attendant was the only living witness.

He had traced her to Sulphur City.

Now Nick poured himself a long drink and settled down, to look again through the album.

Taking a deep breath, like a diver about to enter an underwater world in which he knew he would soon find himself engrossed, he stared down at these pictures intensely, aware that behind every incidental image lay a story, a truth untold: as if the past pressed against each one, straining to get out to him if only he could reach into it.

The photos were a record of his mother's life with Stanley Freeman: there was no reference to any life before. Most of them were taken on their holidays together, those precious moments when they escaped the working lives which defined them so tightly: Stan Freeman, clerk in the Electricity Department, Tizz Freeman, wardsmaid.

The photos appeared mildly celebratory as his mother lifted her bottle of beer up to toast the camera. In these shots, he noticed, she showed an almost seductive relaxation in relation to Uncle Stan: she smiles, she poses, unconsciously taking on the body language of a thousand models posed against glittering automobiles. The fact that Uncle Stan's car is only a Baby Austin, or later a two-tone Zephyr, makes her statuesque inclination more tender, more intimate in her relation to the man behind the camera, who was modelling her, changing her as he gazed through the lens, into the beautiful and seductive woman of his imagination.

This Aunty Tizz was patiently, even passively, willing to contribute, gazing back at him - at Nick now - with a knowing female look on her face, softening her features even as she posed, placing her limbs together in mimicry of thousands of film stars. That she was not beautiful was defied by her air of happiness, her graceful size, the urbanity of her dress - in the wilderness she wears earrings, bracelets, slacks, turban - she exists in these photos with all her characteristic city persona intact.

They are happy. The images are bathed in Uncle Stan's adoration of his wife: he recreates her in each photo as his madonna, his Madame de Pompadour, both wife and mistress.

Rarely are any of the photos taken away from the road, whether sealed or roughly metalled. It is as if these two almost rootless people needed the invocation of movement, of speed – transience – to soothe them. And their buried nights together, alone in the landscape with their caravan and gramophone and bottle of scotch.

Nick took another sip of his drink as he gazed down at them, feeling suddenly so close. Next door he heard a suppressed groan of pleasure, male, and a sudden silence.

He looked more closely at the photos of Uncle Stan, because every picture of 'Aunty Tizz' is answered by an image of Uncle Stan. Yet the photos of him were all subtly different. In none of them does he look completely relaxed. Rather he is caught, mid-explanation as he tells Tizz how to hold the camera, and look through the viewer, focus and press the button. But this multitude of directions unnerves Aunty Tizz so the image is nearly always slightly skew-whiff, as if in her very nervousness to capture the ordinary she cannot help but imprison and explain her own uneasiness, her *need* to fabricate an unreal image of domestic peace, an ideal of happiness with this man she had married so late in her life. It is as if behind her, invisible, stands her past.

So Uncle Stan is caught, always a little peeved and strained, not holding the bottle or glass of beer up as Aunty Tizz does, laughing into the camera, toasting her good luck: with him it is the posed unease of a statue who must hold an action longer than the muscles will allow. Nick saw, now, how his 'uncle' looked back into the camera with the uncertainty of a man who does not know the full history of his wife's past: instead he must mimic an action of celebration, all the time showing in every part of his body he is unsure, bravely quiet.

Nick felt a kind of tenderness towards this man who had rescued his mother as she had got older: she had found a kind of peace with him, a plateau of rest. He adored her, that is plain from the photos, but whether this adoration was a subtle burden, the images did not reveal.

Nick was drawn to one matching pair of snaps in particular: Aunty Tizz and Uncle Stan, each in turn, taken against a 1940s car with a background of a wild open beach. It is clearly in the early days of their relationship, and the wildness of the wind lends a kind of poetry and eloquence to their emotions, as if they will both be blown away, disappear, vacate the image itself. They are city people in the country, in Aotearoa, inside an invocation of the mystery of pohutukawa, sea, land.

Nick glimpsed, looking down at these two images, his old romance that his 'uncle and aunt' were perhaps the Duke and Duchess of Windsor on the run, an ill-fated pair who lived only for romance, who had challenged the world with the very unusualness of their relationship. For in the conformist early 60s, it was as extraordinary to see an older woman attached to a younger man as it was to see a small man wed to a much taller woman. This tacit breaking of gender rules made them as much outlaws as the fact they appeared in that most pitiable of all conditions for people enduring the years of the baby boom: they were childless.

Now, looking down at these photos, on the other side of time itself as it were, himself a kind of gender outlaw, childless, homosexual - like his mother and his 'uncle' seeking to make in a relationship its own virtue, its own meaning, outside of imperatives like children or the law - Nick felt an accord with his mother, a sense of being her child, of her being a forerunner as much as an accomplice: this divorced Pakeha woman who had married a Maori, the woman beloved of Hollywood, *a dark horse*, a woman with a past. And the wind booms around them, as if sucking them in through the vortex of time, away into that invisible world in which only the present is left behind, both hell and heaven because of it: and these images remain - imprints, footprints on the sand, windwhipped.

Next door a shower sounded as the man, or the woman, or both, washed away the scents of sex. In the drain directly outside his window, the slithering sound of water disappearing.

Nick looked back at the photos. He saw how they showed the enclosed nature of her life, of two people without children, and how, in that relationship, all the feelings of a larger family become encompassed. She is mother, wife and daughter to Uncle Stan in the photos, slipping invisibly between roles so that, when Nick gazed at a stiff and formal image of Aunty Tizz with Uncle Stan and his mother, set in the suitably formal layout of a botanical gardens, he saw Uncle Stan's mother, a stumpy working-class woman arrayed in her Sunday best as stiffly as if she seeks the protection of armour, it is she who seems the intruder in the relationship, for she is already supplanted by Aunty Tizz as Uncle Stan's mother, a mother who sleeps with him.

So, in this rare photo, Aunty Tizz stands a little way from Uncle Stan's mother, supposedly leading her along but in fact turning her back on her, expressing her disdain in physical distance: Tizz is caught, mid-stride, as if the very length of her limbs expresses disdain for the smaller, older woman behind her. Aunty Tizz, in this photo, is dressed in the formal clothes in which she came to visit his grandmother: they are *her* armour: yet there is something almost defiantly sexual in them, in the freedom of her legs in the trousers, the lowness of her bodice, in her easy appropriation of her outsized body.

So, in this photo, Uncle Stan's mother is already defeated, disapproving no doubt, like Nick's grandmother, of this mysterious woman with an *unknown past* - a woman who would defy explicit questions about when and where she had lived at a particular time, whose only defence was to create a confusing and conflicting cloud of dates, places, times so that, like a jellyfish emitting a cloud of sand, the air would clear only to reveal that she had already gone.

In fact, Nick began to realise as he gazed down at these photos, Aunty Tizz's celebrated confusion was a defensive strategy which allowed her past to remain untrackable, unknown, like a mazed garden in which, once you entered, you moved along at your own risk and chanced being lost forever, while she gazed on without comment, her eyes as unseeing, and unforgiving, as those of a sphinx. This dishwasher for a fridge company, wardsmaid in a hotel, usher at the Civic - wife of Stan Freeman, a clerk in the Electricity Department.

4

Nick woke with a stranger beside him.

He had gone out, on impulse, to the Polynesian Pools, site of international cominglings of sulphur and male scents and glances. He had met there a young man who had come back with him to his motel.

The young man was not even handsome. He was a memory, Nick thought in the middle of their recital of passionate attitudes, of Paul, the grocery boy he had first had sex with: the same broad nose, the same almost dull eyes, the same ability to suddenly break into giggles, deflate. His name was Paul, too, though this came later, after the hunt, the find. And Nick, who believed himself to be a set of red elbows with awkwardly coloured hair, too tall, a nose set like a beaver to quarry out facts - the truth - now found himself being Paul's idea, or memory, of arousal.

So, in an anonymous motel room, site perhaps of any number of sexual acts, Paul and Nick had made frenetic love, as if within the flesh of the other lay some more transparent form - an angel, perhaps - of redemption, or forgiveness, or absolution for a few hours in which each might be whoever they chose, with each other, alone: those occasionally magic human moments.

At least they certainly aimed at magic. Yet with this stranger's cock now rhythmically moving up and down inside his mouth, the balls banging warm on the bridge of his nose, Nick wondered, with a quite objective sense of distance, how Alistair, his lover, might be back in Auckland. He saw his house, his cat: he saw the phone.

Up above, in the dark, this stranger, Paul, memory of his Paul of long ago who talked of his dork and that fabulously fecund word *rooting*, was now crying out a whole litany which Nick realised, releasing Paul's cock into the air, so he momentarily gasped, was from a famous American porn video. Paul was so sweetly clichéd that his words of imploring, his beseeching for comfort, for relief, for removal from that temporal zone of the flesh known as pre-orgasm, was rehearsing the dialogue of a porn king from the city of angels. Who was he, this actor of extraordinary intimacy?

Afterwards they had smoked a joint, talked a little with that silly, non-sequitur dialogue that follows sex: after an enormous intimacy, the barest limning of facts. For some unknown yet spontaneous reason, Nick made up a name for himself – Eddy – and became instantly a commercial traveller in Sulphur City for a conference. Paul was local, working at a legal office (Nick later found, the local unemployment centre). He played rugby league, had a large family, all straight. His mother, recently widowed, kept asking him when he was getting married.

They drank a little more, paused.

Paul said to Nick he would get into trouble staying the night.

Everyone knew everyone, Paul said, lying there naked, spunk just drying on the hairs of his belly. It was dangerous.

Nevertheless Nick and he had found an imperative which lay beyond danger: they both needed each other, that night, to survive.

So, they had made love during the night, it was true, but it was as if both were condemned to a form of ecstasy, as if within that alone lay their means of survival and each orgasm, taken from their bodies, was a flash of semaphore each could read, yet discard, knowing the script they were reading was transitory and not eternal.

In the middle of their transports, half-awake, Nick had wondered whether in his sexual attitudes and aptitudes he was trying to recreate the mother and father who had so savagely gone. Yet, in the midst of purely temporal pleasure of hairy and muscular thighs, or that strange boy's tongue seeking out his own, or his cock so tensile under his fingers, Nick knew he was celebrating nothing so much as the fact that he was alive, and they were dead.

It was that primitive: that stark.

And so Paul, memory of Paul, had come in the dawn, crying out as he bit Nick's shoulder, allowing Nick to see, to feel his own personal need so Nick, placing lip to lip, kissed Paul into silence and, gummy with semen, slick with sweat, heartbeat to heartfleet fading into darkness, each fell asleep in the other's arms, both, perhaps, rehearsing a formula of eternal love, yet both erstwhile warriors of the moment who knew that those moments – *now* – were what counted.

So, both in the hades of the present, felt heaven momentarily under their fingertips and were happy.

5

They woke late, with Lapidus creating a stage-effect outside the door to signal the return of reality: a jingling of keys, a hearty greeting to unseen customers with advice about that day's weather (a raincoat advised if seeing outdoor attractions).

Paul's eyes had opened to find 'Eddy' beside him. 'What was your name again?' Paul said as he tucked his foreskin inside his shorts, artless as a schoolboy in a gym. His figure had an endearing looseness around the stomach, an incipient sag of age which, in someone so young (Paul admitted to 24), had almost the air of an affectation, like an assumed air of knowledge.

Nick gave his false name, feeling a slight remorse.

'Busy after work today?' asked Paul, coming over to him and looking at him with eyes from which any judgement was withheld, yet behind them was a silent question.

'I've got an appointment today,' Nick said.

The pause between them was fragile in its intensity.

'Would you . . . would you like to see me . . . later?'

'Can I?' asked Nick, who felt like his grandfather.

Paul nodded, without smiling, affecting a casual dismissal of emotion. 'I'm easy,' he said.

'I know.' Nick said.

They laughed, Nick hitting him companionably on the arse.

'D'you want to come to the Buried Village with me?' Nick asked suddenly. He did not want, now, to be alone.

'*Now*, you mean? Today?'

'Yes. Today,' said Nick. 'When else?'

'Yuk,' said Paul. 'It's so boring. What do you want to look at that for?'

Nick paused. 'Come along for the ride. If you like.'

They looked at each other then, both speculating whether the night's attraction could last the light of a day: whether, in fact, it wasn't a crazy misuse of their attraction for each other.

Then Paul went to the phone and called in to work. He said he was off 'with flu' for the day. His boss said there was a lot of it about.

Nick and Paul laughed.

6

*'Who gazing at the green and verdant valley of today could guess at what had gone before? The horror of that night - a rain of fire, mud and death - and before that, a vision of celestial beauty, unequalled in the world - a sight people travelled from all corners of the world to see - and marvel at.'*

The Story of the Great Tarawera
Eruption, 1886

'What a dump,' paraphrased Paul, who was not open to the miracles of nature. 'The only thing I like is that old sewing machine stuck in the oak tree out on the road. And that bit's free.' He was smoking a cigarette and looking around him with professional disdain. After all, he was a local.

Nick and he were sitting on a rude wooden bench high up in the cleft of a hill. The hill was covered with scrub and the view was down the valley. Small tufts of vapour twisted through manuka. The sky was a hard white sheen.

They had stopped, en route, to look at Hell's Gate and Nick had taken Paul's photo then Paul had taken Nick's photo (with directions) in front of the mud pools called Sodom and Gomorrah. Somewhere, behind a cloud of steam, a peacock shrieked with mocking laughter.

Now a Japanese tour party emerged up the track, all happily chattering as they moved along, looking around them with sharp, interrogatory interest. For a moment Nick and Paul became an object of interest in several videos. They watched impassively as the bush swallowed up the file of Orientals.

'Reminds me of those men who never knew the war had ended and lived on in the jungle for years. You know. Caught.'

'Why?' asked Paul, non-plussed by this stranger.

'I don't know. Does there have to be a reason?'

Paul's answer was a joint of hallucinatory intensity which he passed to Nick. The dry pungent scent filled the air. They were silent. The valley grew particular.

'Who are you?' Paul asked suddenly, with a freshness of interest, as if he had just met Nick.

'Oh, I don't know. Just your average kind of fuck-up,' Nick said then, long and slow. 'You know. Adopted kid. No father. Brought up by my grandmother. Fucked in the head. You know. Trying to make sense.'

He was looking at the valley in the distance and thinking of his coming meeting with Lulu and what it might bring. He was also thinking of his life up till that moment.

There was a stoned pause, then Paul burst into laughter. 'Just your average fuck-up,' he repeated, rolling it around in his mouth as if he liked it. Then he turned and offered his hand to

Nick, as if they were just meeting. 'How do you do?' he said, quite serious.

After the smoke they went and looked at the remains of the Buried Village. If there was knowledge, it was not in the shards of pottery placed inside rooms, or the old ploughing implements, or the faded whares. This was a site abandoned by memory, ransacked by seekers. It was barren.

As they left, two men of shatteringly blond Nordic beauty dismounted from their bikes and walked, stiffly, into the tearooms.

Paul and Nick watched them in silence. Buried beauties.


7


Nick was running late by the time he pulled up outside Lulu's house. He was aware that he had only washed himself partially and that his face, it seemed clear to him in the mirror – that repository of images, as if within itself lay a whole index to his personality, issued forth day by day as a maxim, 'today you will be happy', 'today you will be uncertain' – was ridiculously happy. It was a joke, of course, at which he could choose to laugh.

Lulu Short's house was a small cottage shaped by a handyman into an approximation of deco. It was painted an unusual and intense orange, almost a challenge to the pastel houses nearby. And it had a luxuriant garden, which Nick could see had once been magnificent but was now going speedily to seed.

He paused for a moment to collect himself, then knocked.

The door fell open. A short, highly painted elderly woman looked straight into Nick's eyes.

Immediately he was engaged by the watery blueness of her gaze, as well as by the extraordinary painted quality of her face, so wrinkled and aged that the folds of flesh concertinaed around her eyes, mouth, forehead, giving her a curiously shrunken yet highly animated appearance. She had plucked eyebrows, painted none too accurately in a high arching quaver. A gauzy chiffon scarf was pinned round her throat: she wore a cardigan, bangles, bri-nylon slacks, scarlet pompom slippers.

She gazed at Nick for a moment as he stepped inside and, like animals, their smells intermingled. Her hall was very narrow, quite dark and elaborate with pictures, photos, ornaments. In fact, as he glanced quickly around, he could see the entire hall was almost a mosaic in its intensity of icons. Nick immediately longed to look at the photos in more detail but the woman said, 'Call me Lulu, love, everybody does.'

She caught hold of his arm with a surprising firmness. They had to touch: she wanted that. Nick squeezed her arm back, then saw a spasm of pain cross her face. 'Old bones,' she said with a throaty laugh, heading off down the passage-way. 'Follow me, follow me.'

She led Nick into a long, very narrow room which faced an enclosed garden which ran to the back wall of a motel. It was clear she spent most of her time here: there was a television set, a vinyl lounge suite covered in peggysquare rugs, a very old shaggy cat which opened one eye as Nick walked in, looked at him almost drunkenly, with a serenely hostile gaze: then, dismissing him seemingly as an interloper of minimal threat, the lid of the eye shut Nick from its dreams.

'That's Tyrone,' Lulu informed him with a theatrical gesture, throwing open her fingers as if she were introducing a lead act. 'After the late great Tyrone Power,' she continued, indicating on the wall behind her one of those magnificently contrived studio photos on which Nick saw Power's signature, 'To Lulu, My Favorite Fan in Maoriland'. The wall was studded with framed photos from all the major stars of the 1940s, many signed as if to a familiar and especially persistent fan.

'He was a gorrrrrgeous man,' Lulu said, drawling out the consonants, ending on a slight sigh. Then she subsided down to his substitute, the old and moulting cat.

'Sit yourself down, sit yourself down!' She seemed impatient to begin.

When Nick sat down she looked at him closely, shrewdly. 'So you're Tizz's boy,' she said, nodding slowly.

Nick nodded dumbly, overcome by his sense of, not shame, because that was not correct, but of gratitude, almost, at being finally recognised by another human being who knew, however coincidentally, some part of his past.

She leant forward and poured out some tea. Shakily, she handed him the cup. Softly now, softly: 'I figured as much. I figured as much.'

They sat in silence, both sipping their tea. There was an entirely peaceful feeling of contemplation in the air. For one moment Nick felt that he was sitting with Aunty Tizz again, that he was a child.

'God rest her troubled soul.' There was a kind of conclusive sadness in Lulu's voice. She almost whispered.

'She never told me,' Nick said then, shocked by how aggrieved his voice was, how fresh the hurt. 'Till she died. In fact not till after. She left a letter.'

Lulu let out a sharp, almost smacking tsk, but sadness fought the outrage, overwhelmed it like a wave coming in. 'Tizz always loved being a bit of a mystery woman, a bit of a Mata Hari, you might say. I knew her, of course' – she said the 'of course' as if it were historically evident, something you might read in history books, 'from when we was both down at the Civic.'

She paused then, her eyes moving to the left, as if she were visualising the past at that very moment. 'Dress circle, rows F - P, 26 steps up, 26 steps down. She was a looker, Tizz Ngere - not what you might call a beauty but, boy, she could carry off the blokes.' Lulu croaked then with laughter. She reached down and grabbed a packet of Pall Mall.

Nick watched as she lit up, sharing the same beautifully exaggerated choreography as his mother. Like a vestige of beauty in a ruin, this elegance remained.

Lulu blew out a fan of blue in contemplation. 'Her and her stately walk. Queen of the Nile, we used to call her. Like she was carrying one of them vases on her head.'

She paused, lost in thought. Then she looked at Nick sharply, a little surprised to find him there, in her sitting room, right by. 'You take after your father.' She said this as if it weren't entirely a compliment. 'I can see that.'

'I never knew him.'

She nodded then, as if she was remembering. 'He let her down something terrible.'

She glanced at Nick, then her eyes moved again towards that unseen distance, as if up there remained, in a cloud of knowing, all the tinctures of the past. 'Cause, she wasn't exactly no prize, with that baby in her background.'

Nick said nothing. He thought then about the photo of the unhappy child staring up with questioning eyes towards the camera.

'Thelma Mae,' Lulu said after a time.

Nick looked at her and she could see in his eyes, his face – his father's face with his mother's nose, his mother's eyes – that he was anxious, racked.

'I'll tell you what I know, pet,' Lulu said suddenly, reaching out to pat, then squeeze, Nick's hand. Nick thought for one dangerous moment he was going to cry.

'She was living with your father in a caravan, out of the city. They're a regular pair of turtle doves, know what I mean? One day she rings up and I says how are you Tizz and she says he's gone. That's all. He's gone. Gone where I say. Gone, she says. Gone.'

Her face was almost imperially vacant as she entered the empire of memory.

'So I went out there on the bus, catching two buses to get there, and it was a Sunday, so everything's closed, not even a dairy open. So we go and sit down on the railway station. She was carrying you then. It's too late to get rid of it, she says. Do you want to? I says. I don't know. I don't know what I want. Look at me, she says, a woman going on 40 pregnant to a man young enough to be my son. I could just die. I could just die.

'Now, you don't want to get like that. Nothing's as black as it seems, I says. Nothing's that bad. She just looked at me: I got the stuffing knocked out of me this time, Lou, she says.'

Lulu stubbed out her cigarette decisively and looked down at it for a moment. Then she took up her story again.

'So I ring up the Salvation Army; I ring up your grandmother. Your grandmother says she made her own bed, now she must lie in it. Tizz goes into Bethany; she's in an odd mood, won't talk, won't lie there, just driving everyone mad asking if he's turned up, this is a woman nearly 40, not 16.

'Then the news comes through, your father's gone and got himself killed. A boy. A boy to the end. Got himself killed on some crossroads.'

Silence.

The cat beside them suddenly woke up, began an agitated inspection of its fur, cast a malignant look at Nick, as if he were to blame for upsetting its reverie, then subsided again.

Lulu went on: 'I go to see her and she's down in the kitchen now, she's totally changed, she's working and singing and it's like a wedding. It's not right, Tizz, I say, it's not right. What's not right, who are you to tell me what's right. I'm going to have it adopted, she says, someone'll want it. I don't care. I don't give a tinker's cuss. Her exact words. I don't give a tinker's cuss. O she was bitter alright, she was as hard as nails that woman. On the outside. On the outside. No Tizz, I says, one day you're going to regret it. You're going to regret it. One day.

'Next thing I know she's given birth, it was premature, and I'm in there and she says I don't want to touch it, I don't want to touch any part of him ever. You can't be like that Tizz, I say. Oh can't I, she says. Oh can't I? She was so angry, it was like it was burning her up. She says I'm out of this dump as soon as I can walk so help me God.

'You can't come back to the Civic, I say, all the girls know, the boss, everything. They like us to be of good character, you see.

'I don't care, I don't care, she keeps saying. But I know she does. Next time I go she's gone, just walked out like she said she would. Up and went. And I go in and see the matron. What's happened, I say. I want to know about the little one, who's looking after him? I sort of felt sad. That was when your gran turned up. She swallowed her pride, she came straight back from burying your Dad and she says, I'll have him. I'll have the baby. I want him . . . so that's it. That's it.'

They rocked to a complete silence now, together.

A sudden wind shook the house. The cat's fur shuddered briefly. Then a slow groggy purr started up.

Lulu looked at Nick closely.

'These things I'm telling you, don't take them to heart, boy. People do things . . . do what they have to do.' She shrugged. 'You don't know what it was like then,' she said shortly. 'It wasn't easy. A woman on her own. Abandoned. No. It wasn't easy.'

Nick thought about all the things Lulu had mentioned: the station, his mother and Lulu sitting side by side, Bethany, his grandmother.

'I can see your mother in your eyes, she's in your eyes,' Lulu said suddenly. She reached out to pat Nick's hand and then, unexpectedly, he turned to her and tears began slipping and splashing down his cheeks. Yet he was, oddly, smiling too, a strange fixed rictus of a smile, whether of embarrassment or joy he could not work out. He kept seeing his mother and Lulu, a younger Lulu, sitting down on an empty train platform, on a Sunday, with everything closed.

Lulu finally wiped the tears off her own face and offered him her handkerchief – a sensible man's handkerchief, beautifully washed and cleaned. 'I figured we might be needing this,' she said, smiling at him. 'A good bawl does everybody good.'

Nick wiped his face clean, and it was like he was wiping away some tissue below which lay a cleaner skin, one which breathed freely, was shiny, like skin after a burn, when the protective callous comes off.

She looked at him now, his new face. 'I think this calls for a good stiff gin, don't you pet?'

They sat then and talked about themselves. Lulu told him of her life in the theatre, of her two husbands – one bad, one good. She delicately never asked Nick if he were married, or had children. She accepted him as he was.

Lulu then described the registry office wedding of Stan and Tizz Freeman, the strained celebration in the dining room of a local hotel. By this stage Tizz Ngere was definitely 'damaged goods'. Lulu only ever saw Tizz at odd moments after that, like when Tizz and Stan drove into the main street and parked their car and, two suburbanites, watched the nightlife of the main street. 'She looked like she was missing it,' Lulu said.

Nick was aching throughout all this to ask about Thelma Mae. Who was she, where did she fit in? Was she still alive? But delicately, almost as if Thelma Mae were an issue she chose not to cover, Lulu never approached her.

Finally she said, gently, both having had several almost-hallucinatory gins, 'I've given you lots to think about. Maybe you should come back tomorrow.'

As Nick stood at the door, Lulu said: 'She wasn't a bad woman, she just had to fight her own way.' She seemed about to go on, to divulge a piece of information which troubled her. Tyrone the cat appeared sulkily behind her, glanced at Nick with the temper of someone disturbed from daytime slumber, then padded past him towards the light, shedding the mysterious aura of his name as he emerged into ordinary daylight, at which point he leapt away, suddenly freed.

'Can I call you tomorrow,' Nick said. 'I want to, need to stay in touch.'

8

Paul and he were in the shower when the phone went. It was Lulu speaking with the direct imperative of the old: those who do not have time to waste. 'I've been thinkin' about it,' she said, without pause, as if they were mid-conversation. 'And I couldn't rest at night if I didn't tell you . . . tell you . . .'

Her resolution faded away.

'Thelma Mae. She lives the other side of town. I know who she is and she knows who I am - *I think* - but we only ever nod in the street. Let bygones be bygones, I say . . .' She left a long pause.

'Thank you,' Nick said.

Paul came up behind him and tried to embrace him but, after a moment of stilted harmony, Nick bunted him away abruptly. He turned round to see hurt written all across Paul's face.

Sulkily now, Paul padded over to the bed, threw himself down on it and turned on the television. It was a game show and a dazed woman was being shown a glittering automobile which revolved on a platform full of flashing lights. 'You're so lucky to win,' the MC was saying to the audience, who screamed and clapped. 'This could change your life.'

'I couldn't rest if I didn't tell you,' Lulu said then. She sounded exhausted by the battle which had led her to ring him up. 'If I didn't give you the chance . . .' Her voice was fading away as if some vast pressure at the other end of the phone was dragging her away from him.

'Turn that fucking thing off,' Nick said to Paul, putting his hand over the receiver.

With a click of disdain, Paul, a Caravaggio nude, turned off the television. He began to dry his hair with a towel.

'Lulu,' Nick said then, turning his back on Paul. 'Thank you. Thank you. You don't know what you've done for me.'

'Yes I do,' she said frankly. She read out Thelma Mae's address.

Paul was meant to be with his rugby league mates. He was meant to have the flu. Instead he was spending time with Nick, a man he called 'Ed', preferring it to 'Eddy', which he said sounded like an old-fashioned musical comedy.

To Nick, 'Ed' conjured up images of a television series about a talking horse - one whose testicles were wired to produce mouth movements. Nick was not sure if he approximated that image.

Paul seemed to luxuriate in his presence. While their sexual relations were purely between two men, Nick had a sense that his own caresses and kisses were healing, not exactly in a motherly way, because that was to name an object or an action incorrectly, but because all his motions in relation to Paul were those of a nurturing nature, just as Paul, swiftly changing the nature of their discourse, became his name, feeding him his cock, his nipple, soothing him with the sweet flavours of flesh, of sex.

Nick had come clean. 'I live with someone else,' he had said in a voice which was careful in its lack of emphasis, either negative or positive. 'And my name's not Eddy.' He went to a piece of paper and wrote down his full name and phone number.

Paul meanwhile was looking at the three photos, propped against the wall. 'What are these old photos of?' Paul said waving them at him.

*Old* photos. The past.

'*My family*,' Nick said succinctly. My family. Nick gave him the piece of paper.

Paul looked down at the paper and then up at Nick and his dull eyes, the eyes Nick saw as those of Paul, his first lover, smiled as he said, 'You cheeky bugger, Mr Average-Fuckup, I always wondered who you really were.'

'So did I,' said Nick, but Paul didn't get it.


9


On the front door was a galleon in full sail upon an improbable sea. It rode the crest of the wave so precipitously it was as well it was frozen in glass.

A figure moved behind. The door opened.

Nick felt an almost physical blow of recognition, for there stood a woman, aged about 55, with greying hair a little yellowed by cigarette smoke, yet the living image of Aunty Tizz crossed with a softer Maori strain, giving her brown eyes, not hazel, broadening Aunty Tizz's beak of a nose to a flatter, slightly squashed prominence, her lips fuller, more generous.

She wore trousers, an oddly dated outfit, and she was smoking a rollie.

Nick realised later that he must have been looking at her so intensely without saying anything that she - clearly his half-sister - was about to ask if he was all right. But a large Alsatian appeared behind her, putting up a ferocious display of warning, hostility.

Nick didn't know who to look at, his half-sister, the dog.

'I'm . . . Tizz Freeman's son,' he said out loud for the second time in his life. And, each time he said it, his heart was eased and softened and some terrible knot within him unwound.

Now it was the woman's turn to gaze at Nick, so intensely that it was as if her eyes were staring straight back through him as *she* was carried back to that one joint point, the woman from whom they had both, yet separately, come.

As the perception hit home, and her eyes finished travelling swiftly across Nick's face, down his body, back to his eyes, the door opened wide and she murmured, 'Stone the bloody crows.' Then she turned around and yelled companionably to the dog, 'Rusty! Shut up! He's a friend!' At which, almost magically, the Alsatian changed from being a fierce guard-dog into a kind of swooning tail-swishing pet, with moist eyes, who came forward to sniff Nick, to add his scent to the catalogue of smells that would identify the known from the unknown. And the door into Nick Burns's past opened wide.

They were sitting having a cup of strong tea. They were both, for the moment, stiff. Thelma Mae, or Johnny, as she said to call her, asked Nick how he came to be down in Rotorua.

'I sort of got obsessed,' Nick said with a small painful smile.

She shot a look at him, hard, enquiring, then her face softened a bit.

'Yeah, well, it gets to be a bit like that.'

Nick stood up. 'I only found out she was . . . she was my *mother*' - he said this at a rush, like a horse at a fence nervous about jumping, except this time it was easy, he sailed over - 'after she died. You know, I kind of grew up with her. I thought she was my aunt. Not even a relation.'

'More than you could say for me.'

'My grandmother brought me up,' he repeated, numbly, as if it were a catechism, the final form of his penance: it was the last time, the very last time, he would ever have to explain it. 'I called her . . . Aunty Tizz.'

'The cow abandoned me.' There was a bitterness in Johnny's voice. Now it was Nick's turn to wait.

She shot another look at him, noting her mother's eyes, her mother's nose. 'I've got no reason to feel sorry that she's dead,' Johnny said then, rolling herself another smoke. 'She walked out of my life. I never so much as knew her.'

They were talking about their mother in this impersonal way, yet there was a necessity behind it, a cleansing.

'Trying to give up,' Johnny said then, making a face at Nick as she lit her rollie, breathed in deeply, held the match up and, blowing out tobacco smoke, extinguished the flame, and lowered the dead match to the tray where she dropped it, useless.

'The bitch ran out on me when I was 15 months. Walked off with the boyfriend of the girl next door. *Girl* next door. She was 30. She must have been wild,' Johnny said, a little softer then. 'She disappeared downcountry with the horse crowd, a pretty wild lot, drugs, booze, parties, the lot. Then the coot dumped her in Auckland. Got sick of her, I guess.'

But then Johnny was hard again. 'I got no brief with her, ever.' With trembling fingers she now pointed her cigarette at Nick, almost accusingly: yet the haunting thing was she held it exactly the same as their mother.

Johnny did not notice, in her passion. 'I'll tell you the God's honest truth, no bullshit,' she said then.

She sat down hard in her chair, hunched forward, as if the memory was a physical pain, her body a shell nurturing it.

'After she took off, I got left with Dad who worked in the meat factory and what could he do? I got farmed out to family, first one lot, then another. They were hard-working people, kind enough but I always knew I was the kid that got left behind. Dad got religion and I didn't fit into the picture. She certainly didn't.'

There was a pause as she breathed out, thinking, a long almost painful silence.

'Once I tracked her down, up in Auckland.' She looked at Nick aggressively then, as if he represented the city. Then her gaze dissolved into reflective memory – painful memory.

Suddenly she laughed.

'She got the fright of her life, I can tell you. She was living in a hotel down Freemans Bay – not what you might call a good part of town – and I followed her down the street and I thought, yes, that's my mother, that's her. I kind of knew it. And I followed her and knocked on her door. And she looked at me and said yes, and it was kind of like she knew it might always happen: what she might fear.

'So we sat in this room, it had a bed, washing drying on the line. I was straight then, I mean I had on this outfit, I was thinking of getting engaged and . . . I couldn't sleep wondering what kind of person I was, came from . . .' Their eyes met then, acknowledged each other, melded. 'Yeah,' said Johnny knocking the edge of her cigarette carefully on an ashtray in the form of a race horse's head. 'I wormed it out of my aunt where she lived, and I came up on the train, first time I been to Auckland. I sat in the movies all day getting up my courage then I went up to her digs.'

Johnny paused, her voice had become bitter. When she took up again, her voice had a lighter quality, but it was, Nick thought, only an attempt to cover the pain.

'She sort of says it's nice to see you. People are walking in the corridor outside and each time footsteps stop, she gets tense and I get tense. This little runty chap' – Uncle Stan, Nick thought to himself – 'knocks, ready to take her out. She jumps up, lets him in; suddenly she's this 15-year-old all giddy as hell and she says not now pet please. I'll come down in five minutes. *Five minutes.*

'The door closes, she says sorry. *Sorry.* Then she goes over to her purse and empties it on the bed. She goes to the drawers.

162

She starts emptying all this stuff onto the bed. I just sit there, I don't even, can't even call her Mum. I can't. I want to. And she just does this like it's what she'd been thinking of while I was sitting there. And then she lights up a cigarette and she says, Take it. Take it all please.

'I said, I don't want your money.'

Again they looked at each other. Nick nodded slightly.

'She says, no. Please. Take it. Take it. Then she says, almost to herself: I know I done wrong. She looks at me, this hard old bitch who left me when I was 15 months old. I had half a mind to take it, I can tell you. But it wasn't what I wanted . . .

'Then I says Mum - it's the first time I says it. She looks at me, she doesn't quite like it, she even glances at the door. She is upset and disturbed all at the same time. I think: *five minutes.*

'That's not what I want, I want to say but I can't say it. So she says it again: help yourself. Take it. And when I don't move - *I can't move* - she shrugs, she says suit yourself, it's your choice, then she picks up her handbag and says I'm going now, leaving it on the bed and the door shut and I looked at it and I thought of how I wanted to ask her advice on getting engaged and everything and I just looked at the lipsticks and the banknotes and little bits of crystal and I walked out quietly, went down the stairs and I walked back to the station crying all the way, bawling my eyes out. And I sat on the station and waited for the train home and came back here and that . . . and that was the last I ever see or hear or know of the bitch. And I am not sorry to tell you the God's honest truth.'

Then she smiled a little, crooked smile. 'Till you turn up on me doorstep, half-brother.'

They talked desultorily then, moving about the house while Johnny did the dishes, fed the dogs - there were four altogether, with names and personalities. Then Johnny showed Nick her horse trophies: she was a trainer at the local racecourse.

All through this discourse, which was fragmentary, brook-like, now passing over boulders, then rushing quickly down a fall, each had the surprise of looking up and seeing the other person who shared the same nose, the same jaw, the way they held cigarettes.

They were talking when her friend came in. 'This is Doris,' Johnny says po-faced. 'This is Nick, he's a cousin, well,' she paused. 'A brother, sort of.'

Doris, who appeared oddly like Johnny, except that she had a head of wild frizzy untameable hair and the face of a weatherbeaten fisherman, looked at Nick in silence for a moment, looked at Johnny, then looked back at Nick. 'Well whaddyerknow,' she said then, with a not unphilosophical whistle.

The Alsation stood and looked between all three of them.

## 10

'She was a strange one, all right,' Johnny or Thelma Mae said later that night, as she made Nick a bed in her spare room. 'I don't know. I often used to think of her and what it was that made her tick.'

'Didn't you ever want to, well, look her up again?' Nick asked, a small smile on his lips.

'Hell no. I heard she visited her folks once but, you know, they must have been kinda like a hairshirt for her. They were methos – Methodists, hard people, they don't forgive and they, you know, they felt she put a stain on the family name. Primitive times,' she says, 'I'm not saying they're not primitive now, but in those days, the choice was, well, strictly limited.'

Johnny told Nick then that their mother had been married at 15 to a man 14 years her senior, with a young family, who ran a local boarding-house. She did it to get away, but ended up being a skivvy. It was from this man that she had run away with Johnny's father – Johnny Ngere.

Doris came in and Nick watched how the two women related. He saw that Doris had the warmth of a mother, a kind of serenity or content. Nick let slip about his lover, Alistair, in Auckland. They had all laughed. Nick said: 'Snap!'

They talked at length about the discovery that was their mother, then, as he was about to go to bed, Nick stood up and stretched. Johnny stood up too. It had been a big day.

Just as she was about to leave the room, Johnny took one look around it, as if she was searching for something. Then, as she stood by the doorway, about to go out, she asked Nick shyly: 'Do you think she ever . . . thought about me?'

Nick looked at his half-sister – Tizz's daughter – the daughter she never knew. 'Yes,' he said.

He thought then of his mother's eyes bulging in their sockets, as if they were previewing alive what only the dead can see. What did she see as she sped towards her extinction, as her end rushed towards her? Nick did not know, would never know. But 'Yes,' he said. 'Yes. I'm sure she did.'

'Figured as much,' Johnny said as she went out, not entirely dissatisfied.

Nick went to his window and opened it and immediately, from outside came the sulphurous smell, the warm dampness of steam which he could see, outlined in streetlights as white wisps, chimeras which took shape and changed, fading into night.

Further away, on the main road, a truck passing, its lights carving out a spectacular curling whirling rainbow of light which searched everything it passed over. Soon only the pale imprint of its sound remained, fading away as the silence of the small town gathered its forces and re-settled. Nick heard down below a woman begin gargling in the bathroom. A milk bottle was placed out, glass onto concrete.

And just as he fell asleep Nick murmured to himself, Bum to you, chum. Bum to you. And he thought he could hear Aunty Tizz laugh.

# OF MEMORY AND DESIRE

## PART 1

## 1

SHE WAS A short, slightly bow-legged woman who looked older than her 28 years; though this may have been the clothes she chose which were drab, poorly made on the whole and looked as if they had come from a factory shop. In fact she was one of those rare people who look better without any clothes: naked she was a smooth ivory shade all over, with pleasantly shaped breasts which were neither large nor small. Naked she was unselfconscious, most herself. She was a computer keyboard operator for the Suseychi Corporation, she was newly married and her name was Sayo.

They were an odd couple, everyone on the tour remarked on it. He was so handsome in an almost cinematic way, with perfect cheekbones to catch the light, a full sensuous mouth chiselled, it seemed, into his face. He was tall, particularly for a Japanese, as if he were part of the new Japanese race that, with better food and living conditions, was growing to outpace the Americans, the Germans, the Australians. But if Keiji were tall, he moved a little diffidently. In fact he was most at ease in a most peculiar position: standing on his hands. This was his party trick and even, stranger to relate, a form of relaxation.

Keiji was a tense young man, as perhaps befitted someone who was doing well in the same Suseychi Corporation as his wife: aged exactly 24 on his wedding day, he was within several years of being made a junior executive. Whether his marriage would help or hinder this, no one was quite sure. Sayo was not the usual kind of woman an executive's wife should be: she was no beauty; she came from a poorer class than Keiji, whose father had served in the Imperial Army and whose mother, a proud and somewhat overbearing woman, laid claim to descending from a noble, if impoverished, lineage. Keiji came to his marriage a virgin.

Sayo and Keiji had decided to get married in New Zealand, on a package tour, because it seemed easier. Keiji's mother had only grudgingly accepted the match, and then only because her son, her only son, had uncharacteristically refused to budge. In fact it was the first time in their intense life that his widowed mother had found her son obdurate. Perhaps it was this that had made her accept Sayo, whom she saw as common, ordinary in every way: incapable, indeed, of sustaining an intelligent conversation, uncertain about important matters of etiquette, and altogether what she expressed to herself as 'tarnished', 'second-rate', 'possibly even Korean'.

With a woman's intuition she saw that her son's bride was already sexually experienced. There was something in Sayo's level gaze which told her this, the somewhat indecorous way she sat; even, indeed, the way Sayo touched her son, which Mrs Nakajima, the mother, regarded as appropriating, casual, too confident. Living with her son in their tiny Tokyo apartment, Mrs Nakajima felt sure he was a virgin. She saw Sayo as a kind of temptress, a perception which sat at odds with Sayo's ugly clothes, lack of refinement, even her rather ordinary face with widely spaced eyes and clichéd haircut.

Yet Mrs Nakajima sensed that the two young people were intensely in love: it was one of those accidents which happen. Privately she would have preferred Keiji to educate himself sexually with this young woman then move on to the kind of woman who would be useful to his career, provide handsome children and look after her in her dotage. But Keiji would not budge: in her view he was foolish and naive to propose to Sayo. She was a mere computer operator in a room so full of them that Mrs Nakajima, who had seen the room once, visualised it as a paddyfield viewed from a train, with the bent backs of workers intent upon their labour. Naturally Sayo had accepted. Mrs Nakajima had received her, done honour to her in a way which was calculated to make her feel miserable and uncomfortable: for example she unconsciously held her fingers under her nose, as if she perceived an unpleasant odour emanating from Sayo, a thing unforgivable on such an important occasion.

It was perhaps for this reason that Keiji decided, with Sayo's collaboration Mrs Nakajima was certain, to go to New Zealand, get wed alone and experience at least one week on their own before they returned to take up their residence in Mrs Nakajima's tiny apartment.

2

They were married on the front lawn of a colonial New Zealand church which had been shifted to a transport museum as an exhibit. It was a common place for Japanese weddings, and in fact, that day, there had already been two others. Confetti speckled the lawn like lightly trampled daisies, yellow, pink, pale blue.

Sayo wore a hired bridal gown, all white, while Keiji was handsome in his own dinner suit. Sayo thought of the brides before her who had worn the dress, wondering to herself what had happened to them, whether they were happy or sad. But she cast these ideas out of her mind and decided, according to the European custom the dress itself was her something 'old'. Keiji, in her eyes, had never looked more handsome, pale beneath his taut skin, his eyes gazing at her with what seemed an almost fanatical intensity of desire.

They had had to ask a passer-by to take their photo.

Standing together, against a lake which had once been a reservoir, they posed, smiling into the bright, almost iridescent New Zealand sunlight, arms around each other's waists, tense with the happiness which was about to descend upon them like a storm, leaving them, hopefully, happily drowned.

3

They began their honeymoon tour that afternoon, right after a celebratory lunch in the most expensive hotel in Auckland.

They had each had Chivas Regal whisky, which went straight to their heads, and Keiji, who liked to talk, entertained Sayo with a vision of their future, when they might have their own flat and perhaps go on foreign visits and Sayo could even stop working. Sayo did not feel comfortable talking when Keiji was outlining their future. For one thing, he was so much better spoken than her: indeed, in public with him, she often saw people turning to gaze at her speculatively, as if seeking to diagnose her relationship with a man so handsome, so well-dressed, so suited to success.

Besides, Sayo hardly talked much at all: she had learnt when she came to Tokyo from the provinces – her father was a railway worker till he had an accident and was forced to retire – that the less she said, the less people could learn about her and, hence, look down on her. It was true that her mother had died in Sayo's infancy and her father, who was too fond of pachinko parlours and sake, had found another woman to take her place. This woman was not unkind, but she never regarded Sayo as anything other than an impediment in her relationship with Sayo's father. Her father and the woman liked to get drunk, and laugh a lot, and play cards late into the night.

Sayo had escaped by working in two jobs and training herself to be a keyboard operator. Unlike Keiji's mother, to whom it was menial, Sayo saw her job as something which had removed her from an unhappy situation in which she was always in excess, and she even felt uncomfortable when Keiji mentioned, as a matter of course, that when he became more successful in the Suseychi Corporation, she would certainly give up work.

This was the only small cloud on their horizon as they went towards the hotel where the bus tour began. It would take them, in six hurried days, around the small islands that people back in Japan talked about as so green so clean so empty. Together they had agreed they would tell no one they were newly-weds. It would give them more privacy.

4

The tour was made up of 23 people, all Japanese: Keiji and Sayo were allotted seats which they would keep for the duration of the trip. In front of them were two younger women who already, as they looked from Keiji to Sayo and back to Keiji again, more lingeringly, broke out into giggles as if Keiji and Sayo had written all over them the almost guilty fact of their wedding.

Behind them sat an elderly couple who rose, bowed to them pleasantly, indeed courteously, the elderly man, who was deaf, offering to help Sayo put her luggage into the rack.

Across from them sat a rather beautiful young woman whose hand was held possessively by a powerfully built man who did not shift his gaze once as Keiji and Sayo came and sat down, preferring to look ahead and say to his companion, they were already running, by his watch, 4 minutes 30 seconds late. He then said things were not done that way where he came from, mentioning a small provincial city which Sayo could remember seeing from a train and thinking how ugly it was and how her spirit would die if she had to live there.

The bus slid away as Sayo and Keiji settled back in their lambswool seats. Sayo let her leg bump softly against Keiji as they turned a corner. Keiji turned his face to her for a moment and Sayo felt for the first time a misgiving that he could direct such a passionately driven glance at her, so powerful with love. She smiled at him softly, as if to intimate the pleasures of the night ahead. He let his leg rest against hers and so, bumping each other with each accidental motion of the landliner, they caressed each other's bodies, exchanging a duet of silent glances, each of which was full of answering affirmation and promises that the night to come would be a memorable one for them both.

Sayo hardly noticed what was outside the window. When she did so she gazed at it almost without comprehension, seeing it through the reflection of the man whom she was amazed she had met and whom, in a few short hours, she would divest, like a spirit which would be freed, of his virginity.

To everyone about them, apart from the man opposite, to whom nothing was apparent apart from the young woman to whom he was explaining the relative merits of the other bus tours, it was clear that Keiji and Sayo were newly-weds.

## 5

They could hardly wait to be alone. The last-minute arrangements took an eternity, during which they had stood apart, as if, almost decorously, they chose to be separate so that they could better enjoy that moment when they were alone behind the door.

Unfortunately there was a mess-up with the rooms and the elderly couple who had sat behind them ended up in a room with two single beds which, to the amusement of everyone on the bus, they indignantly refused. Sayo and Keiji had to wait around while the rooms were reallocated. They spent their time taking a short walk out into the crisp clear air, looking at the rough graded soil around the motel, marvelling at the unnatural greenness of the pasture all around them. For them the landscape had an eerie prescience, unsoftened by human form. There were hardly any animal forms either apart from a few distant, almost cosmetically placed, sheep. Neither talked as they returned to the motel. They were given their key and made their way down anonymous corridors towards their bridal suite. They were almost numb with desire and apprehension.

## 6

'Go slower, go slower', she had to beg him as she began to realise that he was, indeed, a virgin and, in a common mistake, was trying to roughly impress her with his love-making skills which she imagined he had picked up off pornographic films he had watched with his male friends in a bar. She had wanted to gaze upon his body which she longed to see naked: she wanted to take his cock into her mouth and tell him how much she loved every part of him. But he would not allow her to move much, he was intent on lavishing upon her a somewhat brutal passion which did little for her: though she realised, through love for him, she could not hurt his pride by not showing desire.

Everything went as he seemed to want it until the crucial moment when, murmuring with a rapture which to Sayo herself seemed completely false, Keiji attempted to penetrate her. Sayo had had an experienced lover before - just one - a kind elderly man, somewhat like her father to look at, she felt ashamed to admit to herself when she thought of him in hindsight. But this elderly man had been a knowledgeable lover, educating her in pleasure, the ways to seek and maximise pleasure between two humans.

The elderly man had travelled the East during the war: he had even spent time in the pleasure houses of Shanghai. Sayo, though no promiscuous woman, had gained the knowledge of the many actors in love whom her elderly lover had known: thus, in her one lover, she had as it were experienced many others. This gave to her love-making a sense of greater experience, just as it gave to Sayo that undeniable thing in a human being who has experienced early pleasure and who knows how to obtain it: the sense of being centred in oneself as a healthy animal being.

He who could talk so well, knew so much, now rolled off her, panting, sweating. He lay with his eyes closed and Sayo, raising herself slightly to touch him tentatively, heard a groan escape from him, almost a sob. He had lost his erection, and she looked down at it for the first time in the relative calmness and objectivity she knew she would come to in relation to this most vital part of his being.

Keiji's cock was slightly smaller than her elderly lover's, but her elderly lover had given her to understand he was well-endowed. Her husband's cock, though, was sweetly shaped, almost cherubic within its glans, lying there on his stomach as the de-escalation of his breathing continued.

He turned his face away from her, deeply shamed.

She slowly began to kiss Keiji, beginning first at his hairline, which, as was natural in a young man, was strong and marked, down to his brow, fierce and frowning, across the two rigid lines on his forehead: she kissed his eyelids which he kept shut, tight with shame, no matter how she tried to caress them, with light bird-like kisses, to open: she kissed down his nose to his lips which she touched with the very lightest of caresses: and so, down his body she adventured, touching him, kissing him, accustoming herself to his form with her lips till finally she reached the instep of his foot, which made him suddenly curl upwards, begin laughing involuntarily, even as he called out angrily for her to stop. Suddenly they were fighting, naked, and she was almost stronger than him until he suddenly pushed her aside and they kissed long, long and deep, their first really intense kiss, a promise almost of the pleasures they would eventually find: a kind of pact.

Later in the night Keiji again tried to penetrate her. She woke from her light sleep to find him astride her. This was not pleasant – he had, as it were, penetrated her dreamworld – but she relaxed under him, seeking to offer him every assistance, through unguent movements, small cries in his ear, caresses on the inside of his thighs. But again, at the climactic moment, he did not remain hard. Instead they kept kissing as if nothing much had happened, or rather, as if they both expected this to be the outcome, which, for their mutual survival, they agreed to accept for the moment. So they fell into a slightly uneasy sleep, both aware they were revealed to each other in a particularly vulnerable state: she did not want to intervene on such vulnerable territory, but she knew enough to let him know he could relax: things would find their own course, it would be worked out.

She did not say this in words: rather, her kisses and caresses, and the way she held him as he slipped into the darkness of sleep, told him. And thus he was saved from being enormously unhappy.

Daylight brought them their faces almost as if the sun were a servant who had sneaked into their room and, on a tray, carefully laid out two dishes to welcome them back onto Earth. Yet they tousled, sleeptorn: both seeing each other for the first time as they knew they would see each other again, time after time. Oddly enough, the night had made Sayo appear beautiful, tousling her rather prim hairstyle, loosening her body, while Sayo, gazing silently at Keiji as he gazed back at her, saw there were small lines on his face which would manifest themselves as he got older: it was as if, for a moment, she saw what Keiji would be like as an old man. This oddly comforted her. That morning, together, they simply kissed, as if it were agreed, and each obtained great pleasure from it.

They showered, dressed and presented themselves to the others, who all gazed at them significantly, as if testing how their night of love had been. Most people concluded that they were drugged on a surfeit of love. Yet the elderly couple, to anyone looking closely, seemed the more happy.

8

That day Sayo took more interest in the scenery. They had been taken to the sulphurous district and Keiji talked to her knowledgeably about vapours, gases, energy, power. It was his opinion that the people of the country did not know how to harness the riches which were so evident about them. Indeed, the small town in which they found themselves had a certain dispirited air, as if, through its century of tourism, all that was genuine had been worn away, replaced by a gimcrack unreality of 'authentic' tourist experiences.

They went to look at a sheepshearing exhibition, gazed at charmingly naive and low-tech displays of how New Zealand gained its agricultural wealth. They walked over a small plastic wooden bridge where a recording played bellbird tunes and papier-mâché trees imitated a forest. Sayo was fascinated by a mechanical cow which illustrated how a cow eating grass turned out milk.

Keiji looked at all this with an uninterested air. He took out his video-camera and, while pretending to be filming the exhibits, turned it instead onto his new wife, observing her obsessively, possessing her through the camera. She pretended not to notice this, not out of conceit but because it was only by appearing not to be conscious of her husband's intense regard that she could relax with it. Thus she played to the camera at certain times, directing a coquettish gaze at it as they took in another sight. At other times she simply gazed back at him hungrily, as if she wanted to possess him then and there. She observed Keiji did not seem noticeably upset by what had happened the previous night: though whether this was simply keeping up 'face' she could not tell, she felt she did not know him well enough yet.

Keiji certainly seemed to be less obsessive about touching her all day. In fact she observed him, during lunch, flirting with a small group of schoolgirls from the bus who, unanimously, burst into thrilled laughter at his somewhat feeble humorisms. He did not look at her while he was doing this and Sayo assumed that Keiji was used to women finding him sexually exciting and that it was part of his personality, almost, to flirt and flatter these people's expectations. She did not feel jealous.

After lunch they went to a place called Hell's Gate where, in blinding white light, they walked over what seemed like a miniature desert, made up of boiling water and mud. There was a strong smell of sulphur in the air. As the guide explained the different names of the pools, 'Sodom and Gomorroh', 'Hell's Fury', 'Hate and Revenge', Sayo played hide and seek with Keiji's camera lens as he found and lost her again in drifting veils of white smoke.

9

That night, alone in their motel room, they were each struck by an attack of shyness. It was as if they knew each other both less and more than ever before. Yet Sayo recognised she had to take charge, to a certain extent: besides, she was driven mad by a desire for his body, his strong thighs, his sweet small nipples so cherrybrown on his pale pillowy chest. She went up to him and kissed him deep, on the mouth. He tried to pull his head away but soon he was kissing her as passionately and Sayo heard, as if from a long way away, Keiji making small supplicating sounds, almost subconsciously, like a small animal begging and calling and crying out for her to continue.

Their love-making now was both brutal and affectionate. They made love on the floor, right by the door, with footsteps coming and going beside them. This time she took his cock into her mouth and made love to him long and elaborately. Yet no matter how much he enjoyed this and their other mutual caresses he did not stay hard enough for penetration. Yet this fact, so baldly stated here, had become a mere incident on a longer journey, like something they had passed, fleetingly, outside the bus window: quickly seen, then gone. She encouraged him, then, to bring himself to orgasm, revelling in seeing his body stiffen, his thighs tauten, his toes even digging into the soles of her feet as his breathing grew faster and more hurried until finally, quickly, his eyelids fluttered closed and he jetted against her stomach warm and sticky.

He fell immediately into a deep sleep, in her arms, which lasted for a few minutes, possibly ten: then he awoke and kissed her with an almost dazzling degree of passion and love. Although she still had not achieved orgasmic satisfaction herself, or indeed even been penetrated, she felt a deep tenderness for Keiji, a profundity of feeling which was greater than any she had had with her older lover, or indeed any feeling she had known since her mother died. In fact, as she slipped off to sleep, in bed with Keiji, she dreamt of her mother for the first time in over 10 years. In her dream, her mother was washing her.

She woke up feeling blessed.

They went to some hot pools, the whole busload. There was much merriment looking at the body-shapes. Sayo and Keiji, playing together in the hot pool like a pair of languorous fishes, laughed at the elderly couple as they padded, very carefully, over the tiled floor then slowly lowered themselves into the warmth. The old woman had a body made slack by child-bearing and age, skinny legs and soft, loose flesh. The old man had once had a fine physique, you could see that, but over-indulgence had weakened him till his body looked like jelly-white baked flounder.

Sayo and Keiji, lying in each other's arms in the water as delicately as possible so that, on the surface, it suggested that they were not even touching, exchanged whispered sentences about the old couple and rather unkindly laughed at them.

Later in the dressing-room, the man who sat opposite Sayo and him on the bus was changing beside Keiji. Keiji could see him comparing their bodies, the size of their penises. While they both dried themselves, the man - standing in ostentatious nakedness, displaying himself so all could see - talked about virgins, boasting about his sexual prowess with his new wife, making various indelicate puns and innuendos. The man, called Tatsuro, then ran his hand with mocking pleasure down to Keiji's buttock, which he squeezed appreciatively, all the while telling him how the women on the bus couldn't keep their eyes off him and all Keiji had to do was slip out of his room, late at night, and he would find any number of other - and here he used a crude word to describe women's private parts.

Keiji felt deeply uncomfortable but, being used to male chatter and the necessity for boastfulness, and the homoerotic voyeurism it signified, laughed but said he and Sayo were happy with each other. Whereupon Tatsuro, now fully dressed, said as a man he could never get enough. Keiji left the dressing room feeling oddly sad.

They went to a huge and powerful waterfall after this. The gush of water was so exhilarating that everyone rushed off the bus, chattering and holding their cameras, pushing into one another in their eagerness to get outside where they could hear the young schoolgirls already screaming in excitement as they ran down to the narrow bridge.

Keiji and Sayo walked together, silently, holding hands. It was as if they were unwilling to lose, for a moment, bodily contact. To the elderly couple behind them, they were touchingly in love, offering them a kind of memory of their own passion, from a time when they themselves had waited almost dumbly for all the company to leave so that they could be where they desired most: alone together, naked.

Keiji and Sayo walked towards the deafening roar: a fine mist rose around them. There was an almost erotic power in the drone of the water. Holding hands tightly now, because the sheer volume of the water frightened Sayo, who came from an inland area and could not swim, Keiji and Sayo walked across the narrow swinging bridge, then started back again. Halfway across Keiji forced Sayo to halt in the very middle of the suspension and pressed his body hard against hers, forcing her, half-crazy with fear, to turn to him, her lips trembling, dewed with water while he smiled into her face, cruel with love.

Miming because of the roar, Keiji got the deaf elderly man to take their photo. Standing in the mist, they posed, bodies hugging each other, Sayo's face white, her hand gripped tight as death around Keiji who, at that moment, looked paradisically happy.

When they reached land on the other side of the bridge, Sayo felt faint. She had a sudden longing for food. Abruptly removing her hand from Keiji, she walked alone to the bus and quickly went and sat down. Keiji came and sat beside her and in silence they travelled along till Sayo fell into sleep, her head coming to a natural rest against Keiji's shoulder while he sat there, looking beyond the somewhat brutal profile of Tatsuro, who was talking to the man in front of them. Keiji was unaware that the young woman opposite was stealing glances at him, as if she was wondering what it would be like to make love with a man as handsome and tender as Keiji.

## 12

They looked down at the plate in front of them, the round shelled peas the same unreal green as the pasture, the potatoes the same white as the mountains, the thick slice upon slice of beast, still bloody in parts, lying in a pool of gravy the colour of their mud pools.

Keiji turned to Sayo, and Sayo turned to Keiji as all around them the buzz of conversation took up, about what the food was, how to eat it correctly, what its taste might be. Already their guide and translator, Kaoru, was telling them it was 'New Zealand's national dish': this did not exactly recommend it. Keiji was beginning to see the islands as unevenly civilised, with the small cities which closed too early at night, and the large pink people looking at them with an unreal too-smiling courtesy and, beyond that, an outer ring of people looking at them with cool dislike. He did not know exactly what these hairy, uncouth people were saying but it was implicit in their eyes, in the way their mouths moved, that they were not saying complimentary things about them. Keiji, whose father had been in the Imperial Army and was in fact in Singapore when the British Army was forced into ignominious defeat, realised that history was full of hidden clauses: they were all existing in an uneasy juxtaposition, full of ironies: he a person from the land of Hiroshima, they a newly poor country dependent on the largesse of strangers.

Keiji and Sayo ate their meal, or as much as they could bear to, when the tastes were so unvaried and mild: only the meat, of which there was an unreal superabundance, had the necessary quality of fresh kill. Politely they ate, made appreciative sounds: but their plates were half-full when a rather surly waiter whisked them away from their table. Then they

179

had watched a Maori dance group during which both Keiji and Sayo were aware of only one thing: how close their bodies were to each other, and how long it would be before they were freed from the seemingly interminable stretch of time which separated them from falling onto each other's bodies and beginning, afresh, that exciting voyage of discovery in which each could exchange personality with the other and so assume the transubstantiation which is the basis, and strength, of all love.

At last they were alone. The succession of bedrooms in which they met provided them with new scenery each night for the theatre of their passion. That night it gave them an oblong woody room, a large flat double-bed impersonal as to the conquests and defeats which had earlier happened there.

Alone, Sayo and Keiji began to undress each other, fumbling and furious in their passion to reveal each other, as if to test whether, during the infinite duration of the day which had kept their bodies muffled in clothes, the other had changed. Now they were naked, it was almost frightening the power they had over each other's bodies, the intimacy. Keiji led Sayo quickly to the bed and, not even pulling down the covers, kissed her so passionately that they both fell, in a slow delayed topple, back onto the bed, where lip found lip then broke apart, after a certain period of violent pleasure, both gasping as if for celestial air, then each mouth began to travel, frolicsome and flirtatious, about the body of the other.

Sayo found that the smooth stretch of Keiji's body, between his nipple and his thigh, was so tender that she only had to lick it, delicately, with her tongue, for him to crease down into helpless silent laughter. Keiji, to whom the business of a woman's body was new and hence full of marvel, found that gentleness was as persuasive as vigour, and that Sayo's hands, placed gently on his, educated him as to what gave her pleasure. Thus he ravaged her with tongue and fingertip till she was equally yielding and wanting, as if he were the most masterful and penetrating of lovers. This continued for an almost unendurable amount of time till Keiji, finding this so erotically charging that, gazing down at his lover, looking at her flushed face below his, the beads of sweat moistening her upper lip, the way her head tossed and turned from left to right, he pulled her arms crudely apart so that he might enjoy, unhindered, the full theatre of her passion. He pushed his stiff penis towards her and she now, as if a curtain had swiftly gone up, revealing before his eyes a fabulously gilded light, arched her body back and began raining a storm of kisses across his face, his chest, his nipples, all the while issuing sharp cries of desire, want, need.

Yet a terrible thing happened: just at that moment when he should penetrate her, his cock would not obey him. So it was that, suddenly retiring, but still kissing her so she did not understand his signals and, for a fatal moment, continued on her full theatrical performance of enticement, while he continued to make love to her with his tongue and fingers, he abruptly dropped away from her onto his back. He lay there silent, as if he had dropped back down a deep dark well into sleep – so far, indeed, that there was no way she could reach him.

Humiliation, shame for her performance, disappointment meant that for long moments they both just lay there, in the now profoundly silent room, listening to the diminishing duet of their panting breath, Sayo alone keeping contact by placing her hand on that part of Keiji's belly which she knew to be most susceptible to touch: and she let her fingers lie there, hot, sweaty, still.

When she kissed him, he returned her kisses, but they were lacking the full depth of passion. They were automatic kisses, instantly full of regret. They broke off and Keiji said to her, after they lay for a while in silence, Sayo playing with his pubic hair, matting it thoughtfully with her fingers, that he would have a sauna in another part of the hotel. She did not ask him if he wanted her to be with him..

When she was alone, she lay there and thought of her old lover. Instantly she recalled images of their love-making, which occasionally had been quite bestial. This aroused her

181

and alone, quickly, even crudely she drew herself to orgasm. Then she rose, showered, gazed at herself in the mirror wondering who that stranger was and how she had come to be in that strange room, on her honeymoon, alone. She crept under the cool covers and slept.

Coming back to their room much later, his skin tissue-thin from all the vapour, Keiji made the mistake of going to the wrong door, so identical were they all. For one moment he had had a terrible presentiment, for, behind the door, he could hear quite plainly the panting of a man rising up into orgasm, accompanied by the relentless shoving of a bed against a wall: a lower diminuendo was a woman's voice begging him to hurry, to finish, it was painful, too painful. Yet this seemed only to increase the fury of the man's actions for, as the woman began to issue a strange cry, pleasure inseparable from pain, Keiji realised it was not his own door but that of Tatsuro and his new bride. Keiji stood there, slowly losing the exact jab of his pain. Yet as he drew away a silence had fallen in the room, followed by the ugly snore of Tatsuro, clearly already in deep sleep, and the softer sound, almost plaintive, of a tap being turned on, ablutions made. Was he imagining it, or could he hear the sound of a woman crying?

When he found his own room, Sayo was already lost in sleep. He crept in beside her, not touching her, alone, bruised. Yet Sayo soon, as if the magnetic proximity of their bodies was too much, rolled towards him and fitted her body neatly to his side. Keiji felt a pure and hard erection. Alone he masturbated, then fell into profound sleep.

13

The following day they walked, as if in a trance, around a vast and echoing museum full of artefacts of a culture which appeared to them both, in the state they were in, as threateningly dark, primitive: signals of chaos. The schoolgirls asked Keiji to take their photo on the steps and for the rest of the tour Keiji hid his face behind his video-camera, filming indiscriminately every room, as if he did not possess the power to take away his eye from the lens.

Sayo looked down at some cruel combs, blunt pounders, filagreed spears of unusual refinement: she felt a moment of pure misery sweep over her. From behind the museum glass case, she saw the elderly couple looking down at the exhibits. Their cheerfulness lifted her spirits. Yet she followed around silently behind Keiji, almost like an unnecessary attaché, ignored. She saw the young wife of Tatsuro looking at her: she did not understand it was with complicity. She too was ignored; Tatsuro was in the middle of the flock of schoolgirls, making an embarrassment of himself by ostentatiously examining the penises on certain Maori carvings.

## 14

They sat on the bus as it travelled ever southwards. Keiji had fallen into a deep sleep, his face whitened and strained. Even in his sleep, he carefully did not allow his head to fall upon her shoulder. He removed his leg when it accidentally touched her own. Thus reprimanded, deeply unhappy, Sayo sat there, gazing at him with a saddened erotic intensity, allowing her eyes to caress his body, memorising, as she looked at him minutely, every detail of his flesh and hair and hands: as if she might one day lose him.

So she sat there, gazing, erotically moved into a state not unlike a trance, absorbing into her brain the whirl of his hair at the back of his neck, the way several strands of hair fell down across his forehead; the way his hands lay together and his perfectly manicured nails rested so lightly on the palm of the other hand. The bus rocked and lulled and shook their bodies and she longed, oh longed so much to simply disappear down onto the seat and worship his body with her face, her lips. Yet when she carefully placed her thigh against his, his leg, even in sleep, swerved away, as if her flesh burnt him, and not too soon after he woke up, glanced at her resentfully, turned to look out the window.

They were passing along a coastal road bordered by an ocean beach. Small rudimentary houses faced the sea. Turning his back on her, he stared out at the sea in silence.

## 15

They had had to pretend a certain modicum of tenderness towards each other in order that the others on the bus might not notice, and hence feel free to enter into their personal drama. Both Keiji and Sayo felt themselves observed, however, and it was singularly unfortunate that the very first time it was clear everyone knew they were newly-weds came now. Kaoru, a male busybody who enjoyed putting people into queues and telling them details they never wanted to know about the strange country they were in, called out loudly, 'Make way for the newly-weds,' as Keiji and Sayo filed off the bus.

The mortification Sayo felt for Keiji was profound.

They separated in their room, Sayo going to the bathroom, carefully closing the door behind her. The door had bevelled glass, which soon steamed up with the vapour from the shower. She stayed under the shower quite a long time, singing to herself, trying to lose her feeling of misery. Quickly she made her mind up: she stepped from the shower, aware Keiji was standing near the door, looking at her reflection through the glass. She moved back and forth in the range of the glass, giving him a small, almost geisha act, full of reluctance, displaying her nakedness. He had drawn closer. He was fully clothed still.

Now she came closer to the glass, pressed herself against it so the full outline and shape of her body was clear. She pretended that he was the glass and she made love, for a few pleasurable moments of sheer theatre, against it. After some moments' hesitation - he had less imagination than her - he moved closer to his side of the glass, his breath misting it, then his lips kissed it through the steam: for several moments they sent *billets-doux* to each other, safely separated by the strength of the glass between them.

This artificial barrier acted as an almost physical statement of what had occurred between them the night before. She waited, willing him to open the door. She would not open it. He opened the door, on his knees. She entered, still moist from the shower, steam rushing into the bedroom. He buried his face in her cunt, kissing her with a fierce, even angry passion. She cried out with the pain, he caught her round the hips, pulled her down onto the carpet. His face was white with passion or anger or strain. He cut her vision out by kissing her eyes shut, he smothered her with kisses so harsh and terrible that she was forced to fight him back so that, purely animal for several long minutes, they wrestled and attacked each other on the carpet, combatting each other with all the delayed passion of the hours they had been forcefully kept apart, Keiji moaning and crying out as, in successive waves, his passion attacked her body while Sayo banged her body into his and clawed his back, his thighs, his neck.

Erect, he would not penetrate her. Aware of the night before, she did not perform a choreography of desire for penetration. Achingly now, they kissed long and luxuriantly, as if the decision not to penetrate yet were a pact between them which would only escalate their love. Almost drugged with passion for him, Sayo lay on top of him and possessed his body, every inch of it, with her lips, turning him over, licking down between his buttocks, burrowing even into his arse with her tongue. He tried to resist but eventually played along with her passion so that finally he was pliant, erect, sensate over every inch of himself. Sweating and panting she lay beside him and began to masturbate.

This took him by surprise until, after several moments, he began to realise what she was doing. He turned on his side, then placed himself fully above her, not touching her, yet arched, his muscles straining while he looked into her face and every so often, gently, gently as the lap of purest water edging in across a beach, dipped a flick of his tongue between her lips. As she rose into orgasm, he began showering a storm of kisses over her face, encouraging, easing, affirming her passion. After she had come, he kissed her very tenderly, then, going to the bathroom and bringing back a soft, warmly wet towel, he bathed her all over, turning her over and around, lifting her legs, her arms, under her breasts, her chin, cleaning her.

That night they fell asleep in each other's arms.

## 16

They sat on board the ferry which took the tour party down towards the south. All around them ranged an enormity of sea. It was as if they had been cast off, into ocean. Because the boat was so large, Keiji and Sayo could be away from the tour party. They sat together on the upper deck, on a chair, looking out at the sea. Under their coats they held hands. Occasionally wind whipped spray onto their faces. Either Keiji or Sayo, laughing, would wipe it away. Keiji told Sayo, between kisses, they were at the bottom of the world, a place where humans could go hardly any further, 'not without dropping off the globe'.

Sayo laughed at this, then held tighter onto Keiji's arm as the boat suddenly went into a deep moaning fall. But, as if in a dream, the boat rose upwards again, bearing them up towards the sky: gulls cried, departed and everyone, sensing the couple's great happiness and peace, left them alone.

## 17

They had seen cities, farms, valleys, glaciers, motorways, tourist shops. As they went further and further south there appeared to be even fewer humans, so that for long hours they passed through a landscape which seemed miraculously devoid of any human or animal habitation, even though there were fences, lamp-posts, powerlines and the occasional letterbox. Kaoru, the busybody, talked a lot about Antarctica while Sayo and Keiji waited to be alone and gazed through glass at spectacular mountain ranges which lacked all meaning.

Occasionally Keiji got out his video and filmed the passing landscape: he also filmed Sayo, who had now lost all camera-consciousness. She no longer wondered what Keiji's mother would think of so much video being devoted to a portrait of her: Sayo had a feeling Keiji's mother might never see this video. She felt so safely alone with Keiji, further from Japan than she had ever been before. Behind it all, of course, like a vast dark curtain lay their return to Japan, and their taking up residence in Mrs Nakajima's apartment. There they would have no privacy. This frightened Sayo, because she and Keiji were still so much like illegal lovers, not newly-weds.

## 18

That night they came to rest at a coastal beach near the far south of the South Island. It had a spectacular coastline, almost Japanese in its calligraphy of cliff and cutting mist, of swifting birdfleet, crashing wave. They had a day of rest at the beach: those who wished to shop could go by landliner into a small town nearby, specially set up for the avarice of tourists; the others could spend the day as they pleased.

Thus it was that the people left behind formed almost a complicity among themselves: the elderly couple, one of the schoolgirls, the wife of Tatsuro who pleaded a stomach ache, Sayo and Keiji. The busybody, Tatsuro and most of the others had cheerfully gone off to conquer new artefacts.

Sayo and Keiji had stayed in their room, made rather languorous love after their own fashion. Now penetration had been forgotten and both Keiji and Sayo brought themselves, then each other, to orgasm in a way which was mutually satisfactory. Sayo, who looked forward to having a child some day, was willing to allow the mechanical act of fertilisation to happen whenever it would. She was confident it would follow naturally. The experience she had with her elderly lover had prepared her for some of the odd demands that humans make, in order to find a parallel between emotional and sexual satisfaction.

Exhausted, Keiji had begun an almost cruel form of love-making, one not inseparable from a delicate and pure pain, in which he inflicted on Sayo an extremity of pleasure, rising at times into an almost intolerable ecstasy. Sayo, at first, had been taken aback. Keiji's vigour, his passion, was almost terrifying. Then she answered his angst with her own. At its end, both felt – not shame, because they had done nothing to be ashamed of – but a kind of animal weariness, both pleasant and soporific, rather as an animal must feel after it has successfully attacked, killed and devoured another.

So, blitzed a little with each other's satisfaction, even glutted by their appetite for each other's flesh, they closed their motel door behind them and wandered out, dazed and amazed at finding themselves, not within the cave of a thigh, not under the bowl of a breast, but before an endless aura of sea, beneath an infinite sky.

Nearby, Hitomi, the schoolgirl, was sitting hunched, writing cards to home which she had neatly piled beside her, working through them methodically. Others from the tour party were sitting around, or making the first tentative moves across the sand which seemed, after the confinement of the bus, dauntingly empty and large. The surf itself emitted a harsh but satisfying growl.

As soon as they reached the sand, Keiji flipped up onto his hands and began to walk across the beach. He did this expertly for quite a few steps, causing everyone to stop and look at him, cheering when he managed a long stretch upside down, clapping sardonically when he folded down, very neatly, like a diver into water leaving hardly a ripple. He seemed full of animal spirits, like a small boy, an adolescent, showing off his muscular power. Several of the tour party took photos of him, the click of their cameras acting like a soothing murmur of approval.

On the beach itself surfers in wetsuits were sliding along the waves, wavering and waiting for a major roar of surf then rising unsteadily onto their feet, coasting along majestically with each opening sash of wave.

Keiji walked on his hands, upside-down.

The sun bore down. It was as if Sayo and Keiji had found paradise, at the end of the world there, where humans could go no further.

Sayo and Keiji walked along the beach further, investigating its wonders. They found an immense cave, which they entered and did not emerge from for a long time. Then they found a stream of clear water. The elderly deaf man was already minutely inspecting its marine life, putting some vegetation in his pocket. When he caught sight of Keiji and Sayo he inclined his head in a bow. Keiji bowed back. The old man's wife sat on her own, on a sandbank: she waved at Sayo, who waved back. Everyone seemed to agree: this was paradise.

After this, Sayo had to reconstruct for herself what happened.

She did this in the many months which followed, prompted not least by police, family, friends – even onlookers who felt they had a right to know the details from her.

She had separated from Keiji for a moment, they had walked apart with the happy satisfaction of those who know they are together: they could trust each other. He, it seemed, had wanted to look at the rocks at the end of the beach; she was more interested in the cliffs behind, in getting an overview of the beach. It was she who had made the decision to separate.

Once she had begun climbing she had kept going, seeing always a better viewing point, a more distant platform. At each point they had connected, waved at each other across the growing expanse of space. This space in itself had an erotic quality, as all their actions did, signifying the distance they were apart from each other yet telepathically connected. Then there was a long stretch of cliff for her to climb: there was a track of sorts and as she went on she fell into a reverie in which she reviewed their love-making and imagined their future, when they might live alone, away from Keiji's mother and able to make love whenever they felt like it. Perhaps an hour went by, she did not know.

She reached a plateau, she was breathless. She sank down, sat for a while, waited for her sight to equalise itself. Gradually the line of ocean, curl of beach settled into a fixed form and she began to search for Keiji.

Her first sight was a curious one: from all over the beach people were running towards one spot. For a second it reminded her of ants when they suddenly find a delicious piece of sweet food. Yet while most people ran towards the water's edge, one person ran away, faster than the others: this person was racing straight towards the motel, calling out, it seemed, as the people had come out of the motel, were standing stiff with alarm, hands shading their faces.

She looked now with more intensity at the small, distant scene down on the shore. There was a boat there, a sort of surfboat, people were carrying in a body, laying it on the sand, face up. She watched as someone crouched beside it, and began to lay the limbs out. She stood up now, searching among the onlookers for the familiar bodyshape of Keiji. She could not see him. It was this moment, more than any other, that she would recall later: the moment in which she grasped that he might no longer exist.

She could remember nothing of coming down the cliff except, in separate images, like stills in a film from which the remains had been cut away, flashes of their love-making that morning, igniting, flaring, fusing. Then, abruptly, she saw in the distance the action of a man trying to resuscitate a body. At this stage she did not know whose body it was: yet the very fact of a death happening on the beach filled her with foreboding. As she came nearer and nearer to the scene the actions of the person resuscitating grew increasingly desperate, almost flagellatory.

Now she was running towards the small crowd, people were turning to look at her. The lifesaver was pounding the body, as if it were a piece of obdurate machinery which, if only it would respond to the blows, might be reanimated. Then she was looking down at the body of Keiji: he was fully clothed, drenched, his neck at an odd angle as if it had been broken. Seaweed was wrapped around his body, like a funeral wreath.

She could remember nothing more: not the way she let out a scream so profound it had chilled the spines of everyone there: not how they had to drag her away from his body which she tried to hold and warm and bring back to life by kissing by calling by touching: not how she was lifted away, still calling out to him, and carried back to the motel where she had fought whoever was trying to hold her, and abused them and used language they did not know she possessed. None of this would she remember because a doctor came and, as she was held down by men and women who had suddenly grown much older, gave her an injection. The next she knew she opened her eyes and looked at a ceiling, wondered why Keiji was not there, then lowered her gaze and found the elderly woman sitting very quietly dozing in a chair beside her. For one moment she thought she had refound her mother.

Perhaps the abrupt arpeggio of her breath awoke the elderly woman. But while Sayo looked at this stranger who had come to share in her grief she suddenly recalled Keiji lying on the beach so cold and dead and her first thought was to get out of bed, to go to him: she was convinced he still lay there. Then she thought to herself that it was all an ugly dream; it was impossible. But it was there, written on the face of the old woman opposite who had begun to weep very softly, as if she were weeping for all the losses and deaths which had occurred in her own long life; from before the war, then through the war, then at the end of the war, at Hiroshima. Yet Sayo hated her briefly and unreasonably, she could not see what these other, more vague tragedies had to do with her own intolerable pain.

Everything from here became blank.

19

Now began the time of questions. The bus tour had moved on, speeding away as if it couldn't wait to remove itself from Sayo's ill luck. The other passengers had come forward individually and pressed her hand and murmured condolences. Sayo had gone to the nearest city, where she found herself completely alone, in a place she hardly knew the name of, in a foreign country whose language she did not speak. Sayo unpacked only what was strictly necessary, and awaited the strangers who came with an interpreter hurriedly obtained from the nearest university, a small earnest man from a different part of Japan from herself.

She had never felt so alone. The strangers were all gravely courteous, but this made it more unreal. She said what she knew had happened. After all, she did not know much. She turned it over and over in her mind, what had happened? It began to attack her that perhaps she had been a cause of his death: had she, perhaps, pursued him with her own unreasonable sexual demands? His drowning was without explanation. Why would a young man perfectly capable of swimming end up mysteriously drowning? Were there reasons for him to be unhappy? the interpreter had asked, carefully keeping his eyes lowered so as not to offend her. Was her silence too elongated, was the pause before she replied criminality itself? In the end the interpreter had had to repeat the question. She had whispered, so people had to strain their ears to hear, 'No.' Yet she felt she lied, for all humans have cause to be unhappy.

Then the strangers gave the interpreter their explanation of the tragedy. Keiji had gone for a walk along the rocks and, unfamiliar with the way waves could suddenly surge in, had been swept out to sea by an errant wave. (It was simply bad luck.) One of the surfers had seen him. Sayo could not bring herself to ask: was he calling for help? It was death by misadventure, the interpreter told her, pleased as if he himself had arranged what was, in the circumstances, a satisfactory solution to what was, after all, without solution, without resolution. Sayo could go back to Japan now. It was all over. Keiji's body would follow. His funeral obsequies would happen in the homeland.

## PART II

### 20

The door had fallen open at Mrs Nakajima's apartment and the two women, widow and mother, looked into each other's faces as if to see, written there, some explanation, some final confidence. But Sayo was very tired by the long flight, then the trip in from the airport: she also felt acutely uncomfortable coming to the apartment of a woman who, after all, she hardly knew. Yet she was Keiji's mother. For this reason, Sayo decided, she would try to love her and find what in her was of Keiji, the man who had disappeared.

Yet as soon as the door slid open she knew in her heart she could never love this woman: there was some chemistry between the two which would never cohere. Besides the anger Mrs Nakajima felt about her only son's untimely death was all directed at his bride: without her, there would have been no honeymoon, no walk on the beach, no death. Nevertheless Mrs Nakajima was sufficiently of the old school to know how to dissemble her true feelings: she returned the profound obeisances the new widow made before her and their greeting of each other was an acceptable expression of mutual grief to everyone apart from themselves. For Sayo's discomfort was increased by the presence of Mrs Nakajima's sister, her sons-in-law and daughters who were all sitting in the room, as if a jury waiting for a prosecution witness to take the stand.

Sayo felt intensely watched. She wondered if she was not expressing enough grief: she to whom grief had quickly become, as it were, a mode of breathing. Mrs Nakajima's relatives, however, had begun to talk about Keiji, reviewing his life in intimate detail, talking of his father, his noble forefathers of which Mrs Nakajima was inordinately proud. Mrs Nakajima's sister, a stout fiercely respectable hotel proprietor, told a story about Keiji as a boy fishing at the beach, and how he had astonished everyone with his love of swimming.

Other stories quickly followed. Gradually Sayo began to feel she knew very little of Keiji: she had known only the complete intimacy of those six days and nights in motel rooms in New Zealand. This other Keiji, she did not know: except perhaps, conversely, in that one act of his he could not bring himself to complete.

So Sayo had sat there, a terrible headache clouding her mind, frightened even to put her bags away in a corner because it might not be where she was properly meant to go: Mrs

Nakajima was a stickler for order and the tiny apartment, eerily clear and arranged as if for a piece of arcane, even vaguely cruel theatre, was like an obstacle course for anyone unfamiliar with the territory. Keiji had already told her that his mother was also extraordinarily 'economical', which Sayo translated into a wary, obstinate meanness.

Eventually the relatives departed and the two women were left alone. Almost immediately it became clear they had nothing to say to each other; nothing, that is, apart from the directions a person who controls a confined space needs to give to someone who is staying as a visitor. As Sayo fell into sleep that night, the sounds of Tokyo all around her, she thought she heard waves calling, calling and she strained her ears to listen. Then all was black.

21

Sayo took up her old life. There was in this, if not pleasure, at least relief. She took up a job in another corporation, doing the same kind of work. The work was so numbing that it stopped her thinking of the beach, that day, Keiji lying in the sand wreathed around with seaweed. She tried to accommodate herself to the patterns of the old widow's life, which were mercilessly cut-and-dried, running like clockwork, terminating always in an early night during which Sayo would lie awake listening to the older woman's breathing, its slow rise and fall. At times like this Sayo would listen for the waves which would come and retrieve her, and caress her and soothe her as they pulled her back like a tide to those few days and nights she had spent with the man she loved.

Life never goes according to an easy pattern, however. Sayo was deeply disturbed one day when the widow served her a bowl of miso: as she stared down into it, deeply depressed, she suddenly saw in the whirls of vegetable configurations an horrific vision of Keiji in the tide, his body rotting, unclaimed, a living mass of sea organisms, tossing and flopping with each lull and pull of the waves. This vision was so complete that she dropped her chopsticks and cried out. When the older widow enquired what was the matter (she did not like waste), the younger widow simply said that the soup was a little hotter than she had expected. Then, feeling she had been rude to her host, who was quick to take offence, she explained that day she had had some noodles which had scalded her tongue. The elder widow bowed slightly.

This horrific vision awoke in Sayo a further stage of grief. She now began to sleep badly, tortured by visions of their love-making intertwined with hideous visions of decay and putrefaction. She found at last she could not bear the silence of the apartment any longer and quietly, like a thief, she dressed and went out into the night and, lacking anything better to do, simply got on a train and began to ride the subway.

Thus began the time in her life when she constantly sat on the trains at quiet hours, soothed by the travel which, in its way, was not unlike those moments on the bus when, tired and hardly thinking, she had lowered her head onto Keiji's shoulder and gone into blissful sleep. She found she was not doing her job so well, she could not concentrate. And the sympathy which her workmates had initially had for her evaporated, as people cannot continue to feel sorry for someone over a great length of time.

One afternoon Sayo took the video Keiji had taken of their holiday and, because she was too embarrassed to show it to Mrs Nakajima, who, after all, knew so little of their passion, she went to a love hotel. There, alone in a room decorated like a Memphis brothel, complete with a shell-shaped vibrating bed, she watched the video alone, obsessively returning, in slow motion, to the one small moment when she had taken up the camera and trained it on Keiji.

This was when he was standing on his hands, in the hotel room at Rotorua. She watched over and over again as he evaded gravity, walked, toppled, fell, then righted himself, laughing directly at her. Then he walked towards the camera, his hand out. The camera fled across the ceiling, down a wall, quickly, quickly, in a fleeting vision, across their bed which was unmade and had all the pleasant squalor of their love-making: then the camera showed her, pleading with him to turn it off. A television was on in the room, showing a news item about a flood. When she slowed the image down to almost frame-by-frame point she saw, on the television, animals floating along in dirty torrents, people standing on roofs, water rushing through living rooms. She looked again and again at this footage of Keiji, and felt at once soothed by his presence, the evidence that he had lived. Yet when she packed away the video and walked out of the love hotel, the receptionist staring with banal curiosity at what she had in her bag, she felt more bereft than ever: as if in the very act of locating Keiji she had only experienced, again, the completeness of his loss.

By now the two widows had, without any particular incident inspiring it, reached a tacit understanding whereby neither spoke to the other more than was strictly necessary. When Mrs Nakajima had her family around, which she did more often now that Keiji was dead - as if Keiji's death gave them all a common bond which, before, had been lacking, or was divided in rivalry over material success, a very strong motive with both sisters - Sayo felt a complete outsider, incapable of joining in their stories of other days before she was in Keiji's life. Subtly they negated her, even while they continued to treat her with an almost extravagantly uncomfortable degree of politeness. This only highlighted her provincial origins and made her feel inferior.

Sayo knew she must leave.

Mrs Nakajima had, anyway, confided in her sister that Sayo, whom she never called by her name but referred to as 'the young madame' - as if Sayo alone, with female sorcery, had enticed Keiji to his death - had another lover already. She mistook the long hours Sayo spent riding the subway for lurid hours spent in unspeakable acts. Sayo did not dispel these rumours, for she often looked both vacant and exhausted; she seemed to be listening to another sound, more distant, deeper, as if emanating from inside the hollow globe of the world - which she was: she could not get the sound of waves out of her head.

So, dazed, suffering from lack of sleep, pursued by the siren-call of the sea, Sayo went to her bank, took out whatever money she had saved, went to a travel agent, walked past the door twice before going in. Then, suddenly and exhilaratingly turning into an actor, so for the first time since returning to Tokyo she felt absolutely alive, she booked a return ticket to New Zealand on the nearest available flight. It left in three days.

She went home to the widow and broke their silence. She was returning to her home village, she lied. Her father had become ill, asked for her. She regretted leaving but that was that. She went into her room and began packing.

The widow Nakajima felt a fierce exhilaration. Her every fear had been confirmed: the young madame, the little slut, 'our friend from Korea', was going to live with whatever male it was who would have her. It meant that she, Mrs Nakajima, was freed from the burden of a woman who served only to remind her that her one son was dead.

She went into the tiny corner Sayo used as a room. She would make a celebratory feast for Sayo, asking all Keiji's family and Sayo could ask whoever she might like. It was not to farewell her, she hastened to add, but to do honour to Keiji's widow. Sayo tried to say she did not want this, indeed, she hinted it was in poor taste since her father was ill. Yet Mrs Nakajima would not be stopped.

Sayo said, in confusion, she did not know anyone to ask. Mrs Nakajima understood that her acquaintances might be of a type that could not be introduced into a family celebration. She went away, superbly confident that she would splurge out, make a feast such as she had not made before, certainly better and more extravagant than the one which greeted the news of Sayo and Keiji's wedding.

This meal was a form of torture for Sayo. Keiji's relatives all condemned her in their own minds for her lack of feeling, her seeming absence of grief. Indeed, she hardly seemed to partake of the meal at all, having barely anything to eat, explaining she was undergoing a fast, which they all considered was, in the circumstances, in extremely poor taste. Nevertheless, gorging themselves to excess – in particular the widow Nakajima who suffered acute indigestion for days afterwards – they took little notice of the curious mood Sayo was in, attributing it to her 'flightiness', her 'moodiness'. So, ignored at her own celebration, Sayo was left alone to concentrate on the sound of waves which in her own head sounded celebratory, welcoming, dancing with a lightness of relief: it was as if they were welcoming her home.

## PART III

### 22

Her return to New Zealand was almost joyful to her: here, in this foreign country which now meant everything to her, she saw sights familiar from her honeymoon in an entirely new light. Whereas before they had been essentially meaningless, novelties of landscape or city, now they were invested with the sacred integrity of memory: they fitted within her own interior landscape. And as she took her seat on a landliner, with entirely different people aboard, another driver (only the explanations were the same), she felt a kind of solace overtake her, a serenity, peace.

She loved in particular looking at the water which, in these islands, was always in abundance, insisting on changing sides on the bus when they travelled along the coast, following the same route as the landliner had taken before. Only occasionally did she risk recognition, as they stayed in all the same hotels, motels, hostelries. She was protected by the fact that all Asians appear the same to undiscerning Europeans: besides, she had lost weight already with her fast, and she had cut her hair differently, more severely, in preparation for her forthcoming life.

All the time sitting on the bus she was poised, prepared, like a young novice about to undergo some sublime experience:

every moment on the bus was spent in appreciation of the world outside the windows, the activity on the bus. Only at night would she find the proximity of the rooms where she had made love with Keiji almost overpowering in their magnetism: she would walk by in the corridors outside, hoping that by chance the door would open and she might refresh her memory, already indelible, of their honeymoon rooms.

One morning she had crept into such a room, vacated by some other passengers. The bed was unmade, it still looked exactly the same. This was the room, she remembered, where she and Keiji had made love by the door. She saw this vividly before her, on the carpet. When one of the passengers had come back into the room, unexpectedly, having left something behind in the bathroom, Sayo had not been confused, and had explained with serenity she, too, was looking for something she had lost.

By this time the other passengers on the bus left a small cordon around the young widow. They knew nothing of her story, yet her strict dietary habits, her seeming dislocation from the intense mood of people insistent upon having six days' holiday-and-fun, meant she was always a little to the side, unattached, almost untouched.

Finally the bus drew near the motel and the beach at which Keiji had died. As they came closer Sayo's mood underwent a subtle change. She became painfully upset by the thought that the owners of the motel, possessors of memory of the incident – possessors, even more so, of memories about her own responses, which were only now occurring to her – might still be there. This would complicate things considerably. Yet, when the bus pulled in, there was no sign of the old owners: there was a bright young couple determined to succeed in their new job. Sayo overheard the bus driver talking to them, and understood the original owners were having a much-deserved holiday in Queensland. A recent spate of drownings had cast a slight pall over their business.

Her plan had been prepared all along: during her tour of New Zealand she had been collecting matches, noodles, a grill.

The following morning, before breakfast, she told the driver that she must return to Dunedin as soon as possible. It was nothing bad, she hastened to add: it was a monetary transaction in Tokyo which required her personal supervision. The day before she had, with considerable difficulty, arranged for a message to be sent. So it all seemed convincing: besides, nobody was directly concerned with her. And it was only as the bus took off, leaving her behind, that a general lightness of spirits overcame the entire bus, as if an invisible weight had been dropped off. But because nobody was really aware the widow had been left behind, it was attributed to nothing more than a general excess of good spirits.

## 23

The beach that day was peaceful, still. The enormous waves disgorged themselves onto the sand, ran in on great glassy floors, only to re-spume in another torrent. Further out on the horizon fishermen in boats plied their trade.

Sayo took her single bag, and suitcase, and appeared to head off to the bus-stop where another landliner, travelling in the opposite direction, came by within an hour. Certain countryfolk, travelling into the local town, noticed the rather odd sight of an Asian woman standing alone at the bus-stop. Some commented darkly on the penetration of 'the Asian invasion', while others, with heavily mortaged farms to sell, were thoughtfully silent. Nobody noticed that, when the bus came by, she was no longer there. Thinking back on it later, the wife of the motel proprietor (who liked to think it was one of her professional qualifications that nothing escaped her eyes) noticed the bus roar by, unstopping. But she simply assumed some good-natured passer-by had offered the visitor to New Zealand a lift. The hospitality of the local district was famous.

Sayo cut along the beach with her bag, so light that anyone seeing her might have easily mistaken her for a day-tripper, part of a package tour, simply having a rather adventurous walk on her own. She had carefully stowed her suitcase behind a flaxbush. In her daybag were the necessities to get her through the night. She was heading towards the large airy cave she had noticed on her first trip to the beach. She and Keiji had walked into it together, wondering at its height, its suggestion of a majestic Gothic cathedral: indeed, they had taken advantage of its darkness and obscurity to make quick and pleasurably illicit love. Throughout their kisses Sayo had heard the boom and roar of waves: the very sound which had echoed in her head in Tokyo, drawn her back.

Now it was, as if for the first time, the sound of the waves fell into focus: it was as if, at last, the echo she had heard so troublingly in her head met with the actual, soothing roar, fell into rhythm, found peace. She felt both determined and happy as she made her campsite in the cave. She waited till dusk, then retraced her path back to the flaxbush and under a hugely refulgent moon walked with her case back along the beach. She felt deeply happy for the first time since Keiji had died. She was at home.


## PART IV


## 24


She had been living in the cave for over two weeks now. Her food supply had almost gone and though her fast was continuing as much as was humanly possible, she needed to eat. In fact her fasting had changed her consciousness of time, place, reality. The waves still lulled and soothed her, though occasionally their call was harsh, and strong. She had taken to going down to the water's edge and standing, looking out to sea, at the particular point where Keiji had drowned. This was dangerous as she went into such a trance that she failed, one day, to notice some fishermen walking along the beach towards her. Their voices, carried on the wind, reached her and she listened acutely, like an animal raising its nose into the air, scenting danger. But she was used to hearing voices by this time: in fact she sought the sound of the waves to drown out the voices and relocate her silence.

Suddenly the men were quite close to her. She turned quickly, hurried back towards the flax beneath the cliffs, carefully not heading directly towards her cave. The men walked by, talking among themselves, laughing: yet one turned over his shoulder and looked quizzically in the direction she had taken. She told herself they were so distant they would not pick that she was Japanese. After an hour she returned to her cave and was henceforth much more careful.

She had a particular ritual she followed, where she went down to the sea and paid homage to the man she had loved so intensely, then lost. At these ceremonies, of both abasement and atonement, Keiji would appear to her out of the sea, at times refulgent with love, at other times, depending on his mood, angry as a kabuki demon, terrifying. The weather, too, was deteriorating. One night there was such a strong wind that the very heavens seemed to be screaming with agony. Dust whipped along the beach, obscuring the sun in the sky so that the day, when it dawned, had an odd, ominous white glow to it, the waves broken, sharded with seaweed, tossing out of the ocean as if driven by torment.

Sayo had walked out into this storm, driven by hunger. She tried to find on the beach anything, a bird which had been blown down from the sky, a fish washed up. She returned to her cave with her treasure, a small fish, some pippies, a gull. With shaking fingers she lit a fire made out of driftwood and slowly, oh slowly, the tiny flame fluttered and she waited for the wood to catch fire and burn. But the wind changed direction suddenly, flung sharp and bitter sand into her face. She could only retreat to her mat, cover herself with a few sacks she had found on the beach, and wait for the morning.

When it came she was awoken by Keiji kissing her so tenderly on her lips, running his soft hot tongue lightly along her lower lip, then trailing it across her top lip before, softly, gently, he probed into her mouth, cradling her head in his hands so his tongue might enter her mouth more fully. He kissed her then luxuriantly, his hands so warm and gentle passing down her body, animating her breasts, her stomach which he lingered over, softly caressing, massaging so that she stretched out flat and peaceful, issuing a long deep sigh as he entered her. It was as she knew it would always be: he whispered in her ear, delicately biting on her lobe as his other hand slid to her breast, softly, again and again, stroking her nipple while his cock smoothly slid within her, her insides parting, almost with relief, completely relaxed so that, once inside her, it was as if he fitted perfectly and so, locked together in a timeless configuration, they made sweetly rhythmical love, both their cries simultaneously rising up. At which point she awoke and found herself almost covered in sand, and the dark crease of the cave cut into an inverted V of light, down which the sound of the waves poured towards her, streaming their sound now slightly mocking in their presence, their insistence on reality: almost, too, as if they had been witnesses to the act of love and mocked it with their laughter.

Yet she had no doubt, as she rose and went and washed in the sea, which was more peaceful now, as if replete from its night of fury, that Keiji had come to her and made love. Indeed, as she bent over and washed between her legs there were unmistakable signs of his presence, a sort of rash where his legs had rubbed most urgently against her own. There was even a lovebite.

She returned to the cave, preparing for the daily advent of the fishermen who, each day, now walked past her cave in the early morning, then returned at night with their catch.

But that day something different occurred. After she emerged from the cave, in the evening, she found a single fresh fish laid out very carefully on a rock, cradled on a large leaf of some unknown vegetation. In the distance she saw the fishermen walking away, lost almost in sand, in mist. She looked again at the fish. Its mouth was open, a small slash of blood bubbled from its gill. The fishermen were now lost from sight. But she did not touch the fish.

The following evening, however, she waited in the flax for the fishermen to walk by. It was a beautiful evening in which the winter sun, the softest possible pink, had infused the entire sky with light vapours of pearl, aquamarine, with bruises of amethyst falling away, in the far far distance, to a few charcoal strokes of bruised black: far out at sea, leaving the islands untouched, a storm was moving by.

The fishermen walked along, their rods frail in the light. As they came nearer to her cave, she watched as one of them covered head to foot, in wet-weather gear, which gave him an oddly martial appearance, separated from the others. He was an old man, by his gait, and he went towards the rock where the other fish lay untouched. He stood there for a moment, thoughtfully, then, removing the stale fish, substituted for it a magnificent fish so fresh it curved in his grasp, even giving a last flick of its tail as it lay there, sacrificial on the rock.

Sayo stared at the old man, taken aback by the sudden knowledge that it was Keiji, now an old man, Keiji as he might have been if he had lived. His eyes connected with her own: he smiled at her, a smile of perfect serenity, even good-humoured charm: there was a twinkle in his eye. For the first time since coming to the cave, Sayo looked down at herself: she was aware her clothes had become like rags, stiff with salt, her hair was matted, her face bloated. She felt deep shame and buried her face in her hands till he went.

When the fishermen were gone she emerged, took the fish back to her cave and there lit a beautiful, crackling fire and cooked the fish and with her bare fingers devoured the flesh, whiter than the most beautiful skin in the world, stuffing the food into her mouth as she realised how deeply hungry she was. It was as if her whole soul was crying out for food. She finished the meal, lay there, then was sick.

She waited now for Keiji to return to her. Yet it was as if, in her very act of waiting, she had frightened him away: as if, in her hunger for him, she was again doing what she had done on her honeymoon, forcing on him, as she saw it now, her own appetites and desires. Another old man - not Keiji - was it perhaps her old lover? - now came and left her fish: she ate it more sensibly, in small delicate meals, more like rituals of remembrance than a placating of hunger. She would go down to the sea and sing songs to Keiji, chorusing along with the waves, joining in their eternally restful song: yet he would not appear.

These were her hardest days. She forced herself to review, in her mind, every day and night she had spent with him on their honeymoon, going into every act, providing in her mind alternative endings, more elaborate scenarios. She left her most precious possession, the video, down on the beach one morning, before high tide, hoping this would placate him. And sometimes, late at night, he would come to her: but at these times of loss, his love-making was cruel, vengeful, humiliating. Yet she still longed for him, because she knew that this form of love-making was an expression of his anger and that, if only she could have more time with him, she could cure him of this sadness and they could return to their more peaceful style of love-making.

One day she was observed by a youth on a land windsurfer, one of the many conveyances which, with the changing weather, had begun to make miraculous, slightly eerie appearances on the vast beach. Sayo was standing, looking out to sea; the windsurfer had tacked towards her, veered away.

Later in the pub the surfer, after a few drinks, announced he'd seen an 'abominable yeti' down on the beach. He did not know that the fishermen had seen her for over a month now, and since one of them was in fact the man who had pulled in Keiji drowned, they both knew who she was and had decided amongst themselves, since she was doing no harm - except possibly to herself - to leave her there. This surfer, however, could not allow such a good opportunity for self promotion to pass. Later that evening, made brave by many drinks and having told themselves innumerable stories about ghosts, curious coincidences, actual murders, three young braves crept along the beach, heading towards the cave from which an eerie light issued.

They were ready for unearthly apparitions and indeed, inside the cave, they observed a young Asian woman dancing by herself, to her own odd tune, reminiscent of Chinese operas. The shadows caste on the walls were so strange, her tune so weird, that the youths, hitherto brave and feckless, fell silent and gazed upon her, then crept away, chastened by what they had seen. Later that night they got completely drunk and their actual vision merged into tales from movies, pulp novels, hearsay. The following morning the wind changed direction, the surfers all packed up their boards, took off to the other side of the island. Yet over breakfast, the least hungover, most garrulous of the three found time to raise a deliciously erotic frisson (in his view) in the breast of the young Maori woman serving sausages and baked beans from a huge stainless steel bin in the kitchen.

To this young woman, ghosts and spiritual presences were not the subject of jest. But a co-worker beside her, more attuned to television, overheard the conversation and thus word quickly spread around the small community that there was a weird Asian living in a cave on the beach.

Surreptitiously at first, Sayo was spied upon, to verify these reports. So little happened in that hospitable district that things like accidental deaths, traffic accidents, unplanned pregnancies took on the scale of international events, talked over, discussed, looked at from this angle and that till finally, every aspect of the subject exhausted, it either entered into folklore, to be inaccurately recalled at communal events, or it simply dropped from view, overtaken by a new, more pressing sensation.

People soon realised the young woman was the widow of the 'Jap' who had drowned there the previous winter. One of the men called in to restrain her, in her grief, verified that the woman was her. This gave her presence a sort of poetic symmetry which even the most hard-hearted could not fail to recognise. People uniformly felt pity for her, the more banal imagining she had gone crazy. Some people felt she had entered under the aegis of the district and, as such, they were all duty-bound to keep her anonymity protected. Others felt that her discovery might give the tourist image of the area a bad name, already under a cloud after the spate of recent drownings. This latter group, who talked on the subject more tirelessly than the others, insisted their point of view was activated by concern. 'It just can't go on': 'she's doing herself a serious injury': 'it just isn't right'. The implication of possible death was even talked about, in terms of injurious headlines.

Yet, oddly enough, the possibility of a community response was made slower by a recognition of the very depth of grief of this thin, determined woman, speaking another language, coming from another country entirely, who had chosen their district to come and mourn her husband in. It was unavoidable, this figment of intense love, this calligraphy of human tragedy happening on their doorstep. Yet it was also this very intensity which frightened some. Grief occurs in everyone's life, it is inseparable from our being human: if someone grieves to an excessive degree, is this not a comment on the absence of tears in those men and women whose mothers, fathers, children, lovers have all died? She could not be left alone, it was not right. Something had to be done.

So finally, a few phone calls were made to the nearest city police, a surveillance discreetly took place. And because the woman was known to be Japanese, and Japan was a powerful, even feared, client of New Zealand, it was felt correct that an interpreter accompany a policeman when they made their now inevitable visit.

## 25

Sayo was now so habituated to her life in the cave, it was as if she had no other. Keiji came and went in her life, much as he might have in his real life: sometimes moody, at other times affectionate, occasionally staying out the whole night, returning in the morning to make groggy, slightly soiled love. She had even begun to wonder whether she was pregnant, a subject which worried her as a cave was not suitable for a child to grow up in. All the time through this the waves kept up their continuous and powerful music, playing in rhapsody, as it were, an accompaniment to the emotional states of her husband.

A sole policeman, who had cut down hanged men from beams, pulled sad housewives out of gas ovens – a man who took grieving relatives in to view corpses – now walked along the beach feeling a deep discomfort for the task ahead of him. It was fortunate, in a way, he had as a companion the same small earnest man who had earlier translated for Sayo. The two figures walked through the salt mist, one large, tall, ungainly and distinctly weird in his blue suburban uniform; the other slight, his glasses constantly fogged by salt, slipping slightly on the sand, hurrying to keep up with the taller man. Because the policeman was embarrassed he talked about fishing, a subject about which the small man from the university knew nothing, so that subject dried up. The sergeant fell back on his conversational backstop: travel and the respective merits of overseas countries compared with New Zealand.

Sayo saw the thin shape of the interpreter outlined against the sky in her cave. She was startled, as she was cleaning the cave, making it as tidy as possible for her husband who was returning that night. Yet she welcomed him courteously, as a housewife might welcome a fellow employee of her husband, bowing to him ceremoniously and enquiring after his wife. The shadow of the policeman now hovered at the cave entrance.

The interpreter then said to Sayo that she could not stay here; it was a contravention of passport laws. She looked at him as if he were quite mad. He took in another breath and explained to her, in Japanese, that she had entered the country on a visitor's permit and she was already over the limit by two months. It was a criminal offence, he added. She looked at him without expression: as if, indeed, he were talking a language entirely incomprehensible to her. Her eyes only moved slightly, to take in the sergeant who now bent over and entered the cave. She made a small, courteous movement with her hands, indicating he should make himself at home. The sergeant later embarrassed himself by recalling, as he went over the event in detail before falling into sleep, how he had responded in as courtly a way as he knew how, indicating he preferred to stand.

This was the odd thing, he recalled later, because the entire event disturbed a widower like himself: the way she, a gaunt woman, dressed practically in rags, with hair matted, had stood so straight, intimating that she was interviewing them as much as they were talking with her. She had a kind of dignity, he told himself, which was troubling. Standing there he did not immediately see how the situation would resolve itself. He hoped it would not have to be resolved by force. An immense weariness had overcome him at this thought.

The small interpreter had then raised his voice slightly and was speaking to her very quickly. He told her it was a serious criminal offence, she could go to jail: she must return to Tokyo immediately. It was causing problems between New Zealand and Japan.

She lifted her eyes from the interpreter then, and looked at the sergeant to whom she smiled, quite graciously.

I have no wish to cause problems between New Zealand and Japan, she said, bowing slightly to the sergeant who could not help his head, of its own accord, jerking slightly. Then she shifted her eyes away from them and was silent. It was as if she were suddenly listening to something else entirely, another music, another sound. She did not look at them again.

So, taking her silence as agreement, first the sergeant, then the interpreter began gathering up the few items among her possessions they could see were worth saving: her carrybag, an empty video case, an overcoat. While they were doing this, Sayo had silently, as if magnetically drawn, moved out of the cave, walking very slowly towards the water. It was a shock for the sergeant; he turned around, she was not there. Then he saw her, a diminishing figure against the brilliantly lit sea. It was one of those days when everything appears white. It seemed for a moment that she were moving into the sea. He quickly dropped what he was carrying and hurried down to the beach.

But the woman had just stopped by the sea. As he approached her, she, with her back towards him, performed a complete and deep bow before the waves. He stopped still behind, silent.

The interpreter now came out of the cave, carrying her few possessions. It was as if she was now waiting on them.

And together now, the three of them began their slow walk back towards the settlement, the young woman walking slowly because she was weak, the other two following yet accompanying her, almost like courtiers beside some rare captive princess.

In the mist on the beach, figures stood, watching this apparition move by. Nobody spoke.

## PART V

### 26

Rush-hour Tokyo: there are people everywhere, hundreds, thousands, millions of humans rushing and pushing from one side of the immense city, trying to get to the other. Noise, dirt, pollution. One train is full, the doors are pushed shut, everyone within is squashed so tight that faces, limbs, bodies, briefcases all form a wall, pressing against the glass, like fish in an aquarium, threatening to burst out.

One of these faces pushed against the glass is a woman. It is Sayo. She looks much the same as she did before her marriage, her widowing, except she has a slightly different haircut, is older. And as the train disappears from view we see her face, and in her face is embedded all the haunted hidden richness of memory, written in lines which can never be replaced: yet there is also something else in her face, a blankness, a deep and utter silence. *Nothing.*

# DARK AND LIGHT

THERE WAS A time when he would never have done what he was now, gladly, doing. He would have preferred to stay, unhappily, in love. Or been tormented in a kind of late-Visconti way, hearing in his mind a lyrically tearsome soundtrack by Mahler. There were any number of ruses which might have, once, kept him from his fate: which was to enter, gladly, that dark zone of pleasure known as a sex club.

It was on a busy anonymous road where there was almost no foot traffic. In one of those triumphs of city planning, the street had such a severely deracinated look that it might have been subject, in some war, to blanket bombing, then indifferent renewal in times during which aesthetics had been conveniently forgotten.

Besides, of course, the sex club only came alive at night. Night - the dark - was its true essence, as if the absence of light - or daylight - accelerated its mystery, deepened the power of its sway.

What had happened to Eric, a successful acrobat in the showbiz of living, to find himself in that dark place? He was not economically depressed: he was not one of those straitened people who eek out their dole by sitting in saunas for almost an entire day, as if to extend the duration of cruising was to increase its impact. No, Eric was lucky: his sophisticated cooking books, ever so slightly ironic, managed to be always one step ahead of the aggressively *nouveau riche* bourgeoisie who dominated the city's social life (or imagined they did). Of course, since the Crash, Eric had had to spend more time on inventive ways of cooking: *cuisine minceur* had come to be as unseemly as Marie Antoinette's rumoured opinion about the socio-economic status of cake.

For Eric, though, passing quickly under that dim red light - the only thing in the darkened street to indicate the place was a zone of freedom for those seeking sexual pleasure - the Crash was but a stale echo of that other, more vast concatenation.

Perrin, his oldest friend, was now dead. Finally, utterly, completely. No amount of romantic theories of the hereafter could persuade Eric - a pragmatic kind of person, given over to the pleasures of the palate (of which there can be few more immediate) - that dear, utterly crotchety, in the end tragically aware Perrin was still present in the city in which they had both spent - or was it misspent? - their youth.

Eric had tried to tell himself that some vapour of Perrin, some essence, still resided in the streets they had both so often pioneered in sassy fashion. The fact was that Perrin's presence was there only as an ache, a sting of absence so forlorn it was almost impossible to address. It was as if doors had sealed shut behind Perrin, cutting Eric off from him forever - or at least until, Eric guessed, his own moment.

He pushed open the door with brio. At 38, Eric knew enough about making entrances: it did not do to let the world see your indecision. People despised those caught in quandaries. All anyone wanted was the hard prize of victory; and fake victory, like life, was miles better than its reverse: death.

Yet it was this that Eric was escaping - or was it embracing? - by coming to the club. He wished to forget: he also wished to remember, to recall, to sound out some almost forgotten emotions on himself. He was like someone who both has lost something and is searching for something he cannot quite recall.

The-man-in-the-window - he to whom one showed one's ticket - varied. Occasionally it was a man who wore a hard hat as if he were a left-over member of the Village People who had toured the country and like so many shows, shed a person or two when the circus moved on. At other times there was a handsome muscular Polynesian with a voice so soft it was like lying on a lilo and drifting out, past the coral reef, into a possibly dangerous pale aquamarine sea.

Each time Eric came - and he tried to restrict his attendance so he felt at least a little of the excitement of the unknown - he put on a ritualistic performance of being completely at ease with the situation, even familiar with the men-in-the-window, addressing them as if he knew their names, their lives, their moods. There was a kind of camaraderie in this. He had arrived one night to find a hopelessly drunk, effeminate fat man trying desperately to get in and, standing ironically to the side, Eric had listened to the fat man being persuaded that he was too drunk to come in or, if he did, he had to be particularly careful of his actions. When Eric emerged from the shadows the man-in-the-window – the Polynesian – and he had exchanged an ironic set of signals. Both understood.

He wanted – what did he want? – he thought as he moved swiftly beyond the bright sphere of light inside the front door. Here several men were languidly playing pool – one, a Maori with long hair and not wearing a shirt, looked like he came from the country. There was a not entirely spurious air of being in a man's club. None of the men playing pool raised their heads to glance at him: the concatenation of balls upon the baize seemed more urgent. In a dim room beyond, where satellite television constantly played, Eric saw one or two faces turn, look at him without expression, turn away.

He did not hesitate. He moved quickly, to the left, towards that darkening corridor beyond which lay, on first impressions, total black. He wanted – he wanted, of course, to meet someone. To meet, if necessary, more than just someone – several people. It did not matter. On the one hand he wished to meet someone he might have a relationship with; this was one option. On the other, he was quite prepared for anonymous sex ending in the relief of orgasm. For Eric, this kind of encounter at least gave him the benefit of knowing that his body existed; that it had not faded away into an unknowing sphere without tactile expression. He felt, at these times in the club, with hands undoing his belt, unzipping his fly, stealing across his chest towards his nipple, as if he were a block of clay which a many-handed sculptor was persuading, seducing, shaping into life, identity.

That this happened under a cloak of darkness, in which the faces of the people touching him, feeling him, 'making love to him' as it might be expressed, were almost invisible, did not

213

matter. There was the Braille of want: the hard indentations, the soft ululations of desire. Like blind men, they were forced to extend their other senses so that, where some people might see loss, Eric possessed an almost hallucinatory clarity and perception – of the other person, not of their life or face or identity in the world, but as a human stripped of almost everything, returned simply to a sentient body to whom darkness gave freedom to express their want: their need.

What better analogue for the human heart than a maze?

Eric slowly entered the oddly jointed corridor, giving himself time to adjust his sight to almost total blackness. He leant against the corrugated iron walls, breathing gently. It was now, he calculated, exactly four months since Matthew had gone. He had left, not indecently – he had stayed right through the slow retreat from Moscow that was Perrin's illness. He had supported Eric through the worst hours. Then, when Perrin was finally rendered down, all of him, his mystery and his passion, his flaws and his anger, to a small plastic box full of pumicey grit, Matthew had gone. He had gone to Sydney. His destination did not matter. For Eric, the single most important fact was that Matthew, the essence of the living in the middle of the dying, had gone.

Eric told himself, and genuinely believed, that it was pleasant to have his flat back to himself, that he need no longer have to watch videos of music he only just, really, tolerated. He did not have to feel constantly parental towards his young lover, whose friends were naturally of his own age, and in whose presence Eric felt not only older than he was, but positively foreign. These were young men to whom the world appeared so much less complex: boys so lucky that politics was an option not a necessity: boys who lived with the disease, but who had not been alive, riotously, triumphantly erupting into life during that phase when nobody knew of the accompanying presence of death, of its silent coursing through the body of one man to another, all around the world.

Eric felt in his jeans pocket. The tip of his finger touched the tight plastic sheathing a condom. *Pour votre securité*. He

214

immediately withdrew his hand. Further in the maze he could hear a rustling of voices, the softer hiccoughing of a man being brought to pleasure. Quickly now, throwing aside his reverie, his caution, Eric felt, by fingertouch, along the wall, and turned abruptly into an intensely dark corridor.

He was hit by the heat of human bodies. The air itself seemed converted into the interior of a man's mouth, hot, rank. He bumped, momentarily, into someone standing still. 'Sorry,' he murmured quietly. A face in the dark turned to his. Nearby, now, a man, surrounded by two men, Eric thought, was crowing out his orgasm. Business-like almost, the two men manufactured his pleasure, their faces, Eric imagined in the dark, almost stern. Now the man, having achieved what he presumably set out to do, sagged against the iron wall, panting. One of the men melted away. The other stood there still, massaging the other's back. Then they spoke and Eric realised, almost with hilarity, that the two men were lovers.

Eric felt a hand move, tentatively at first, up his thigh. The fingers quickly found his fly. He shrugged it aside: he did not want that desperation of desire, cruel, metallic. To give pain is not to be unfeeling.

Eric, straining to see to whom it belonged, carefully but not unkindly took the hand away. He patted a thigh nearby and moved on.

There was a kind of method in it. Darkened lights were positioned at odd intervals, beside cubicles from which, on a busy night, you might hear pleasurings, slappings, all the casual cacophony of men fucking. If you stood still long enough and concentrated your sight, you could make out the shape of the participants of the night. You got a silhouette of a face, ears, haircut, body. To this potent detail you brought your imagination, your desire. Your need.

At times, Eric thought, the maze seemed to reflect a stereotypical vision of lost souls: penumbral sleepwalkers wandering in a daze, their faces sour with lust. Any action attracted a ring of onlookers who watched like lepers forbidden

215

contact. Yet at other times the maze seemed to disappear completely and the space became like that area up by the tin roof, unified into one soundscape, a symphony of men having sex with other men, the very sounds of which – the sharp intake of breath, the man groaning while being fucked, an arse being slapped, the swift arpeggio of orgasm – all created its own persuasive sexual universe, momentarily limitless, a world with its own reality – an illusion, naturally, but occasionally a necessary one.

And the dark provided a softer baize, a textural matt in which these desires could be not so much written, as felt out, touched, grasped and taken.

Eric quickly, efficiently, as if he were sorting through a pack of cards sorted out those men who matched his inner Braille of desire. There were two. One, a young man he had seen in a checkout counter at the supermarket, was wiry, with broad shoulders and an inward-looking face. He moved quickly, distractedly, about the corridors: there was a nervousness about him, a volatility, an excitement.

The other man was short-haired, a thin moustache on his upper lip. His body was neither overtly muscular nor plump: he, too, had seen Eric when he came in and had lingered, momentarily, beside him, as if allowing, animal-like, their auras to mix. Now he came straight towards Eric and, pausing only briefly, placed one hand on Eric's crotch, his other opening Eric's shirt and feeling with professional ease for his nipple. For one moment the two men oscillated in each other's possibilities, looking intensely into the other's faces. Warm breath fanned over Eric's cheekbones as he looked – he did not quite know why – away. His own hands were massaging up the man's back. He could feel beneath the cotton tight muscles moving. The man pushed his face closer to Eric's now, his lips brushed once, twice, against Eric's mouth. His strong tongue quickly moved past Eric's lips.

Eric was almost embarrassed at the way his mouth fell open, as if the stranger had pressed some button which said 'go', at the rush of saliva in the cave of his mouth; then his own tongue, instinctively, sought the stranger's.

For one long moment their tongues performed a ballet, a minuet of possibilities in each thrust, each soft suctioning seduction backwards, each lolling forward and rolling, dolphin-like caress.

It was at this moment that Eric realised he had not been kissed - he had not kissed - like that since Matthew went away. He had thought he had forgotten how to do it; he had thought he would never kiss again. He had, it was true, almost forgotten that kind of kissing, luxuriating, long, sensuous. He relaxed his back against the wall, letting out a soft, low groan.

This had taken no more than 18 seconds, yet both, pausing as if to take stock of the situation and sense whether it was mutually pleasurable for the other, realised they were surrounded by three - or was it four? - onlookers.

At various times of blackness, Eric had been one of the watchers. On certain nights when he had not found the parallelogram of someone else's desire, he had succumbed to that deeply ambiguous, hauntingly unsatisfactory act of watching and listening to other people having sex. This had a particular piquancy for Eric because it was, as it were, the reality of his life being made manifest - this was the relief in it, perhaps - his sense, after Matthew left, that everyone on Earth was having sex but him: that he alone was cast into an eternal darkness from which desire, contact, life had been banished. Matthew's going had placed him there. Whether he was destined to stay there all his life - it felt like that at times - he did not know.

But now the stranger's hand had found his. The touch of his palm was broad, pleasantly dry, his fingers quickly lacing through Eric's. He was pulling him away from the onlookers, towards a cubicle in which they might close the door. Eric briefly resisted, he did not know why: perhaps it was a sudden mad desire to join the onlookers for whom the lack of an encounter held emotional safety. But the warmth of the stranger's fingers, his arm as it banged lightly against his own, quickly told Eric what he must do: he must leave that space behind, abandon himself to the follies, the intricate choreographies of desire.

Inside the cubicle, as if they had no time to waste - indeed, as if the world was about to end within minutes - both stripped naked.

Gladly now, as if a huge weight was beginning to be taken off his shoulders, all the pictures which Eric carried with him for all time - his inhuman burden, his human choice - the image of Perrin as he lay inside his coffin, grey and chill, undertaker's make-up unable to mask the bruise on his forehead where his tissue-thin skin had broken; of Perrin when he lost his reason and, eyes unfocused, called Eric a liar, a fraud: all these evaporated into the exhilarating essence of *now*.

Eric gasped. The stranger's fingers were pincering his nipple. His back arched as he fell slightly forward into the other's body. The man's tongue slid between his lips, Eric's tongue flashed to meet his, and for one moment, gasping with the pain the man was inflicting on him, he hung there, trembling, alive.

The man now explored Eric's body with the hands of a good, a sensual, lover. There was immediately an odd sense that they had known each other for a long time: they were suddenly, even as they discovered it, familiar with what gave the other pleasure: supreme pleasure. The man was now taking charge of Eric's ecstasy; he was delivering to him, in sharp slaps, in slow probings with his tongue, in his hand's exploration of his arse, his soft grasping of his cock, his balls, a kind of inventory of existence for Eric. It was as if, in the trail of his fingertips, Eric was being reinvented.

Eric felt the man's cock, its dimensions and feel as personal as the features on a face, the lines, the curve of nose, the prominence of ears. His cock felt glassy, almost like a plump marble mortar, perfectly shaped.

Eric had the sense that he was being reborn. As the stranger's fingers and tongue and lips moved all over his body, he felt that he was coming into existence again, that he was leaving behind that dead period of his life which followed on from Perrin's death and Matthew's going.

The impact made him realise how instantanous the change could be. It was as if this stranger, in this seemingly incidental situation, had flipped his switch to 'on' - a switch that Eric almost believed had been rusted over. He saw very clearly that he had existed, through all that time, in non-circuit, as it were, all his lights blown out. But now, as the sweat from the man melded with his own, he realised how wrong he had been. He had a delirious sense of his own deliverance, that he was being plugged back into the grid of sexual desire, which lit up the entire globe in great flames of energy and flowed, man to man, woman to man, woman to woman, all over the Earth: a kind of life-force.

It was happening there in the sex club, that night, in other cubicles too perhaps, he did not know . . .

The man's hands smeared some cool unguent over the cheeks of his arse. The action felt like the preliminary to an operation. The man even had a certain seriousness, almost a detachment, as he moved in the dark.

Eric reached for him, pulled him down so their faces were close. He kissed him for a long moment then whispered, slowly, 'What are you doing?'

'I'm going to fuck you,' the man said without any changed emphasis, an erotic nonchalance in his voice, an easy command.

As he spoke - and Eric realised these were the first words they had exchanged: everything up to now had been communicated by touch, by semi-articulated groans and whimpers and sighs and grunts, the whole flittering fleet of pleasure's language - Eric detected a faint trace of a foreign accent. Once an aphrodisiac, this now acted as a warning, almost a symptom. Who was this stranger? Where had he been? Been with? The ghost of Perrin stirred within him, not unkindly, nor with any melodrama.

The stranger rustled in his pocket, Eric heard the sharp rip of plastic.

For a moment he felt the trill of a ridiculous, a surreal, sentiment: 'I don't fuck on a first date.' Yet would there be others? Would he ever see this man again? Or was this his one chance to fulfil the potential of what had been, hitherto, a perfect sexual encounter?

'I don't fuck on a first date.' Could he say this? Or would it date him to a bleak and plangent Connie Francis world: ('It's My Party and I'll Cry if I Want to'?)

Eric sighed, whispered in the stranger's ear, almost as if it were assent, kissing him between each word, which held in its own way an epiphany, a bead of memory forming, 'No. . . no . . . no.'

They kissed again slowly now, with a sense of sadness, as if each were taking time to think of how they could solve this conundrum satisfactorily. For it meant too, at that moment, another world had entered that cubicle, where other men had probably exchanged body fluids not even an hour ago; ghosts upon ghosts. As if to dispel this sudden intrusion, Eric gathered the man's head in his hands, pulled his face lightly away, and passed dry hot lips again again again over the other man's slack, open mouth. While the stranger pleaded with him to meet the next day - he was only in Auckland for two days, they must meet again - Eric offered his brief, crude invocation: his solution.

Almost immediately hot splatters, like butter on an element, almost sizzling, fell across his chest.

Later Eric moved out of that dark zone of pleasure. They would meet - or maybe not meet - again. As he walked back out through the door, the man-in-the-window nodding over yesterday's newspaper, Eric realised with a shock that already it was dawn, the night had ended and there was light, trembling like a membrane, all over the world.